John Harris was born in 1916. He authored the best-selling *The Sea Shall Not Have Them* and wrote under the pen names of Mark Hebden and Max Hennessy. He was a sailor, airman, journalist, travel courier, cartoonist and history teacher. During the Second World War he served with two air forces and two navies. After turning to full-time writing, Harris wrote adventure stories and created a sequence of crime novels around the quirky fictional character Chief Inspector Pel. A master of war and crime fiction, his enduring fictions are versatile and entertaining.

D0873436

BY THE SAME AUTHOR
ALL PUBLISHED BY HOUSE OF STRATUS

ARMY OF SHADOWS
CHINA SEAS
THE CLAWS OF MERCY
CORPORAL COTTON'S LITTLE WAR
THE CROSS OF LAZZARO
FLAWED BANNER
THE FOX FROM HIS LAIR
A FUNNY PLACE TO HOLD A WAR
GETAWAY
HARKAWAY'S SIXTH COLUMN
A KIND OF COURAGE
LIVE FREE OR DIE!
THE LONELY VOYAGE
THE MERCENARIES
NORTH STRIKE
THE OLD TRADE OF KILLING

PICTURE OF DEFEAT
THE QUICK BOAT MEN
RIDE OUT THE STORM
RIGHT OF REPLY
ROAD TO THE COAST
THE SLEEPING MOUNTAIN
SMILING WILLIE AND THE TIGER
SO FAR FROM GOD
THE SPRING OF MALICE
SUNSET AT SHEBA
SWORDPOINT
TAKE OR DESTROY!
THE THIRTY DAYS WAR
THE UNFORGIVING WIND
UP FOR GRABS
VARDY

JOHN HARRIS

THE SEA SHALL NOT HAVE THEM

HOUSE OF
STRATUS

Copyright © John Harris

All rights reserved. No part of this publication may be reproduced, stored in a
retrieval system, or transmitted, in any form, or by any means (electronic,
mechanical, photocopying, recording, or otherwise), without the prior permission
of the publisher. Any person who does any unauthorised act in relation to this
publication may be liable to criminal prosecution and civil claims for damages.

The right of John Harris to be identified as the author of this work
has been asserted.

This edition published in 2001 by House of Stratus, an imprint of
House of Stratus Ltd, Thirsk Industrial Park, York Road, Thirsk,
North Yorkshire, YO7 3BX, UK.
Also at: House of Stratus Inc., 2 Neptune Road, Poughkeepsie, NY 12601, USA.

www.houseofstratus.com

Typeset, printed and bound by House of Stratus.

A catalogue record for this book is available from the British Library
and the Library of Congress.

ISBN 0-7551-0219-3

This book is sold subject to the condition that it shall not be lent, resold, hired out,
or otherwise circulated without the publisher's express prior consent in any form of
binding, or cover, other than the original as herein published and without a similar
condition being imposed on any subsequent purchaser, or bona fide possessor.

This is a fictional work and all characters are drawn from the author's imagination.
Any resemblance or similarities to persons either living or dead
are entirely coincidental.

"The Sea Shall Not Have Them"
was the motto of Air-Sea Rescue
High-Speed Launch Flotillas.

During the war 13,269 lives were saved from the sea by Air-Sea Rescue – often under the enemy's guns. Of these, 8,604 were aircrew.

"Your superlative ASR Service has been one of the prime factors in the high morale of our own combat crews. This organisation of yours has picked up from the sea nearly 600 of our combat crewmen since we began operations in this theatre. This is a remarkable achievement made possible by only the highest efficiency and the greatest courage and fortitude."

LIEUTENANT-GENERAL IRA C EAKER
(Commanding 8th US Air Force in Britain)

PART ONE

Across the wide Suffolk fields the wind blew with the coldness of winter, bringing with it the varied sounds of the aerodrome. Faintly, the men working on the sooty-painted night bombers dispersed round the perimeter could hear the scream of steel on steel from the workshops by the hangars and the noisy revving of an engine from the Motor Transport yard. Then, brittle and staccato, cutting sharply across all the other noises came the sound of a Browning machine-gun firing – like the sharp tearing of a huge cloth – as armourers lined up sights on the range. The echoes seemed to carry more clearly on the wind than usual, as though held close to the earth by the low clouds that folded layer upon layer towards the horizon, where the trees stood prematurely bare of leaves in the shivering lace of winter dress.

The day was bright, but only because it was noon, for the gathering clouds seemed already to be pressing the light out of the day with their threats of rain. The cows beyond the perimeter were huddled in the lee of the hedge, their square sterns to the weather, their sad eyes staring mournfully in front of them. The swallows had long since disappeared and only the iron-songed crows remained, wheeling above the aerodrome buildings, their tattered wings black against the sky.

There was something that spoke of winter in the very air – the smoky blueness of the distance, the sharp angularity of the aerodrome buildings clustered behind the hangars. You could smell the chill in the wind from the stark way the windsock by the Control Tower stood out against the barren sky, a pointing finger to the frost and the not far-distant snow, and from the way the group of uniformed figures clustered in the shelter of the tall camouflaged building from which the aerodrome traffic was directed

The Wing Commander's jeep stood behind the Control Tower and, at the side of the building, out of the wind, the Wing Commander himself waited with his second-in-command and the Flying Control Officer. Beyond them the ambulance and the fire-tender were drawn out of their garages, their drab camouflage matching the grey day, their crews watching the sky. A few other figures bunched in the doorway of the crew-room, slouching figures in flying boots and leather jackets – flying personnel who had abandoned their chute and poker and their numerous trivial jobs. They, too, were staring at the sky.

About them all there was a tenseness, an expectancy that was not missed by the crew doing the inspection on the Lancaster parked in front of the maintenance hangar. The fitter, sitting by the starboard outer engine on the dun-coloured upper side of the main plane, his big boots hanging in space, watched them for a while, hardly aware in his thick jersey and overalls of the cold wind that buffeted against his back.

The Wing Commander was talking quickly in an outburst of nervous energy, his hands deep in his jacket pockets, walking about as he spoke, still staring hard at the sky, and the others were staring with him, so that the whole group had a heroic cast of urgency.

The fitter looked down at his flight-mechanic below him who had just returned from the flight stores.

"What's going on down there?" He indicated the group by the Control Tower with a jerk of his spanner.

The flight-mechanic, fumbling in a toolbox, stared up at the fitter who craned forward to look at him.

"Kite overdue," he said.

"A kite? Who's flying?"

"Harding."

"What's *he* doing flying? Thought his crew just forced-landed in France."

"He's flying a Hudson back for a write-off at the Maintenance Unit. There's only three of the crew coming back."

The fitter tightened with his spanner the nut he'd been screwing down with his fingers and began looking for another among his kit. He was uninterested, dejected, like all Servicemen working overtime for no obvious reason. Then he lifted his head again, looking over the sprawling camp in which there seemed no sign of its vast life, beyond the tense figures by the Control Tower and a toy lorry charging round the perimeter in the distance.

"Who's coming back with him?" he asked.

"Sergeant Ponsettia. Flight Sergeant Mackay. And a passenger. They're bringing some big shot back. Air Commodore Waltby, the rocket merchant."

"Why Air Commodore Waltby?"

"VIP. He's been visiting the rocket sites and he's coming back with a load of gen on rocket-launching. He's the Group Captain's brother-in-law or something."

"Who told you? Groupy himself?"

The flight-mechanic pushed his hat back. "Keep my ears open, chum. That's all."

"Think Harding's had it?" The fitter's voice was lacking in compassion. Its owner had known too many aircraft fail to return during the long course of the war. He felt a certain amount of unconscious sympathy for human beings unluckier than himself. No more.

"Well, he's overdue," the flight-mechanic said. "That usually means only one thing. He must have got the chop."

"Hard luck. Nice bloke. Wonder where he is?"

In the Operations Room in the camouflaged headquarters building beyond the hangars the Squadron Leader Controller placed a flat counter on the middle of the blue patch on the plotting table that represented the English Channel and pushed it with his pointer to a spot near the coast of the Continent.

"That," he said to the Group Captain, "is Harding."

Squadron Leader Jones had a soft Welsh lilt in his voice that spoke of wild blue hills and gentle valleys, and he had a friendly confidence which made Group Captain Taudevin feel better as he thought of the missing aircraft and the men in it. He was a small slight man, typical of Wales, going bald and younger than he looked. He glanced at Taudevin and tapped the counter again. "There's still time, of course, to hear they've forced-landed somewhere," he pointed out.

He stared reflectively at the long plotting table in the centre of the room, set out in the form of a map of the United Kingdom, the Channel and the Continent, and bearing movable counters to plot aircraft belonging to the station or flying in its vicinity.

Behind him, a corporal WAAF scratched with a piece of chalk at a squared blackboard on the wall which carried the numbers of aircraft, their pilots' names, their destinations and their estimated times of arrival.

The machinery which covered the destiny of the missing Hudson had slipped quietly into motion, each individual piece fitting jigsaw-like into the others. Signals Traffic Room at Group Headquarters had received reports of an emergency signal from an aircraft over the sea shortly before Taudevin's Signals Officer had originated a message to them indicating the absence of a Hudson Coastal Command machine piloted by Flying Officer Harding, stationed under Taudevin's command. There was no excitement. Indeed, there was still no alarm – for Harding might yet turn up elsewhere, might even still be flying – but the cogs of a normal search for an overdue aircraft had already begun to click into place. Coastal Command had been informed in routine fashion and, through them, the Naval Captain in command of the Light Coastal Forces in the Channel. A hundred separate individuals stationed in a dozen different places were already concerned with Harding's absence.

Jones tapped with his pointer to the sea in the vicinity of the marker, which represented the missing aircraft.

"I gather there are Air-Sea Rescue launches north and south of this area approximately," he said. "And at least one naval launch. There are also two Walrus amphibians in the area. It's only an approximate position, unfortunately, because we're not certain what happened. But Felwell and Harbry picked up a weak Mayday signal without a call-sign and managed to get a rough bearing on it, which placed it in that area. Unfortunately, it didn't last long enough for them to get anything accurate. That was probably Harding's last cheep before he ditched."

Taudevin looked round the long room with its tall windows, its WAAF plotters, and the bulldog clips on hooks which held sheaves of paper containing operations directions and weather reports. He was a wiry little man, young for his rank but with the old eyes of command. He had been a famous fighter pilot in the early days of the war but a crash at Malta had finished his active flying career in a vivid burst of orange flame that had left him a little older, and with bright mottled hands twisted into claws by burns which wrenched at the skin until it was folded into creases shiny with newness. He was a man of nervous mannerisms and sudden stillnesses that left you wondering if he were listening to you; his pale eyes tranquil, silent, busy with his own thoughts to the exclusion of everyone else, alone in spite of the business of the aerodrome around him.

He stood still now, apparently unhearing, staring through the window at the low clouds which hung, sick and heavy as a wet blanket, over the fields. As far as he could see there was no break in them anywhere.

Jones was still speaking. "Aircraft are flying over the area, sir, of course, and any one of them might pick up a signal from the squawk box in the dinghy. Unfortunately, the weather's a bit dicey and that might prove the complication."

"What's the picture on the weather?" Taudevin asked sharply, as though he had suddenly wakened from a trance.

Jones reached for the internal telephone. "I'll get the Met. people to send someone up. He'll be able to give you the general picture more clearly than I can." He spoke into the telephone. "Oh, hello, is that you, Tom? Slip in here and give us the picture on the weather, will you?"

Flying Officer Howard, the Meteorological Officer, who came in a moment later, was a small scholastic-looking man with spectacles. He spoke deferentially to the Group Captain and had the manner of one who hated to commit himself about anything.

"Well, sir," he began, "we're all right here at the moment, but Stornoway, up in the Isles, reports cloud at five hundred feet. Visibility down to a thousand yards. They're ten-tenths overcast there. Heavy rain and a gale-force wind. No flying." He spoke rapidly in short, jerky sentences, as though he were a weather report himself.

"What does that indicate?" Taudevin asked, not turning from the window, his mind still sharply on Harding.

"I'm afraid, sir, we're in for a nasty blow. There's a trough of low pressure moving south-south-east at about twenty to twenty-five miles an hour."

"How long have we got before it reaches the Channel?"

"I think it will be blowing hard here and completely shut in by this time tomorrow – or even earlier. Flying will be out."

The Meteorological Officer put his charts, blue- and green-tinted and marked with the tiny numbers which

8

indicated meteorological offices, on the Controller's table. It was as though he were saying, "There it is, if you don't believe me."

Taudevin was silent for a while. His eyes were still and restful but his mind was racing over the possibilities of what might have happened. He was uneasily remembering seeing at Wattlesham aerodrome in the early days of the war, before he had left for the Middle East, a Blenheim which had hit the water while returning from Norway low enough for a momentary drift of the pilot's attention to allow it to touch a wave crest. It had bent its propeller-tips and lost the airscoops from its engines, its tailwheel and its under gun-turret. And it contained a very startled pilot who hadn't properly recovered from the shock of discovering what the sea could do to a metal aircraft at speed merely with a touch.

Taudevin found himself imagining such a thing happening to Harding, though he knew it could never have occurred through any drift of attention – not with Harding. In the normal way, Taudevin was not in the habit of worrying long about his aircrews when they were missing or overdue. It had happened before and it would happen again, and it was part of his job not to take too much notice of that. And, though he never enjoyed waiting for them to return from operations, once it was known what had happened to missing crews he had taught himself to dismiss them from his mind.

But Harding was not missing on an operational flight, he reminded himself, and in addition he had with him a VIP whom Group and even AHQ and London were anxious to have safely back with them. The fact that the VIP was his wife's brother-in-law and his own good friend did not weigh in the balance at that moment with him. His chief concern was with getting back a briefcase full of important documents.

"This time tomorrow," he said aloud to himself. "It doesn't give us much time. I'll get in touch with the Navy personally and explain the urgency. And I'll contact Group and ask them if they can't spare an aircraft or two for a sweep before the weather shuts down."

"It's a pity the bearing we've got isn't very accurate," Jones said. "I can't imagine why we didn't get a better one. Flight Sergeant Mackay's a good wireless operator."

Taudevin nodded, his expression unchanged. "It could mean a difference of twenty or thirty miles or more, and twenty or thirty miles at sea-level can be a long way when you're searching for something as small as a dinghy. Just a bright day for flying – that's all we want." He turned to the Meteorological Officer. "Are you sure there's no chance?"

"The barograph is falling a little already," Howard pointed out, as though with a vague sense of shame that he was unable to co-operate.

Taudevin studied the charts for a moment, his shoulders hunched, sucking a cold pipe. "Keep us taped," he said. "How about a plot every hour?"

"I'll do that, sir."

Realising he was dismissed, the Meteorological Officer picked up his charts and disappeared. The Group Captain thrust his twisted hands into his jacket pockets and walked slowly towards the balcony and looked at the grey sky.

"I guarantee," he said slowly, "that every time anyone ditches in the sea the weather immediately starts to make things as difficult as possible. It took them two days to find me when I ditched in 1940. Fog patches and rain. I've never felt so damn lonely in all my life. And I've never been so cold. And that was summer time. We haven't as long to get Harding. We can't afford to wait until after this weather blows itself out." His eyes went bleak as he spoke, and Jones could feel a little of the chill that had struck across him that summer in 1940.

He stood in silence, waiting for Taudevin to continue, then the Group Captain turned and came back to the plotting table.

"Group have been on the blower again," he went on. "They're getting anxious. Waltby had some important material for them, I gather."

The Controller remained silent, chiefly because he could think of nothing helpful to say.

"You know who Waltby is, of course?" Taudevin stared at him with enquiring eyebrows.

"Yes, sir, of course." Jones tried to answer briskly and Taudevin gave him a tired smile.

"No, I mean that he's my wife's brother-in-law. He married her sister. Good friend of mine. His wife is coming down here to meet him when he returns. My wife is supposed to be meeting the train. She's been away for the day and I can't contact her until she gets to the station. I shall have to tell them when I go to pick them up. They're bound to know immediately that something's happened. He should have been with me."

"I'm sorry, sir." Instinctively Jones glanced quickly at the plotting table and the lonely marker that represented Harding.

Back in his own room, Taudevin stood by the window watching the ensign which flew from the mast outside his office, rippling in the wind so that the roundel-marked Royal Air Force blue whipped stiffly across the sky. A couple of WAAFs came past, their heads down, each one holding her precarious hat down on thick hair which hung low over her neck, in direct defiance of orders which stated it should be off the collar. Beyond them, the bare trees slowly waved. their topmasts against the sky.

Across the open space in front of headquarters Taudevin could see the guard changing by the main gate. He watched silently during the manoeuvring which removed the old guard and replaced him with the new one, and saw the corporal and his party move off again towards the guardroom, taut and solid-looking in their webbing belts. Taudevin approved with a nod, though he knew very well that the elaborate procedure practised on the main gate was chiefly for show, part of the spit and polish of the Air Force, a paragraph out of the drill manuals, and that at all the other points which warranted a guard the change-over was casual and friendly – and just as efficient. He also knew that his interest in the smartness of the guard was unnecessary – that had there been any slackness on the main gate the Administrative Officer, Squadron Leader Scott, who occupied the next office to his own, would already have been flinging himself across the wide concrete roadway in a flash of the ponderous, frustrated energy which was the motivating power in almost everything he did.

Even as Taudevin watched he saw Sergeant Starr, Scotty's general duty man, march smartly across to the wooden hut that served as a guardroom and disappear inside. The Group Captain sighed and turned away from the window. It was a pity, he decided, that Scotty didn't apply to all the other duties which should have occupied his time the same zeal and energy he expended on guard-mounting, saluting and what he chose to call "airmanship", that outmoded term from official documents which he loved to roll round his tongue.

Airmanship and loyalty were the little tin gods before which Scotty rattled his worshipping beads. For Taudevin it was sufficient to ask efficiency, and he received in return all the things that Scotty never quite managed to inspire in spite of the fact that he chased them all round the camp with floods of orders invoking King's Regulations and Air Council Instructions, and countless little messages insisting that the various departmental officers should do likewise. Taudevin received all the carbon copies of them on his desk in daily batches.

He really would have to do something about Scotty before long, he decided, as he stood before his desk. The old boy seemed to be getting worse, taking it out of everyone else to cover up his own inefficiency, utilising the rank he held – which was still, paradoxically, insufficient to enable him to make a personal decision about anything important – to worry other hard-working men about trivialities.

Taudevin thought for a moment over ways and means with which he might curb Scotty's over-enthusiastic interference, then he decided they might for a while continue picking up the bricks where Scotty dropped them, covering him when he forgot things. He might, however, have a discreet word with the Station Warrant Officer who, after all, really ran the station and always had done. Some of Scotty's work might even be pushed over to that gentleman if he had no objection. And Taudevin thought he wouldn't have.

Even as he considered it, Taudevin realised he was really only shelving his responsibility. It was hardly fair to pass the baby on to the SWO. Actually, the responsibility for curbing Scotty was his own and no one else's.

Then he shrugged and decided again the whole matter could safely wait a while. Scotty had done nothing really violently serious yet – though it was only a matter of time, he reflected soberly. But, for the present at least, he felt he didn't want worrying with trivialities while there was this anxiety about Harding being overdue.

His mind came sharply back to the problem at a knock on his door as Squadron Leader Scott himself entered. Taudevin glanced up at him, on the point of saying he was busy, then he composed his face to register attention and polite interest.

Scotty approached his desk with that peculiar long energetic stride of his which, like his hearty manner and the popular Air Force moustachios he wore, hid the unhappy uncertainty that lay beneath. His face was red and flushed and over his breast pocket below his faded wings he wore two or three medal ribbons from the 1914-18 war and a Distinguished Flying Cross, all of which made him loath to wear a greatcoat, however bad the weather. "I'm not a bloody desk wallah," he liked to point out, "and I don't want people to mistake me for one." As a result of his efforts to avoid the error it was said maliciously in the Mess that he was always in greater danger of death from pneumonia than from enemy action.

Scotty had been for a time noisily in charge of a satellite station but trouble there had brought him to an operations room and, for the same reason, finally in charge of administration under Taudevin and plaguing the life out of his commanding officer with just the fretting trivialities from which he was supposed to protect him.

"*Good* morning, Sir," he began heartily as he burst through the door.

"Good morning, Scotty!" Taudevin sat down at his desk and made himself sound cheerful and eager to listen, but his slight impatience was betrayed by the movement of his fingers tapping the blotter. "What's worrying you this morning?"

Scotty unrolled a couple of posters he had been caring under his arm. "How about these, sir? *Prepare yourself for Civvy Street*. Rather wizard, I think. I suggest we bung one of 'em up in the Mess somewhere. Shall we?"

He had started off his conversation with a boisterous and confident efficiency but that last treacherous "Shall we?", that flinging of the onus on to Taudevin, betrayed him utterly. Scotty always offered his suggestions in the form of a question.

"I think I can leave that to you," Taudevin said, faintly irritated.

"Roger, sir." Scotty smiled in his hearty fashion, relieved to have his suggestion endorsed. "I'm just going over to the canteen to give the boys a lecture on post-war planning. Thought I might bung one up there, too. By the way, sir, I do feel these lectures aren't attended half well enough. There are too many people finding excuses to dodge 'em." Taudevin stared at his desk. Scotty and his lectures were famous. Whatever their subject, their matter was chiefly loyalty and ideals and duty.

"I do feel that since we're all going to get a basinful of post-war planning when we're demobbed it's as well to gen up on it. None of the boys have a clue. Don't you think we might make the lectures compulsory?"

"I don't think so, Scotty," Taudevin answered softly. "Some of these fellows have been running their lives very efficiently for a long time now. Perhaps they don't want to be planned. I'm afraid I can't agree to forcing them – not yet, anyway."

"Well – hm – perhaps not, sir." Scotty spoke a little huffily and Taudevin found himself wishing he'd go away. He put the posters down on the edge of the Group Captain's desk and laid his notebook carefully on top of them.

"Sir," he went on. "Flight Sergeant Mackay – "

Taudevin was reading the notes jotted down on Scotty's pad: "Investigate rate of promotion, Signals Section." "AOC's inspection." "Accommodation in hutted camp." "Bus service to town." "Ensa." "Padre's Church Parade" – and he knew he was going to have to make a decision on every one of them, whatever they were. Then Scotty's words sank into his brain and his head jerked up. He sat motionless, his eyes suddenly hard and still and unblinking – like a cat's.

"Mackay? What about Mackay?"

"Well, sir..." Scotty drew a deep breath. "The Station Police have discovered a jerry-can of petrol in his car, sir."

Taudevin's frown deepened a little but he didn't move, and Scotty continued.

"Police corporal saw him pick it out of a ditch by the dispersal area. Seems it fell off a motor transport. At least, the MT Section have reported one missing. Mackay apparently saw it happen and was picking it up after dark. This morning, when the corporal investigated further, he found the jerry-can in Mackay's car – you know the one, that old Morris he runs about in."

"Why didn't the corporal stop Mackay at the time?"

"Gather, sir, he was a little apprehensive about the result. Mackay's rather a big type and rather given to blowing his top off. Corporal felt it might be a sticky do. By the time he'd investigated, Mackay was flying."

"The corporal's a damn fool. He obviously made sure Mackay was flying first."

Scotty's eyebrows shot up. "Hm – yes, sir. I agree. But pinching petrol's a poor show whoever does it. Court martial offence. What ought we to do? Felt since he was aircrew, and the aircrew types are your particular interest, you might like to hear about it. What do you think?"

Taudevin spoke slowly as he replied. "Whatever we might decide to do, we'll have to wait a little while," he said. "Flight Sergeant Mackay's been reported overdue in Flying Officer Harding's aircraft. We suspect he's somewhere in the Channel in a dinghy."

Scotty was taken aback. "Oh!" His jaw dropped. "Oh! Shaky do, sir! Sorry to hear that. What do you feel should be the drill, then?"

"What do you think it should be, Scotty?" Taudevin said, weary and a little malicious.

"Well – er – after all, it's serious." Scotty, thus appealed to, floundered for a minute. "Can't let him get away with it. Poor show and all that. But under the circumstances – well, sir," he concluded, tossing the decision back into Taudevin's lap, "it's for you to decide."

Taudevin drummed with both hands on his blotter for a while. When he spoke it was to the desk top and not to Scotty. "Mackay's a good wireless operator," he said. "He got the DFM while he was a sergeant. I recommended him myself. I believe he's put in for a commission, hasn't he?"

"Oh, has he, sir?" Scotty's heavy face looked relieved as he saw the Group Captain taking the responsibility. Taudevin frowned for a moment. Scotty had obviously failed to remember Mackay's application for a commission, which must have passed through his hands and it was Scotty's job to remember, if only because he was in charge of administration.

"What else do you know about the affair?" he asked sharply.

"The corporal put in a report..."

"That means it will be all round the station by now."

"Afraid so, sir."

"I'd have preferred it kept quiet." Taudevin still sat with his arms across his desk, those horny nails of his tapping the blotter. He appeared at ease and undisturbed but his voice had an edge to it. "If nothing's done about it they'll be saying there's one law for flying crews and another for the ground staff."

"Exactly, sir. Damned disloyal thought, I might add, considering how the flying boys are clobbering the Hun just now."

Taudevin gave Scotty a sidelong glance, annoyed by the way he seemed to associate himself with the aircrews and by the satisfied manner in which he spoke – as though the decisions being made were his and his alone.

"There was a sergeant at Felwell who took a jerry-can of petrol, I remember," Taudevin said slowly. "Similar circumstances. Stealing by finding, I suppose you'd call it."

"That's right, sir. Court martialled and reduced to the ranks." Scotty had a smug look of self-righteousness on his face. He'd remembered the case and looked up the verdict, and he brought it out triumphantly.

"And then, if I remember," Taudevin went on disconcertingly, "shortly afterwards he was given his rank back and was eventually killed over Essen."

"Er – oh, is that so, sir?" Scotty looked abashed and Taudevin gave him a sharp glance. Just like Scotty, he thought, not to have bothered to enquire *that* far.

He stood up. "I'll think this over for a day or so," he said. "We don't *know* that Mackay didn't really find that jerry-can. He might have done, though I don't honestly think so. There was no petrol in the tank of the car, was there?"

"No, sir – er – I think not." Scotty rubbed his nose doubtfully and Taudevin could see he didn't know.

"Hm. It's a pity the Special Investigation Police should happen to be on the station at the moment, looking into that petrol-stealing at the Maintenance Unit."

"Yes, sir. Poor show that. Glad to know, though, sir, it was a civilian they arrested and not one of our people. Damned unpatriotic business with a war on."

"Special Investigation wouldn't let this charge be squashed if it were made out." Taudevin seemed to be speaking to himself, as though he failed to hear the other's comments. "So just sit on it for a while."

"Station Police say charges ought to be made out by now," Scotty persisted, "if we're going ahead with it."

"Tell the Station Police to wait," Taudevin snapped, suddenly angry.

"Oh – er – yes, sir. Very good, sir." Scotty picked up his notebook hurriedly. "Now, sir, about the accommodation in the hutted camp – "

"You attend to it, Scotty," Taudevin said quickly, pushing his chair back. "I'm rather occupied at the moment."

"Roger, sir." Taudevin winced. Scotty never seemed to have grown up and liked to use slang with the generosity of the youngest sergeant-pilot, curbing it at all only in front of the Group Captain. "And, sir..." Scotty made a desperate attempt to claim Taudevin's attention as he saw him move away from the desk. "This Ensa company who're supposed to be doing a show here on Sunday – "

"You fix it, Scotty. I must see the Wing Commander." Taudevin escaped towards the corridor, aware of the vast difference between the Controller, with his quiet confidence, and Scotty, with his high-powered lack of it.

"Sir." Scotty's voice rose to a broken squeak as Taudevin reached for the door-handle. "This new bus service – "

Taudevin slammed the door quickly and, behind him, Scotty broke off abruptly and slowly began to collect his papers, brooding on the lack of co-operation which seemed, as far as he was concerned, to extend from the lowest aircraftman in the Station Warrant Officer's office to the Group Captain himself.

As Taudevin stepped outside into the wind he knew very well that the queries on the pad, having been rejected by himself, would eventually be pushed into the lap of the Station Warrant Officer, who would give them to his sergeant to deal with – who was the person who should have dealt with them in the first place, instead of them being brought to him by Scotty.

He suddenly felt angry with the older man for plaguing him with such trivialities while somewhere beyond the blue fields and the white cliffs that lay even beyond them four men were probably struggling for their lives in the water, and the fact that he knew so little about it suddenly began to grow in its importance until it nagged like a raw blister on his heel.

t w o

The Hudson had hit the water not with the splash that Air Commodore Waltby had expected but with a harsh shattering crash that seemed to tear great rents in the metal, and he realised in the first instant that slammed him with breath-taking force against the bulkhead that the sea was as solid as a cliff when it was hit at speed.

As the machine struck, in a sheeting wall of green water that gushed in a wave over the Perspex windows and dropped with a noise like violent rain on to the fuselage, it seemed for a second to stand on its nose, then it flopped heavily back again on its tail with the awkward movement of a falling skittle. The cabin immediately seemed full of icy dark green water that came from nowhere, snatching Waltby's breath away, slapping and splashing round him, up to his waist and his arm-pits in an instant, sweeping away into the tail the scraps of signal pad paper that had littered the navigator's table. Frantically envisaging himself trapped in that rapidly rising flood, locked in a heavy aircraft that was bubbling down, down, down into the dark fathoms of the sea, Waltby fought blindly to undo the parachute harness he had put on in the first moment of emergency and struggled against the weight of water towards the escape hatch.

Then, immediately, he realised he'd lost his grip on his briefcase, that precious load of documents he'd collected at the rocket sites up and down the Pas de Calais, and all his own important notes on what he'd seen and how it might be used. It was as important – even more important – than his own life. He had crouched against the bulkhead, awaiting the impact of the aircraft hitting the sea, with the case clutched to him, wondering in a foolish, rabbit-like fashion how much he could remember of it if he were to lose it. With every foot of height they had lost, his brain had churned over with an old woman's fretting nag of anxiety as he had tried to photograph the contents of the papers on his mind.

In a daze of excitement as he recovered from the shock of the crash he began to paw about for the case under the dark water that filled the whole interior of the Hudson, then, as his jostled memory cleared and he felt the case bumping against his knees, he recalled that he had taken the precaution to strap it to his waist with his overcoat belt through the handle.

For the first time, as his mind abruptly dropped the worry of the case, he became conscious of the sudden silence after the roar of the engines and the buffeting of the wind. Now there was only the hard – almost solid – slap and smack of water outside the fuselage and the slosh and hurry of it inside. And everything else was silence – dim, stricken silence that brought home to him more vividly than anything that had happened the fact that the living bird which had carried them was now carrion floating on the water.

The sea was up to his neck now and a small wave chasing along the cylindrical interior of the aircraft smacked him viciously under the chin and blinded him for a second as it filled his eyes and mouth. Panic caught him as he saw the water outside the Perspex window, green and ugly looking, then someone was shouting in his ear in a voice that was high-pitched with urgency.

"Through the hatch! Up above you!"

He reached up, and with the assistance of a violent shove from behind he shot upwards, banging his head viciously on the open hatchway before he emerged into fresh air that struck cold and frighteningly damp against his face after the warm, petrol-smelling interior of the aeroplane.

In the first shock of freedom it amazed him to see the height of the waves outside. He had noticed while they were flying that the sea appeared to be choppy, even rough, its peaks tipped with white, but down here, down on the level of the water, it seemed mountainous, towering high above the wallowing wreck of the aircraft, the waves bearing down on them with a terrifying inevitability, seemingly as big as houses and just as solid.

Conscious of someone behind him also heaving his soaking frame through the hatchway, he shuffled in an ungainly fashion along the curved body of the plane. Its smooth surface was slippery with water and he found it difficult to keep his grip and his balance on it, especially with the bulky briefcase between his legs all the time, impeding his movements. His hat with its gold braid had disappeared – he had no idea when or where – and the wind whipped through his thinning grey hair.

Only half aware of thought, he began to wish he'd paid more attention to his dinghy drill when he'd had it explained to him in the hangar. As a research expert he'd never had much cause to need dinghies until the last month or two when his increasingly frequent trips to the German rockets sites or jet aircraft fields had made someone high up decide he was valuable enough to be instructed how to use them.

The other members of the crew – and he felt with a slight start of surprise that he had never thought of the others as people until now – were all out of the aircraft by this time. One of them, Mackay, the wireless operator, was standing on the wing, his hard, angular face pinched and pale with strain, like a stone idol's. The water was over his feet but Waltby saw with relief that one hand held the rope of the rubber dinghy which bobbed glaringly yellow against the grey sea away from the side of the plane, its frantic heaves in the chop – like the struggles of a young colt on a rein – jerking at Mackay so that he held with his other hand on to the side of the fuselage and scowled bitterly at the sky. Waltby then noticed that the hand holding the dinghy had an ugly gash in it that saturated the white rope with the startling redness of blood, which ran, shining and dark, across his fingers and dripped into the water in hurrying droplets.

While he was wondering which was the best way to get into the dinghy without falling into the sea a wave hit him in the back and he slithered on the seat of his trousers in an undignified fashion into the water. As it closed over him he experienced another of those dreadful moments of panic that numbed his thoughts to everything but the desire for life. He let out a yell of pure fear and choked immediately with salt water that tasted sharp and raw on his tongue, gagging him with its bitter strength. He came up, kicking frantically, spitting, unable to see, then as his panic dispersed once more he realised that his Mae West was supporting him. Alongside him was Ponsettia, the Canadian navigator, his great yellow moustache drooping and wet like a walrus'.

"OK, sir?"

Gasping, trying to nod, trying to kick his way to the dinghy that reared bouncing and buoyant above him, Waltby was fishing instinctively below the surface of the sea with his hands as the heavy briefcase, now full of water, dragged at his body. It seemed to be slipping down, so he got his hand on the handle and jerked it fiercely up and held on to it, aware in the same instant that his watch would never go again.

"The bag," he spluttered. "Got to get it in the dinghy soon or I'll drown."

Ponsettia grinned and he tried to grin back and for his trouble got a mouthful of water that wiped away the gesture like a slap in the face.

"Hold on to the bag. I'll try to help you to the dinghy."

Waltby again tried to smile but worry over his precious bag seemed to be seeping across his mind like the cold across his body, and he found himself panting, fighting, it seemed, against all the vast acres of the sea, against these slow inexorable waves that lifted him about as if he were a feather.

"Keep going," Ponsettia gasped beside him. "I'll help shove." Then a wave swept them apart and Waltby was on the point of crying out again when he once more felt the Canadian's hand reassuringly on his shoulder.

"When you've finished arsing about," Mackay said unemotionally from the wing, "it'd be nice if you'd get in the dinghy. The kite's going down any minute."

The water was now creeping up the wireless operator's flying boots as the aircraft settled lower in the water, grey-green like the sea, silent and still, like a great dead whale. His voice was harsh and impatient, and the blood still fell in dark drops from his hand into the moving water.

"OK, Mac." Ponsettia's words came in gasps. "Keep your hair on, brother. The Air Commodore's got another little life to think of."

At the apt description of himself clutching with both hands at his stomach while the navigator pushed him towards the dinghy, Waltby felt better in spite of his fear and the sickness he felt at the water he'd swallowed.

"Well, look slippy, man." Mackay's face was taut and angry – to Waltby it had seemed to be taut and angry from the first moment he had been introduced to the crew. "The skipper's stopped one or something."

Harding, the pilot, crouched lopsidedly on the cabin top by the hatchway, his face twisted and wrenched out of shape with pain.

"I'm all right, Mac," he said. "Get the Air Commodore in. I only got a bit of a whack across the bread-basket when we ditched. I'll be all right."

As he splashed towards the dinghy Waltby heard the wireless operator muttering to himself in that angry, hostile fashion of his which he had already started to associate with all Mackay's conversation, indifferent to Waltby's struggles or the strength of the sea.

"Bloody chairborne wonders," he was saying, as though he were deliberately trying to throw defiance at Waltby's rank. "More trouble than they're worth." Then his voice rose anxiously and suddenly there was concern in it. "You sure you're all right, skipper?"

"Get the Air Commodore into the dinghy and stop binding about me."

The aircraft was deeper in the water now. Only the trapped air in the fuselage seemed to be keeping it afloat and as this was gradually forced out the machine was slowly sinking.

"Hang on to the rope," Ponsettia said to Waltby as he grabbed for the yellow side of the dinghy. "Then sling your bag in."

Waltby shook his head, his teeth chattering too much for him to speak. At last he managed to control himself.

"Probably lose it. Can't risk it. Get in yourself first. I'll hang on to the bag."

Ponsettia glanced curiously at him, then, splashing and kicking, he heaved himself up and flopped panting over the side of the rubber boat which tilted up on its edge as he did so, water dripping from the canvas sea anchors underneath that held it steady. Splashing like a great stranded fish, his legs stiff and black in silhouette above Waltby as he struggled, he heaved his body into the dinghy at last and it slapped back again on to an even keel in the lifting sea, and he lay there for a moment, panting with the effort until he recovered his breath.

After a moment or two he sat up. "OK," he said, scrambling to his knees. "Pass us your bag."

Waltby shook his head again stubbornly. "Rope," he gasped. "Pass a rope – one of the dinghy ropes."

"Rope?" Mackay said harshly from the main plane of the Hudson "Rope? Jesus, this is supposed to be an emergency."

Ponsettia stared hard at Waltby for a moment, then without a word he passed one of the white ropes attached to the life raft and the Air Commodore grabbed at it.

"Hang on to me," he said.

With Ponsettia clutching his collar in a grip that threatened to choke him, and with the sea slapping him with relentless insistence in the face, Waltby released his grip on the dinghy, passed the rope through the handle of the briefcase and pushed the end up to the navigator again.

"Tie it," he said. "Let go of me. Tie the bag."

"Say…" Ponsettia paused, then he tied the rope quickly to another of the dinghy lines.

"Good!" Waltby felt relief for the first time and, unfastening his belt, passed the bag, now fastened securely to the dinghy, up to Ponsettia. "Just had to be sure," he panted. "It's valuable."

"Bloody bag," Mackay was muttering on the wing. "Lot of bloody fuss for a bag. Haul the bastard in, Canada. The skipper's waiting."

Waltby turned to grasp the dinghy lines and as he did so a wave, slapping its underside, blinded him as it broke outwards into his face. He almost lost his grip and swung away, one hand grasping with desperate hurry for a hold. Then Ponsettia leaned over and, grabbing him by the collar again, heaved him upwards. For a moment they struggled, with Waltby half in and half out of the water, his belt caught somehow on the underside of the dinghy.

"I'm stuck," he panted. "Let me down and try again."

"Get the old bastard in," Mackay was snarling just above them as Ponsettia jerked and heaved.

"What'n hell's catching?" the Canadian panted. "Christ, are you covered in grappling irons or something?"

Waltby's breath, as he tried to force his tired arms to pull him up, was beginning to come in searing gasps that tore at his chest, then unexpectedly the obstruction freed itself and he slid over the rounded yellow side and lay sprawling in the well of the dinghy on his face in several inches of water, his feet helplessly in the air, his hands, trembling with exertion, thankfully on the precious bag again. His mind was stunned to blankness by the confusion and the urgency and by the throb in his head where he'd hit it on the escape hatch.

"OK, Mac." He heard Ponsettia's voice through the daze of exhaustion. "We're in."

"About time," Mackay commented briefly. Then he turned to the pilot who still sat on the fuselage. "Right, skipper. Come on. Let's have you."

Harding slithered down the side of the plane and landed on top of Waltby, smashing all the breath from his body, and half smothering him. "Pardon me," he said with over-elaborate politeness as the dinghy settled again.

Half underneath the other two, his head ringing, his eyes full of whirling lights, his breath an agony in his chest, Waltby felt their frail craft rock violently again as Mackay climbed in from the wing, then it settled back to its lifting, sliding motion on the slow, indifferent heave of the waves.

"Any more for the *Skylark*?" Ponsettia said, his nasal voice – Waltby realised in a shock of shame at his own panic – undisturbed and steady despite the excitement. "OK, bud, shove her off. Let's get goin'. We've a long way to go. There's a hell of a lot of sea, I guess."

three

Aircraftman (second class) Herbert Milliken had never seen quite so much sea in his young life before. Mile on mile of it, acre on acre of it, it stretched away on all sides in a rolling prairie of broken grey- and green-veined marble, the steely waves sweeping headlong from the north, rolling on like the advancing battalions of some attacking army, while the scraps of dark cloud sped past overhead beneath the slaty unforgiving heavens.

It lifted the launch in which Milliken crouched – first the port side, then the starboard side – in a hideous, sickening roll that sent his stomach quivering up to his throat, and set the masthead with its fluttering scrap of bunting clawing mightily across the sky so that Milliken's anxious eyes, watching it, rolled in unhappy arcs with it.

With his experience of seagoing no more than a trip or two to Flamborough lighthouse on his holidays at Bridlington, he had felt himself thoroughly a sailor following in the island tradition of Great Britain. But now, after eight hours – his first eight hours – on a high-speed launch and forty miles out where the tides coming from the Dogger Bank met the tides coming up through the Channel in a welter of broken water, he wasn't so sure.

He was cold and miserable and not at all certain that he was ever going to see land again. His face was green-grey and he was chilled to the marrow, in a way that unmanned him, by the unseen mist that filled the air and made everything sticky to the touch with salt rime.

He had chosen his position near the open door of the sick bay because – in spite of being in the way of everyone who came stumbling past – there he was out of the raw bite of the wind, yet not completely out of the fresh air, without which he felt he would die. Inside the sick bay, from the doorway of the wireless cabin, he could hear the occasional thin cheep of the wireless set or the confused murmur of voices. On the starboard bunk a deckhand lay smoking, his feet rolling port and starboard with the swing of the boat. A second deckhand, rolled in a duffel coat and silent, lay hidden half underneath the bunk among the rippling belts of ammunition for the point-five guns, the spare Mae Wests, and the pigeons which had been dumped aboard by an apologetic corporal three minutes before the boat had left the shore.

From time to time Milliken got a nauseating whiff of paraffin fumes from the alleyway to the forecastle which did duty as a galley and it defeated all his powers of imagination to think that a human being, on this lurching, swaying, rolling monstrosity they called a boat, could willingly labour in that stuffy alleyway over a hot stove, absorbing the fumes with every breath and still not be sick for the rest of his life. At the very thought of it Milliken's stomach gave another nervous flicker.

From the open engine-room hatch he could hear Dray, the second engineer, on full throttle with "Lili Marlene", as he pottered about between the two great 650-horsepower Thornycroft engines that drove the boat through the water. Milliken was already aware, even on the short acquaintance of one day, that Dray fancied himself as a crooner, but again, thinking of the petrol fumes and the heat in the engine-room, he wondered how he could live, let alone sing.

He watched the sweeping, white-capped waves washing the stern round, up and down and round again in sickening arcs that beat the time like the swing of some great pendulum, and tried to recall just what madness had persuaded him to volunteer for Air-Sea Rescue.

Dragged from his bed at first light by the blare of the Tannoy loud-speaker, eighteen-year-old Milliken, fresh from his training as a medical orderly, brand new on the station and still strange enough to Air Force life to treat a corporal with respect and a sergeant with wary caution, had hurried eagerly to the launch basin beyond the sea-plane hangars and climbed aboard High-Speed Launch 7525.

He had volunteered for the duty, he remembered unhappily, out of a desire to aid his country on active service rather than in the passive role of nursing the sick in the station hospital, and his anxiety not to be late had caused him to be tremendously early. The base had been deserted when he arrived and, although the black surface of the river was rippled by the wind, the basin where the launches lay was deceptively silent in the shelter of a group of buildings. The water lay still, oil-slicked and drab, and at the bottom of the slipway the scum and rubbish collected – the sticks, the bits of paper and the orange peel. Its scent was one of brine and oil and rotting wood. The gulls were squatting hunchbacked on the end of the jetty, somnolent and still. And in the air was the sharp frosty freshness of a late autumn morning.

HSL 7525 lay on the outside of the flotilla, her narrow grey deck – to Milliken unbelievably cluttered up with ropes, water casks, guns, fenders, Carley float and crash nets – sloping gently upwards past the bridge and the wheelhouse to the foredeck. She was not as beautiful as Milliken had expected – with none of the low rakish line of some of the launches he had seen – for she was built for longer ranges, but still with the high speed for inshore rescue work under the guns of the Germans. Milliken had felt an odd thrill of excitement at the thought that her powerful engines were going to carry him into operational waters, perhaps even into a brush with the enemy – for he was still young enough to be romantic about war and not long enough in the Service to have been soured by the monotony of it.

He was still standing on the after-deck by the sick bay doors, rubbing his nose in awe, when he became aware of the smallest flight sergeant he had ever seen, waiting to pass him.

"Stop picking your nose and get out of the way," the Flight Sergeant snapped. "Shove over and let the dog see the rabbit!"

Milliken turned quickly. In spite of his smallness the Flight Sergeant had something about him that made Milliken wary – bright eyes restless as fleas and a brick-red face that made him look incredibly alert and ebullient at that early hour. He was not young by any means but he had a youthfulness, an agelessness in fact, with his weathered face, his gingerish quiff and his bright young eyes, that made it difficult to guess his years.

"It's all right," he was saying with heavy sarcasm. "I'll wait. Big-hearted Arthur, that's me. Generous to a fault. I'm good at waiting. I've won prizes for waiting."

Long before he had finished, Milliken had been goaded into life. He leapt smartly to his left, caught his foot against the closed hatch of the engine-room and found himself sprawling on his knees, his feet tangled in a coil of rope.

The Flight Sergeant stared at him as though he smelled. "Go on," he said pitilessly. "Rupture yourself, do. Who the hell *are* you, anyway?"

"Milliken, sir," Milliken yelped, trying to scramble to his feet, collect his belongings, put his hat on and stand to attention all at the same time. It was only by an effort that he refrained from saluting. "Milliken, sir."

"Billycan? That's a silly bloody name – "

"No, sir. Milliken, sir. Milliken."

"Millycan, billycan, what-the-helly-can, I don't give a fish-tit. What are you doing messing up my boat? What are you? Armourer? Electrician? Sanitary wallah? Or just the man who fought the monkey in the dustbin?"

"Medical orderly, sir," Milliken stammered. "Told to report to 7525."

"Medical orderly?" The Flight Sergeant barked the words. "Medical orderly? And what were *you* in Civvy Street? Pox-doctor's clerk?"

Besides fear Milliken was now beginning to feel another emotion. He was a serious young man and had hoped to harry the enemy as a pilot when he joined up but, with the war nearing its end, he had been directed unwillingly to medicine. He had accepted the disappointment bravely and had given his whole interest to nursing – although the most he had had to do up to then was clean up after others – and such was his pride in his new profession that he found himself consumed by a dislike for the little Flight Sergeant which grew until it became utter loathing.

"Medical orderly, are you?" The Flight Sergeant was rubbing the hatred raw. "Medical orderly? As if we hadn't enough to do with one man short in hospital without having to look after bandage-bashers. Just you keep out of my way," he warned fiercely. "On a high-speed launch, you might as well learn now, the medical orderly's the lowest form of animal life. His job is only to look after survivors. The crew's job is to look after the boat."

"Yes, sir," Milliken stammered, not knowing whether to smile or look humble.

"And don't call me 'sir'," the Flight Sergeant said. "Save your 'sirs' for the skipper. His name's Treherne and he's an officer so he knows nothing and is thus entitled to be called 'sir'. He's only a lad, anyway. *I* run this boat but I let him give the orders to give him something to do – see? Mark those." He indicated the stripes and crown on his sleeve.

"Those indicate the most important rank in the Air Force. When you've been in a little longer you'll know that the sergeant is the man on whom the Air Force revolves. And a Flight Sergeant is the man who pushes the sergeant around. The Flight Sergeant is one of God's chosen few. *I'm a* Flight Sergeant."

"I see, Flight."

"Christ," the Flight Sergeant said to the open door of the sick bay. " 'I see, Flight', he says. Just like that. As if we were all pals together and had been for years. And me with twenty years' service on me back. Jesus, what a war does to the Air Force! They give you a number, a uniform and a cup of canteen tea, and you start thinking you're an airman, just because some son of Satan from Whitehall said you were a bit good during a Wings for Victory week in Wigan or somewhere. When *I* joined up, it was 'Yes, Flight *Sergeant*' and 'No, Flight *Sergeant*' and 'Three bags bloody full, Flight *Sergeant*'. Nowadays, you stand about looking as though you don't know whether you want a belch or a haircut. *Stand up!*" he bawled unexpectedly, so that Milliken, who had been listening breathlessly to the diatribe, jumped with sheer nervous terror.

To him, the little ginger-quiffed man was suddenly all the authority of all the non-commissioned officers in the whole of the Royal Air Force, terrifying, awesome, vulgar and noisy, and possessed of that biggest of all big sticks – superiority in rank. He was the parade ground, the drill book, and all the vast secretive, sly knowledge that was vested in every one of the older hands with their wrinkled grey-black uniforms and battered hats which made Milliken's new blue, his still yellow buttons and sleek forage cap look indecent.

Just when his soul was racked by his hatred the Flight Sergeant, his face red, the quiff on his forehead quivering with his anger, a tight, bounding rubber ball of a man, taut and energetic and evil, suddenly grinned, a surprising grin which changed his whole face and put lights into his eyes that Milliken had never expected.

"My name's Slingsby," he introduced himself more calmly. "Jimmy Slingsby. Jimmy the Bastard, they call me. Known throughout the Air Force. I drink blood and eat rivets."

With this last terrifying announcement he disappeared below, leaving Milliken feeling as though he had been swept backwards by a gale of wind.

While he was still recovering he heard the thump of feet on the black wooden piles of the jetty and other members of the crew began to drop aboard, all of them in various stages of untidiness and carrying side-packs, oil-skins and sea jerseys. It was only then that Milliken realised just how incredibly smart the Flight Sergeant had been. Unlike the others, he spurned a jersey and he was shaved immaculately. Every button had shone despite the early· hour, and his uniform looked as though it had recently been washed. When Milliken was to know the Flight Sergeant better he would find out that it had.

While he was still standing in amazement at the thought, Treherne, the skipper, arrived, hurrying down the ladder; young, eager as Milliken, and like Milliken a little dubious about his own ability still. Milliken saluted him carefully, as he had been trained to do on the parade ground, "Up, pause, two, down," but Treherne, in his haste, took not the slightest notice of him and then Milliken saw that no one else took the slightest notice of the skipper in their hurried efforts to prepare for sea, and he felt incredibly foolish.

By this time the deck crew were loosening the ropes which connected 7525 to the next boat in the trot in a bewildering maze which looked to Milliken like a cat's cradle. With an explosion that made him leap round in startled fear, certain that the stern of the boat had been blown off by a mine, the engines leapt to life one after the other and the vessel surged forward for a second at the creep of the propellers.

"Let go springs." Bewildered by the activity, none of which he understood, Milliken turned round, aware that Treherne had reappeared on the bridge, still struggling into a duffel coat.

"Let go springs, Skipper!"

"Let go aft!"

"All gone aft!"

"Let go forrard."

"All gone forrard."

The deckhand on the foredeck, standing alongside the winch, thrust gently at the boat alongside with his foot, and 7525 started to glide slowly across the basin towards the river.

From inside the sick bay the cheeps of the wireless set began abruptly. Milliken took up a position on the after-deck, where he had a good view, and prepared to enjoy the trip. But as he peered into the wind made by the boat's movement, and tried to take in everything at once, he was pushed aside by a red-haired individual minus a front tooth, whose name Milliken had discovered was Corporal Robb. He emerged from the sick bay door eating a colossal corned-beef sandwich and stood on the after-deck, taking in at a glance that everything was in order.

To Milliken, very stripe-conscious still and unaware of the enforced casualness of dress and discipline on a crowded small boat at sea, it seemed vaguely unfair that Robb should wear no badges of rank, no hat, no tunic – nothing, in fact, beyond a thin brown civilian sports shirt, a pair of Air Force issue trousers held up by a length of heaving-line, and a pair of boots which appalled Milliken, fresh from his training, by their lack of polish and the salt rime which gave them a pale grey colour.

"Where can I lay my stuff out?" Milliken enquired as he came back along the deck.

"Stuff?"

"My bandages and things. I brought a few of my own."

"Doc," Robb said, "if you're looking for a table or a dispensary or something, we don't possess one. But, as far as I'm concerned, you can lay your little whatnames out in a neat line all the way from bow to stern if you like. Only I advise you to tie 'em all down separately or you'll lose 'em overboard."

As he disappeared, still eating, Milliken reflected that somebody was pulling his leg.

He blushed a little, classing Robb with the Flight Sergeant, and decided to keep his own counsel in future. He soon recovered from his humiliation and even began to feel heroic and strong in the sharp breeze. Not long from his aeroplane models and *Modern Boy,* he could almost imagine himself – quite forgetting the role he'd been trained for – preparing to give battle to the enemy. He knew suddenly how Drake and Hawkins must have felt as they'd beat down on the Armada, and the emotions Nelson must have experienced as he first sighted the great white warships of France in Trafalgar Bay. Then, just on the peak of his surging excitement, the wind whipped the top off a wave on the port bow and a bucketful of icy water slashed across his face, with a shock that took his breath away, and began to trickle down his neck.

Milliken ducked hurriedly, wiped himself dry with his handkerchief, and looked about him again more cautiously. Treherne was huddled on the bridge now, his cap jammed low over his eyes, looking to the envious Milliken incredibly young to have command of this thundering, powerful boat. He was staring into the wind over the port bow at the spit of land they were passing that ended with the wreck of a ship, red-brown and rusty, its masts at a crazy angle, a gaunt, cigarette-shaped smoke-stack cocked drunkenly over.

"Going to be rough, Flight," Milliken heard him call into the wheelhouse where, he presumed, the terrifying Flight Sergeant was handling the wheel.

He failed to hear the Flight Sergeant's reply above the din of the engines but he decided that if this was what the skipper himself called rough he had nothing to fear.

Even as the thought crossed his mind the launch left the lee of the spit of land and hit the first of the waves that were sweeping across the mouth of the river. Her bow rose abruptly and smashed down in a stomach-catching drop into the valley of the next wave, with a crash that seemed to Milliken to have shattered the whole bottom of the boat to flying splinters of matchwood. For a second his feet were clear of the deck as it fell away beneath him, and a stifled yelp of fear escaped him. While he was still in the air he grabbed for a handhold, and just then his heels hit the deck again with a jar that shook every tooth in his head.

"Throttle her back a fraction, Flight," Treherne said and, to the chastened Milliken's astonishment, there appeared to be no trace of alarm in his demeanour.

The boat continued to plunge into the waves in a manner that set the mast rattling as though it were loose. Milliken glanced upwards and with each shuddering jar saw the stays and halliards quivering and the masthead racing across the clouds. He looked hurriedly away as he felt the first tremors of sickness in his stomach, then, wondering what he had let himself in for, he heard Treherne speak again to the Flight Sergeant.

"All right, Flight, bring her on to course now."

Above the tumult of the engines Milliken heard the groan of planks as the boat swung from south-west to south-east in a ninety-degree turn. She canted slowly over at a forty-five-degree angle, so that the starboard side of the hull vanished beneath the white foam that raced hissing past, and Milliken was startled to realise that the waves washed only a few inches from his feet now instead of five feet as before. As he felt the drag of the boat's swing pulling him over the side, and he imagined himself flung into the boiling foam and lost for ever before they had even noticed his departure, he held on tighter to the handrail and, clenching his teeth in terror, dug in his toes as the boat heeled further over.

For a moment it seemed to hang shudderingly on its beam ends, its masthead along the wave-tops, on the point of turning turtle before it disappeared beneath the water. Then slowly, terribly slowly, it heaved itself up on to an even keel again, and Milliken's breath came out in a heavy sigh of relief.

Dray, in the engine-room, was still singing unmoved, his husky voice rising thinly above the roar of the engines – "Amour, Amour, Amour", by this time, it appeared.

All the deck crew beyond one lookout on the bridge had disappeared below. The cheeps still came from the wireless cabin. No one except Milliken seemed to be at all disturbed.

Long after Milliken had been frozen stiff by the bitter wind that was blowing, the corkscrewing of the boat through the water had continued – long after he had lost the first fine rapture of excitement and was crouched down on the sick bay steps trying to keep warm. It went on through the red blur of sea-sickness that welled up suddenly and left him sprawling on the deck retching his heart up, his blue fingers clutching the lifeline; it went on while he crawled miserably back to the sick bay, wondering painfully how he could ever be expected to attend to the injured feeling as he did, wondering in fact how he could ever even get on his feet again. He suffered it through a period of purgatory in the paraffin-scented galley, whither he was driven by the iron voice of the nightmarish little Flight Sergeant to help cut sandwiches for the crew, chivvied in addition as he stumbled over the high step to pick his bloody feet up. It went on while, his job accomplished, he slowly recovered once more in the sick bay, his head ringing with the metallic howl of the engines.

He had lost all sense of time by now and, as the corkscrewing had continued, all thought had finally disappeared, too, in a misery of cold and damp and weariness. Then without warning, and when he was least expecting relief, the engines stopped in a thankful silence that came like a shock and the boat slowed down as it lost its way through the water. Corporal Robb, on his way aft through the sick bay with a message for the wireless operators, threw a white submarine jersey at Milliken. "Better put it on, doc," he said. "It's cold. Smells like frost. There's a duffel coat, too, if you'd like one."

"What do we do now?" Milliken asked through stiff, chilled lips as he pulled the jersey on.

"Get your swede down, doc," Robb said. "You've a long wait ahead of you. We're on rendezvous now and we stay here till we're sent for or told to go home. This is the exciting part."

Over six boring, weary hours had elapsed since the engines had stopped and since then the boat had rolled monotonously and inevitably port and starboard, port and starboard, port and starboard. Beyond the look-out and a brief attempt by Robb at fishing from the stern, no interest seemed to be shown in anything – least of all in Milliken – by anyone, and the sky seemed to grow greyer and chillier as it pressed lower down on the swaying masthead where the rag of ensign flapped noisily.

As the first violence went out of the motion of the boat Milliken had thanked God for the relief it brought but now, as she swung beam-on to the waves and the roll took the place of the corkscrewing, a short, vicious roll due to the narrow beam, Milliken realised he was worse off, not better.

For a while he tried hard to sleep, but he was cold and with every lurch he had to dig in his elbows to keep himself on the bunk, and in the end he gave it up, more exhausted by his efforts than by the jarring crashes at speed that had wearied the muscles of his legs.

Feeling like a pea rattled round inside a dried pod, he sat upright on the bunk, only to find in his misery that he was obliged to listen to the incessant talking of Tebbitt, the deckhand on the other bunk.

"Never get back to base in time to meet that damned train," seemed to be the gist of what he was saying, and it kept coming across to Milliken like a Greek chorus to everything Tebbitt had to say, in waves of despair that filled the sick bay with gloom. "Blasted tub will never make it back for me to get to the station. Always my lousy luck. Whenever I want to go somewhere, we don't get the 'Return to base' until it's too late." He was reciting his worry like an incantation and even Milliken, young as he was, could see he was trying to invoke good fortune by a reiteration of possible bad fortune.

"It's due in in the early hours," he went on, "and I've got permission to be out of camp to meet it. Gus Westover" – he indicated the man lying among the ammunition and spare Mae Wests below him and to his right – "he's offered to do my boat guard tonight so I can get away. But I never shall. We're bound to be late."

Tebbitt was a big man with a fresh round face in which his eyes seemed oddly out of place. His cheeks were those of a farmer, pink and white and plump, yet his eyes were those of a worried city clerk.

"It's my wife, Hilda," he went on, and Milliken, who had tried to listen at first as a means of taking his mind off the incessant rolling of the boat, was by now silently praying in his nightmare of sickness to be allowed to die in peace. "She's coming down to stay with me in the town for a week or two.

Canteen-worker, you know. Londoner by birth. I met her up in Tyneside when we were stationed at Blyth. Doesn't like North Country people though. And now she's coming down to stay here for a bit. Hoped she might get a job round here, so we could be near each other. But it's a bit near London for her and she might not settle."

It was beginning to dawn on Milliken by this time that Tebbitt was bewailing not a missed train but an unhappy marriage, and he began to take a distinct and hearty dislike to the absent Hilda Tebbitt. "Likes to be called Linda," Tebbitt pointed out, pressing his woes on Milliken as though the sharing of them would make his load easier. "She always did say that if she had half a chance to get back to London I wouldn't see her out of it again in a hurry. And sometimes I think she's in dead earnest."

Milliken began to be certain of it, deciding privately in a burst of bad temper which made him feel a little better that if Tebbitt was the only example of a northerner she'd come across he wasn't surprised.

"Reckon she's been saving as hard as she can for the train fare home for some time." Tebbitt was sitting on the opposite bunk with an ease that Milliken envied, swaying backwards and forwards, his hands miraculously in his pockets instead of gripping the bunk. "Only she's that daft with money. Always blues it on some soft knick-knack. Last time it was a plaid coat to go with a green suitcase I bought for her at Christmas. Daft with money, she is. Dead daft."

The boat gave an unexpected lurch, which slung Milliken sideways on his back to the deck. Tebbitt picked him up, still talking, and helped him back on to the bunk. He was obviously sick with worry and anxious to share it with anyone, even a stranger. Milliken was beginning to suspect that the rest of the crew had heard his story so often they wouldn't listen any more and that Tebbitt had to take advantage of any uninitiated audience whose attention would give him courage. Milliken even began to think the frightening Flight Sergeant might be a pleasant change.

"Says she wouldn't mind the V.1s or the V.2s if she could only get back to London," Tebbitt was saying earnestly. "All she wants is London again – with shelter-life and everything, too! She says she misses the pubs and the dance halls and things. So I've persuaded her to come down here for a bit and see if she likes it. I've got her some digs for a week or two. She'll be on her way now, I suppose."

He fished in his wallet and produced a photograph, which he passed over. Milliken was already quite used to the nostalgic Service ritual of photograph-showing and he studied with over-elaborate interest the picture of a tall handsome blonde whose good looks were marred by her tight mouth and her too strong chin.

"She says if I'm not at the station to meet her she'll get back in the train – it's a London train – and go straight on with it." Tebbitt laughed nervously and mirthlessly. " 'I'm not going to be on my own in some strange town,' she says. 'Not on my Jack Jones.' She's like that. Straight John Bull. Says what she thinks. And it'll be just my luck to get back too late to meet her. I'm sure we shan't make it. Aren't you?"

Milliken hadn't the slightest idea but he nodded and said he thought they'd make it all right.

"Well, maybe we will," Tebbitt agreed gloomily, suddenly cast down into a vast huddled heap of despair, a colossus of unhappiness, so that Milliken wasn't sure whether he wanted to get home in time or not, whether he wanted to meet his wife or be free of her for good.

"So long as I can meet the train, it's all right," he said. "But we shall never make it. The engines will break down or something."

The gloomy jeremiad went on and on, pausing only while Milliken went outside to be sick once more, and starting again like a serial story as he crawled back to the bunk. It did not come to a stop even when he finally turned his back. When Robb entered the cabin, eating another sandwich, and interrupted, Milliken actually managed to raise a thankful smile in spite of his stomach.

"You still alive, doc?" Robb grinned. "How do you feel?"

Milliken gave a nervous, unhappy snigger and Robb went on. "Why don't you go into the forecastle?" he said. "There's some hot soup there. It'll warm you up."

"*Self-heating* soup?" Tebbitt asked as Milliken lowered his feet cautiously to the deck preparatory to a dash, holding his nose, through the galley. "Is that all there is again?"

"Self-heating soup and meat sandwiches. A cup of tea if we can keep a kettle on the stove long enough."

"I'll have another cigarette."

The forecastle had a damp, misty look about it in the weak glow of the deckhead lights that made Milliken wary. He lifted his foot cautiously over the step, only to be flung to his knees into the forecastle as the boat gave a fearsome roll, and in alarm he realised it was heaving if anything even more violently than the sick bay. Robb helped him to his feet with an "Upsy-Daisy" that made Milliken hate him for his condescension, and while he was still having difficulty in wedging himself on a seat Robb thrust a can of steaming soup into his hand and flung a spoon down beside him.

"Here, fill your boots."

Milliken almost dropped the tin as it burned his hand, and he groped frantically for a handkerchief, gasping at the pain in his fingers' ends. With him in the forecastle were only Robb and a man he recognised as Corporal Skinner, the engine-room NCO. The forecastle was silent except for the slap of the water outside and the clanking of a couple of empty soup tins that rolled maddeningly backwards and forwards in the rubbish box on the deck. An oilskin swung in stiff, jerky arcs across the white-painted bulkhead and the smoke from Corporal Skinner's cigarette-end hung in the air, moving in a curiously erratic fashion to the roll of the boat. The forecastle had an oddly crowded look about it.

Milliken glanced about him with unhappy eyes. The low deckhead made Robb stand with his shoulders stooped and, on the table, a loaf of bread slid from side to side with the bread knife, chasing an empty mug round and round the polished surface.

Skinner was looking quizzically at Robb. "When's the 'Return to base' coming through?" he asked. "I'm sick of this bit of sea."

"It's all alike," Robb pointed out. "The other bits are just the same."

Skinner stared at his cigarette, then burst out explosively in a fretful anger.

"Christ, I'm sick of this bloody boat," he said. "I seem to have looked at nothing but these bulkheads for months. I never want to see a boat again after the war. Never as long as I live. Twelve men and a medical orderly" – Milliken noticed the differentiation with bitterness – "to say nothing of pigeons, crammed into this damned tub, all doing nothing just in case some silly bastard falls in the sea. I wish I had an office job. I wish I was a flight mechanic again. If only we could have a spot of decent weather it would make it easier. These bitches roll so much."

"We had some sun a fortnight ago." Robb grinned. "About ten minutes."

"Sun?" Skinner went on with his noisy whine while Milliken watched him with wide inexperienced eyes. "It's about time we all had a bit of leave. That's what. A few hours' sleep at night, without that flaming Tannoy squawking at you fit to bust to get down to the base. Day after day. Week after week. Not even time for a fag in the canteen. It's Saturday today but there'll be no night out for *us*, and there'll be no lie-in tomorrow, Sunday or no Sunday. We'll be staring at the sea same as usual while everyone else's having their breakfast." He paused and jerked a finger at Robb. "And that's another thing, the grub! If we're lucky and it's not too rough, we can have a cup of tea, providing the kettle can be tied tight enough to the stove. And the lid can be tied tight enough to the kettle. And the cork will stay in the spout. And the stove don't break loose with the rolling. Sandwiches and self-heating soup for meals!"

"You can always have corned beef for a change." Robb took a bite at his own sandwich and spoke with his mouth full.

Skinner glanced up sourly.

"What's the matter, Skinner?" Robb asked. "Spit it out. It isn't really the grub, is it?"

"I'll put a spanner in the starboard engine one of these days and have a week up the slip for an engine-change. Then we'd get some time off."

"In danger of missing a date?"

Milliken watched Robb in wonderment that he should know all of Skinner's affairs. He had not yet become aware of the absence of any secrets in a boat crowded with crew. Secrets, like duffel coats and jerseys, were everybody's property among men living constantly on top of each other.

Skinner glanced up at Robb, a look of disgust on his face.

"A WAAF in camp," he said sourly. "You have to have your bints in camp these days. No chance of getting one outside. Issue underwear and brass buttons. Jesus!"

Robb was spooning soup now from a tin, his back to Milliken, leaning with one arm through the forward hatch ladder to steady himself. "And now there's alarm and despondency in the Waafery because there's no sign yet of the great lover, Canteen-Cowboy Skinner? That it?" he asked.

"It's a good job for Air-Sea Rescue there are WAAFS," Skinner said with an odd grin that changed his face. "I don't know what we'd do without 'em, bless 'em. We couldn't live

45

a normal sex life cooped up on this bastard. You have to get what you can." He grinned again and flipped the ash from his cigarette. "When *I* go out, chum, the ASR on my badge means 'Advance, Strike, Retire'. They think I'm out harrying the Huns up and down the ocean from bunghole to breakfast time. It pays dividends after dark when I start harrying the WAAFS. Every girl loves a hero. And I'm a hero who's prepared to love every girl."

Robb smiled in a knowing way that made Milliken suddenly think he'd had more women in his life than he knew what to do with.

"From the day you discovered you were a different shape from women, Skinner," he said, "you were lost to decent mankind."

"Whacko!" Skinner grinned again, obviously unworried by the insult. "I was going to meet her at the station dance tonight," he said.

"You'll be back in time to take her home." Robb pointed out. "If you're lucky, anyway. And that's the only part you're interested in, I'll bet – the bit that follows the dance."

"She promised me last night she'd see me there."

"You with her last night?" Robb glanced sharply under his eyebrow at Skinner and even Milliken saw his expression change. His blue eyes became colder and his smile faded.

"Had a few drinks in the pub outside the camp."

"Thought you were overhauling the oil-feed on the port engine?"

"Oh, that!" Skinner bent hurriedly and drew quickly on his cigarette. "That! Hell, I did that in a few minutes!"

"Thought it was a big job."

"Not that big."

"Bigger than a few minutes, all the same, I'll bet."

"I patched it up." Skinner kept his eyes on his cigarette and Milliken watched them both carefully, aware of a sudden coolness in Robb's manner.

"You'd better not let Chiefy know," Robb said. "He'll shop you if he knows you've skimped the job."

"I didn't skimp it. I taped it up." Skinner looked up quickly, then bent over the cigarette again. "Listen, d'you think I'm going to roll about in the bloody bilges taking jubilee clips off when I've got my best suit on?"

"You've always got your blasted best suit on," Robb snorted.

Skinner grinned, unabashed. "Have to be ready," he said. "Can't waste time, when we do get some off. You know the Boy Scouts' motto. 'Be Prepared'."

But Robb's smile didn't come back. "One thing Chiefy's fussy about and that's engines," he said.

"The Lad said I could go when I'd finished. I asked him."

"I'll bet the Skipper hadn't the slightest idea what you were doing. He's only a kid straight from navigational school, anyway." Robb spoke with the authority of his twenty-eight years.

"He said it was OK."

"How long did it take you? Honestly."

Skinner lay back on the bunk and stared at the smoke he was blowing through his nostrils. The cheerless little forecastle was silent for a while except for the monotonous clank of the empty tins and the slither of the loaf across the table. "Quarter of an hour," he said.

"Quarter of an hour?" Robb raised his eyebrows. "I thought it was a job lasting all evening. Chiefy got us off stand-by duty so you could do it. If it had been a quarter of an hour's job he wouldn't have done that."

"He's too keen. Always wanting to get to sea. The engines got us here, didn't they? They'll get us back. What more do you want?"

"We might want 'em to give us full revs in a hurry and for a long time. Somebody might be in the drink."

Skinner glanced up sharply, his face heavily shadowed by the weak lights in the deckhead.

"God, some of you people! Are you and Chiefy after a gong or a mention in despatches or something? All you ever want to do is fetch somebody out of the drink."

"That's what we're here for, isn't it?"

"Ah, you're too bloody keen! This was a cushy billet before you two were posted to it. Now it's work all the time. I tell you, you're too keen."

"It's a pity you're not *more* keen. We shouldn't have so many breakdowns if you were."

"There's nothing wrong with my engines."

"7526 doesn't get so many breakdowns."

"She's a better boat."

"She's a sister ship."

Milliken, feeling better after the soup, listened to the exchanges anxiously, only half understanding the import of them.

"Listen," Skinner was saying. "This old bastard has had a warp in her ever since she last went up the slip for an overhaul. Chiefy Rollo got her on the cradle wrong. He's not your fussy Chiefy Slingsby. Haven't you ever seen the way the bow whips when she hits a wave?"

"Skinner, I don't care if she's got a granny knot in her; it isn't the boat that makes 7526 smarter off the mark. It's not the engines either, come to that."

"It's the crew, eh? God, all I ever hear from you and Slingsby is 7526. What's the matter – trying to do the same as Loxton, that gong-hunting skipper of theirs? I get sick of you two wanting to know why we can't get more out of her. Chiefy Rollo never bothered. It's just luck that 7526's a faster boat. Their fitter always was a lucky swine. *He's* got his third stripe. *I* haven't."

"Perhaps it's because he overhauls his oil-feed when it goes haywire, instead of taking a girl to a pub."

Robb pulled himself to his feet and lurched towards the galley. He was still crossing the step when the sudden high-pitched squeak of morse from the wireless cabin stopped him in his tracks.

"Hello" – he cocked an ear – "here it is, Skinner. The one thing you can do well 'Return to base'."

"Those joyous words!"

Skinner began to lower his legs casually to the deck, whistling softly, then the high-pitched chirrup of the morse stopped. "Botty!" the voice of Knox, the wireless operator, yelling for his mate came through the open doorway, disembodied and urgent. "Stand by to check!" And there was the thump of boots on a ladder.

They heard the Flight Sergeant's feet hit the deck of the wheelhouse as he leapt up from the bunk up there where he had been sitting. Robb made a dive for the wheelhouse ladder and they heard the Flight Sergeant's voice as he appeared above.

"That's not the 'Return to base', Robby," he was saying. "Knocker can read that before it's decoded."

Suddenly, miraculously, without any visible signs beyond the abrupt silence, the boat began to wear an air of attention that was manifest even to the inexperienced Milliken, now sitting bolt upright in the forecastle watching the taut figure of Skinner, halted motionless by the galley entrance. There was silence from the wireless cabin for a while and Milliken found himself holding his breath and listening to the slap and splash of water under the boat's chine, and the clank of the soup tins in the box by his feet.

Then he heard a pencil rattle sharply in the frame of the hatchway between the wireless cabin and the bridge.

"Chiefy! Chiefy!" The wireless operator's voice came thinly to them, muffled and small, as though he had diminished in stature, and they heard the Flight Sergeant's feet and Knox's voice again.

"It's us, Flight! Kite in the drink. North-east of here. Botty's decoding the bearing now."

"Kite in the drink!" Slingsby's voice came down to them, then it rose to a shout. "SKINNER!"

Skinner, already staring up into the wheelhouse from the gloom at the bottom of the wheelhouse ladder, indulged in a little wishful thinking. " 'Return to base', Chiefy?"

"Kite in the drink. Start up!"

Skinner turned away, his face angry, and stumbled noisily towards the sick bay and the engine-room.

"And wake the Skipper as you go past," Slingsby shouted. "On deck, everybody!"

Milliken dived for the sick bay and, reaching for his bag of bandages and lints was on the point of laying them out and nervously inspecting them when he remembered Robb's words at the beginning of the day, and decided to leave them where they were.

He was filled with an exultant excitement. Here, at last, he felt he was on the point of serving his country. He was really going to war this time.

Then the port engine exploded into life with a roar and a splash of water astern, and the boat began to surge forward a little. The starboard engine crashed into movement a moment later and, as Slingsby in the wheelhouse moved the engine-room telegraph to ahead and the throttles to full speed, the bow of the great boat lifted swiftly and the stern settled to the down-drag of the screws.

As the seas hit the port bow on her swing round to the north-east she canted alarmingly in one of those sickening rolls over on to her beam ends. Milliken hurriedly forgot his heroic feeling of going to war and clutched wildly for a handhold as he was slung in a one-legged dance from one side of the sick bay to the other; then the launch was butting frantically into the waves in a series of shuddering jars as she headed north-east.

four

By the time Waltby and the others had settled themselves in the dinghy they were beginning to realise just how cold the wind blew, particularly against their saturated clothing. The high inflated sides of the raft offered a little protection but they were too near to the surface of the sea not to get some of its reflected chill.

Huddled between Ponsettia and Mackay, Waltby looked round at the others and it seemed he saw them for the first time. Previously, he had had no time to study them in the hasty introductions before taking off, and these men who crouched with him in the rubber boat among the odds and ends of equipment they had managed to snatch up before the aircraft struck the water seemed to be complete strangers.

Harding was a tall fair young man, with the aged look that comes with responsibility, the look the war had inflicted on so many schoolboys. His features were good and about them there was the same easy, unaffected self-confidence that showed in his manners and speech. Ponsettia, the navigator, was small and slight with a serious dry manner which belied an obvious humour. It was as though he had formed his humour into a protective weapon against his own slightness – as though it were some defence against the vastness of Canada where he came from and the heftiness of his Canadian friends. It was like the great yellow moustache he affected, now hanging wetly on either side of his mouth – something that added a little to his stature.

51

Mackay, the last of the three, was a big man, the biggest in the dinghy, hefty and hard-faced, and Waltby remembered, on being introduced, forming an opinion of a man not given to introspection, someone confident in his own size and his own ability to take hold of life and beat the best out of it, and yet someone who had somehow lost his sense of humour in doing so – as though he had never had the leisure to be happy merely for the sake of happiness.

As though to prove his independence, without help from the others, Mackay had taken off his tie and knotted it round his left hand as a tourniquet, so that the black material bit cruelly into his whitened flesh and reduced the bleeding from the gash in it to a mere occasional spot of bright blood that fell into the water sloshing about their feet.

It was in the first few minutes of relaxation, as they were all getting their breath back, that Waltby first noticed the motion of the dinghy. Its bounding, sweeping movements were brought to his attention when he realised in a state of alarm that he was having to hang on with his free hand to stop himself sliding helplessly about the well. It rose slowly out of the trough of a grey wave, as though climbing by its own power up the veins of foam that the breeze dragged down from the crest, balanced for a second on the top, and lurched sickeningly over so that he was flung against Ponsettia before skating perilously down the other side in a stomach-heaving slide.

For a second, as they hovered on the top, Waltby could see across the empty miles of sea the broken surface of the horizon. Mile upon mile, the sea stretched grey and forbidding beyond the curve of the earth, and for a man used to the land there was something awful and terrifying about the loneliness and the absence of other life upon it, something in the wetness and the smell that clutched at the heart. Waltby had never seen the sea so close before. Watching it from an aircraft or the deck of a great ship, he had never realised its power, but down here in the dinghy, as though he were one with it, he sensed its barbaric strength from the ease with which it lifted them. A feeling of desolation crept over him as he stared, so that he was momentarily unaware of the other three, better drilled in how to use a dinghy, settling down and sorting out their belongings from the pile among their feet. Then through the motion he became aware of the ache in his head and, putting his hand up, realised it had been bleeding and the blood had dried to a hard, cracked enamel on his cheek.

He heard Ponsettia speaking to him and the cheerful voice drove his own old-womanish misery out of his mind.

"Tough tit, ending in the drink," the Canadian was saying, without however seeming unduly disturbed himself. "Just think, but for this the Prime Minister and the boys in the Cabinet would have been whooping it up with you for that lot at 10, Downing Street, or wherever it is these guys whoop it up." He indicated the briefcase. "Just our luck to get pooped in the engine by a Messerschmidt when you've got that."

"Christ," Mackay growled. "Anyone'd think it was the plans for the atom bomb, the fuss you lot are making."

Waltby pretended not to hear. "All I heard was the bang," he said.

"Sure, I know. Worst of being a passenger. Can't see a goddamned thing. Still, if it's any comfort, we returned the compliment and Jerry's in the drink himself now somewhere south of us – sitting on his own little rubber platform wondering what happened. Boy, he sure is going to be lonely!"

"All the same," Ponsettia went on thoughtfully after a pause, "his wet behind don't help us none. And me, I had a date for tonight."

"Another new popsie, Canada?" Harding enquired, and to Waltby, concerned with the safety of the briefcase and the wretchedness of their condition, they both seemed empty-headed and trivial in their chatter.

"Not me," Ponsettia replied. "Same as last week. And the week before. It's sure enough the real thing this time. Hell, I didn't pluck up the courage to kiss her for two nights running. Isn't that enough to prove it? No necking. We go for long walks, holding hands – me, Joe Ponsettia, the scourge of the Waafery."

They all laughed, but the laughter died quickly, as though the chill froze it in motion, and Waltby realised abruptly that the banter had been merely to keep their spirits up – empty but more important than he had realised. Then Harding called them briskly together and Waltby, who'd been watching the sea again, was glad to draw his eyes away from the fascinating but frightening movement of the waves.

"Well, now we're here," the pilot was saying, "the first thing we'd better do is try to look after ourselves. Anybody any suggestions?"

"We'd better get the sail rigged," Mackay said quickly. "And make sure the flares work. And there's a hand-operated squawk box here that sends out a wireless signal."

"OK, Captain Bligh, take it easy." Ponsettia waved a hand. "There's no hurry. No need to go busting a gut. We're here for quite a bit yet."

"Think so?" Mackay said fiercely, his words bursting out of him as though they were infected with his own energy. "Not if I can help it."

"That's just the point," the Canadian grinned. "You can't."

"Can't I?" Mackay wrenched off his helmet, and his flattened, greasy hair was ruffled into spikes by the wind. "Can't I? I've been in trouble before, chum, and got out of it. When I was in Greece I'd have been a prisoner if I hadn't killed a Jerry. With my bare hands I killed him." He crooked his fingers and stared at them as though he were suddenly afraid of their power. "When I was in the desert I walked forty miles back from a crashed kite. In that sunshine," he said, trying in his inarticulate way to impress them with the heat and the sand and the flies and the brassy glare which had seared into his memory so that he would never forget it. "I got out of those two, didn't I, with my own efforts?"

"Maybe you did, bud," Ponsettia said quietly. "But I guess this is one you won't get out of by your own efforts – not unless you're a sea lion or something."

"I'll get out," Mackay said with angry determination, as though he were challenging them to dispute the statement.

"In a pig's eye," Ponsettia insisted. "Not by your own efforts, bud. This is one of the times when you've gotta sit and wait."

Mackay seemed to lose patience. "Aw, go to hell," he said. "Let's get on with something. We'd better get the squawk box operating first. At least then we'll be doing something towards saving ourselves."

"If you nip over the stern," Ponsettia said slyly, "you can probably push us ashore. How's your breast stroke?"

Mackay gave him a sharp look, obviously uncertain in his humourless way whether the Canadian was pulling his leg or not.

Harding interrupted. "How about you, sir?" he asked Waltby. "Have you any suggestions?"

Waltby jumped as he realised he was being addressed, and was at once conscious that it was a mere gesture of politeness and respect for his rank. He had been absorbed in the growing friction between Mackay and the navigator and had been crouching between them, fiercely trying not to look at the disturbing motion of the sea which held him like the eyes of a snake.

"I really don't think I can contribute much," he said uncertainly. "I'm entirely in your hands. All I want is to get this briefcase back to where it'll be of some use. Consider me one of the crew."

His voice died away to a croak as he finished and he licked his lips nervously. The lurch and slide of the dinghy over the waves was filling him with a trembling nausea. Now that he had time to think about it, now that the excitement of getting aboard was over, he realised how violent the motion was. Every time the dinghy balanced on the broken crest of a wave and slid down the other side his stomach plunged away with it.

"How about trailing some fluorescein on the water?" Mackay queried. "Makes a big marker."

"Better save it until we see an aircraft," Harding said. "No point in wasting it." He was little more than a boy and he spoke quietly but there was no disputing the authority in his voice. As he finished the dinghy lurched again and he winced and put his hand to his side. Mackay leaned over towards him immediately.

"Skipper," he said, "you all right?"

"I'm all right."

"How's the bread-basket?"

"Oh, dry up!" Harding grinned, faintly embarrassed. But his smile was tight and not very convincing. "It's a bit sore, that's all."

"Sure you haven't broken something?"

"I'm damned sure I have! A rib, I expect. But it's not as bad as all that."

"Skip, let's have a look." Mackay's voice suddenly became urgent, but Harding shoved him away.

"God, you're worse than an old woman."

"Well, you never know." Mackay seemed to feel no resentment at the rebuke. He sat back, his eyes watching Harding, noting with satisfaction that he wore a leather flying jacket and appeared to be warm enough in spite of his pale face. Then he sat up sharply.

"Skip," he said, "you haven't got flying boots on!"

"No, old boy," Harding said. "Nor my winter combinations. I borrowed these from a bloke where we forced-landed. I forgot to swap 'em back. Somebody's going to be a bit browned off, I expect." He stared suddenly at Mackay. "Here, cheese it, Mac. You're making me feel embarrassed."

He pulled himself upright as the dinghy climbed slowly up a moving wave and began its sickening slide down into the next trough. They had lost contact with the aircraft already. It had not taken the tide long to carry them away from the waterlogged machine.

"Well," Harding said, examining the dinghy, "this job seems to have inflated all right. It's hard enough. How about paddling round for a bit? We might find something floating that will be useful. A parachute, for instance. If we could pick up a parachute it would be just the thing to wrap round us. Might keep the wind off a bit. We're pretty wet and exposure's as great a danger as running out of food."

Waltby felt a flood of shivering guilt as he remembered the inexperience which had led him to fall into the sea so that Ponsettia had had to go in after him.

"Blokes have survived days in a dinghy when they could beat the cold," Harding went on. "It's up to us. Besides, any kite that comes near would spot a parachute more quickly, being white."

Glad to have something to do, they freed the paddles with difficulty – for the dinghy was crowded and they had not yet got used to their proximity to each other – and tried to propel themselves through the water, leaning over the maddeningly high sides to scoop at the sea. But they couldn't make the dinghy ascend the waves just when they wanted to, they found – it seemed to prefer to make its own way up – and they had to abandon their plan and lie back, gasping with the action.

Then Mackay pointed to a scattering of wreckage floating a short distance away.

"There's a piece of wood or something among that lot over there, Skipper," he said. "Let's get hold of it. It would make an extra paddle. Then we might be able to get along."

"Looks splintered to me," Harding observed.

"Might bust the old rubber bag we're riding on," Ponsettia agreed.

Waltby said nothing, clutching his briefcase to him in a wretched silence. He felt ill and completely lost and bewildered in this swiftly moving world of young men which, he realised, had left him behind years before, and he became uneasily aware how much more fitted he was to wage war from behind a desk.

He'd been too long away from the squadrons, he thought, too long away from the young men who flew the planes, the young men who were the breath and life of the Air Force. He'd spent too much time among the thinkers and not enough among the men who did the work. He suddenly felt, watching the three young men opposite him taking active measures to save their lives, that his mind had been running too long on the rails of theory, without the refreshing halts when the muscles took over. He'd spent too much time in his office and at his drawing board. He'd grown stuffy and middle-aged too soon, and he was aware of his plump pale face and the incipient stomach, which made his uniform bag uncertainly. I'm beginning to look like a damned shop manager, he thought, instead of an airman. I've been behaving like a city clerk too long to be a soldier. Still, he excused himself, for the scientist – even the Service scientist – there wasn't much chance to swagger down foreign streets and shake off the cobwebs a bit. Someone had to fight the war from behind a desk.

As the thoughts slipped by in his mind like a set of flipped cards in the files in his office, he was watching the others lifting themselves up in the dinghy to see over the intervening waves that came in inexorable phalanxes from the north, in a slow marking time like the seconds ticked silently off by a moving line on the face of an electric clock. Then a wave lifted the dinghy up again and they got another quick glimpse of the piece of jagged wood, green-painted and floating limply a few yards away.

"The ends look pretty rough to me," Harding said.

"And it sure is safer," Ponsettia pointed out dryly, "to have a dinghy and no paddles than an extra paddle and no dinghy."

They settled back once more against the round, tightly blown sides of the raft, which had a comforting hardness against their backs.

"Water's pretty high in here," Mackay remarked, staring at his feet.

"Better bale." Harding started to look about him for something to scoop out the water and his eyes fell on Mackay's hand. "You'd better lay off the baling with that," he said.

"Not likely," Mackay growled. "I can bale as well as anybody."

"Don't be a stupid clot, man."

"I can bale."

"OK. If you like." Harding shrugged. "What're we going to bale with?"

"Use my helmet." Mackay held up the helmet from which he had taken the earphones and wire lead. "Might be some good."

"You're an optimist," Harding retorted, studying it. "If you ask me, it'll make a lousy baler. Still, here goes."

"That briefcase would shift a bit of water." Mackay was eyeing Waltby. The briefcase seemed to be crystallising into a symbol of his ready aggressiveness. "Holds quite a bit. How about it?"

"I think not," Waltby said quietly, already aware of Mackay's hostility towards him.

"You could shove the papers in your pockets."

"I think not," Waltby said again, feeling more than ever like a stuffy old aunt.

"Can't see why not," Mackay persisted.

"Wrap up, Mac," Harding snapped and Mackay fell into a resentful silence, resentful not against Harding but against Waltby and more particularly against his briefcase and all it seemed to him to represent – the brass-hats, the cups of tea from WAAFS, the hide-bound traditions of the Service against which he had always rebelled without ever fully understanding them, the parades and the orders from the high-ups to such as himself, the flying men who were winning the war for the office-bashers. It represented the mistakes and the fumbling and the absence of equipment, everything that had bogged the war down and dragged it on into its sixth weary year while he only wanted to get back to Civvy Street with his plans for the future, plans which he had to keep thrusting into the junk-room of wartime, the place where all the peaceful pursuits had to be stored, gathering dust and growing old, some of them never to emerge again. The plans which drove him on and on to finish his two operational flying tours, the plans which, in fact, had been responsible for his struggles for freedom in Greece and the Desert and even here and now in the dinghy.

Mackay's plans were only trivial compared with the vast machinations of great countries but, to Mackay, they were important. They were concerned only with a little street-corner shop he had started in the last uneasy days of peace but to Mackay they were Casablanca and Teheran and the Freedom of Nations, and he grew more impatient with every day he had to go on leaving them stacked away in the dark.

He stared hard at Waltby, not in the least abashed by the broad ring on each of the shoulders of his saturated coat, then, still nursing his anger to himself, he tried to make himself comfortable among the conglomeration of feet, legs and the odd bits of equipment attached by cord to the dinghy.

"Say, did we have any pigeons with us?" Ponsettia asked suddenly.

"Yes." Harding looked up. "They put 'em aboard before we left. We were flying a Coastal Command Hudson, so we had to have pigeons. The fact that we were flying the thing to the boneyard didn't matter. We had to have the pigeons because there was somewhere in the aircraft for the poor little blighters to sit. Now they're drowned."

"Poor little bastards." Ponsettia sighed. "Me, I'm fond of animals and birds. There was one I remember used to fly with us when we were doing Atlantic sweeps from Cornwall. It had lovely eyes, that pigeon. Just like Betty Grable. I got quite fond of that little son-of-a-bitch before I finished. That bird had got more flying hours in than some of the boys at headquarters."

He glanced quickly at Waltby as he finished, realising he had made a *faux pas*. Waltby didn't resent the comment, but Mackay caught the glance, too, and went on maliciously. "Heard the story about the bloke who brought the pigeons into the Mess?" he asked. "He put them on the table that the chairborne blokes always use. You know the one. He left a notice on the crate. 'These birds fly,' it said. 'Do any of you birds?' They didn't like it."

Waltby caught the sharp inquisitive glance directed at him as Mackay finished but he deliberately looked the other way and pretended not to have noticed.

"Think anyone saw us?" he asked.

Again he caught that fleeting expression of malice on Mackay's face, this time also vaguely one of triumph, and he guessed it was because Mackay took the question to be one of anxiety.

"Worried about that bag of yours, sir?" Harding asked more shrewdly, and Waltby nodded.

"Shouldn't think anyone saw us ditch," Ponsettia observed. "I didn't see any ships or anything. Pity we didn't manage to get a message through."

"Hell, I never got the chance, did I?" Mackay exploded into aggressive resentment again. "The transmitter just fell to pieces in front of my eyes. I'd just time to change to distress frequency and bang out a couple of *maydays*. I didn't even have time to clamp the key down."

"That means nobody got a bearing on us," Ponsettia said. "At least, not a good one."

"I did what I was supposed to do," Mackay snorted.

"I never said you didn't, bud," Ponsettia said mildly. "OK, Mac," Harding interrupted. "Keep your hair on, old boy. Nobody's fault. Who expected to meet a Jerry here at this time of the war? Anyway, it's something that Canada got *him,* too. I never knew you were a dead shot, Canada."

"Skipper, I could hit a sparrow in a loop with a rifle. Any Canadian from River Falls could. That's nothing. But machine-guns – brother, they scare me stiff. I always shut my eyes. It was just luck."

"Anyway, it's some satisfaction to know that he's got a wet behind, too." Harding was watching the waves as he spoke and his eyes were suddenly full of questions.

"Think these things can turn over?" he asked abruptly.

"Judging by the way it's behaving at the moment," Ponsettia said, lurching against Waltby as the dinghy topped a wave, "I reckon they couldn't only turn over – I guess they could turn inside out if they tried real hard. Can we all swim?"

He glanced down at the dinghy. "It makes you think," he went on slowly, staring at the rubberised canvas they were sitting on. "Just imagine, if one of us guys had anything sharp on him that could cut this canvas – rip, zzip – we're sitting on about five hundred fathoms of ocean and nothing else."

They stared at one another for a moment, and Ponsettia's words seemed to chill their thoughts, slowly freezing into the very bones of them, like the cold that was rising out of the sea.

"That bit of canvas," the Canadian concluded soberly, "is all there is between us and the bottom of the deep blue sea."

five

From a position high above the sea you could peer down into its depths – sometimes on a clear day when the sun pierced the dark fathoms it seemed you could see the very bottom and the sad wreckage of ships. But when the water was broken into moving waves and the light was diffused by the uneven surface, you had to be content with what floated. Then spotting was not always so easy.

Ten miles away to the north of the dinghy a Walrus amphibious seaplane – a birdcage of struts and wires propelled by a noisy 750 horse-power engine – butted low over the sweeping sea into the growing wind, as though it were a storm petrel. Below it, the grey waves, oddly diminished and solidified by height, stretched as far as the pilot could see.

Lieutenant Patrick Boyle, RNVR, at the controls, peered through the Perspex in front of him, then turned to his companion who was crouched by the wireless set, his face rapt and strained as he listened to the high cheep of Morse.

Boyle raised his eyebrows but said nothing. Petty Officer Porter, his navigator, caught the gesture and shook his head. "No joy," he said. "It's a launch they're calling up, not us."

Boyle nodded and pushed the controls forward so that the blunt float nose of the plane dropped a little, and he opened the throttle wider. The thin roar of the motor rose and he could hear the wind scratching at the fuselage, as though it were a horde of small animals striving to get inside away from the cold.

Listening to it, his eyes never leaving the sea, Boyle began to sing as the speed of the heavy old-fashioned machine increased. His one great love was speed and his one great ambition was to get off Walruses on to something faster. The fact that Walruses were built to fly at low speeds for spotting carried not an atom of weight with him. He wanted to be rid of them for good and all.

The certain knowledge that he was doomed for the rest of the war to fly these same amphibious seaplanes didn't damp his spirits in the slightest. He lived in hope of being given a Seafire and flying from the deck of an aircraft carrier. There was still a chance, he told himself as regularly as he took off for his daily Channel sweep, that they would give him a conversion course on to fighters in time for the Pacific onslaught against the Japanese which was promised as soon as the German war was over. And though he knew the chances of such a happening were extremely slender, Boyle's light heart never failed to leap at the thought of it.

"He flies through the air with the greatest of ease," he sang contentedly. "The daring young man on the flying trapeze."

Happily, as he finished the song, he changed to "All the Nice Girls Love a Sailor" and then "Wings Over the Navee, Wings Over the Se-ee-ea," until Petty Officer Porter, a heavy, unsmiling, serious individual, frowned at the torment. It was one of the burdens of Porter's life that Boyle liked to sing to pass away the monotony of patrolling the empty-seas – everything he could think of – and even, sometimes, to recite. To Porter's frustrated disgust, Boyle even preferred longer narrative poems Porter didn't know, Shakespeare which sounded like gibberish to his unattuned ears, and the epics of Robert W Service. The longer the better, Boyle seemed to think, as he wrestled with the rolling phrases, interspacing them with "Da-da-di-da" and "Tum-tum-ti-tum" whenever he forgot the words.

As he finished "Wings over the Navy" he swung without thinking into "Dan MacGrew."

"A bunch of the boys was whooping it up," he announced, "in the Malamute Saloon. The kid that handled the music box was hitting a jag-time tune – "

"God's night-gown," Porter muttered to himself.

As Boyle recited he caught sight of a small vessel ahead of him, its wake trailing back across the broken sea, a small dark rolling fragment on the ugly surface of the water, and he swung his machine down to get a closer look.

"Silly, silly people," he pointed out to Porter. "Going to sea in this weather. Ha – " He broke off. "The RAF boys. Bless 'em, they try so hard. It's a pity they'll never make sailors," he ended, with the pitying condescension of the Senior Service for a game but very junior rival.

Below them, the launch's grey decks with the single white-painted star flashed in the poor light then disappeared again as the boat rolled violently. The wake streamed astern, creamy and foaming, twisting over the waves as the helmsman tried to avoid some of the worst of the weather. The ensign at the masthead whipped over the starboard side of the bridge in the wind that roared down from the north.

"The boat boys are taking a beating today," Boyle said.

Porter turned briefly and clumsily at Boyle's words and stared stolidly as the Walrus roared over the swinging masthead of the launch.

He could see, in the brief instant that placed the boat sharp against the silhouette of the landing wheel folded neatly up to the underside of the Walrus' lower wing, a crowded bridge below the tattered ensign, and the upturned face of a man with red hair. The man merely gazed back at him without waving, then the boat slid away beneath the aeroplane and disappeared astern.

Porter's heavy eyes followed it as Boyle swung the machine round towards the south. He could see the great numbers on the black blunt stern of the boat, disappearing from time to time in the wake as a wave rolled away from the boats quarter – 7525. 7525 – and the threshing foam that broke against the bow and fled down the side of the hull.

"In a hurry all of a sudden," he said. "Only just started up.

"Maybe the war's over." Boyle grinned, and he swung the Walrus round in a tight circle and swooped low over the launch again. Then a spatter of thin rain across the Perspex caught his attention and he turned forward again.

"Rain," he said briefly. "Not much. Seems to be shutting down a bit, though."

He glanced down at the launch, away on the starboard bow now, below the wing-tip, hammering through the grey white-flecked sea.

"She's heading up north like a retriever after a rabbit," he went on. "Wonder what she's got?"

As he spoke Porter bent quickly over his wireless set and reached for his Morse key, one hand on the volume control, his body huddled and shapeless in his flying clothes. Boyle heard the squeak of Morse filling the cabin above the high-pitched roar of the motor over their head, attached to the mainplane, ugly and unstreamlined – like a motorcycle engine out of its proper sphere. Boyle glanced up at it and scowled.

"It's us this time," Porter said unemotionally after a while as he bent over his decoding machine. "Kite in the drink. That's what the fuss is about. Just north of here somewhere. It must be urgent, though, because they're calling Larry Smith down from up north to help search the area. Just when we were expecting the recall, too."

Boyle's expression showed no change. There was neither excitement nor anger on his features.

"What's the course?" he asked.

The Walrus flew north in the grey afternoon light, over the lonely miles of the sea, its noisy engine screaming. To Boyle, although in contact with the shore through his wireless set and with Porter alongside him, the sea seemed to grow wider and more lonely as the clouds shut in. It was something he noticed every time he had to fly through the autumn afternoons. With the gradual disappearance of light, the sea seemed to grow larger and more threatening, and he, in his relationship to it, smaller and more insignificant. The impression was heightened by the total absence of shipping, for Boyle knew well that German coasters hugged the shore and travelled mostly at night, and that most of the Allied vessels were further south in the Narrow Seas, in that strait between England and France where the constant heavy traffic of war was kept up.

"Wouldn't like to be in the drink in this weather," he said slowly, staring down at the cold sea, his eyes narrowed all thoughts of singing forgotten suddenly.

"Ever heard of one of those aircraft dinghies capsizing?" Porter asked.

"I should imagine they could if they tried. Give me a Walrus every time, bloody old string-bags that they are. God knows, I'm chokker with Walruses, but to hell with ditching in a kite that won't float."

Porter touched his arm heavily and pointed across the sea at a rapidly moving speck approaching them.

"Keep an eye on him for a minute" – Boyle was cheerfully unperturbed – "till we find out what he is. I don't believe in mixing it with a Messerschmidt in a Walrus."

"OK, it's a Thunderbolt! It's a Yank!"

The other aircraft grew rapidly as its great engine flung it low over the water towards the Walrus, and they heard its snarl as it flashed by underneath them.

"There's another on this side," Boyle pointed out excitedly. "I do believe they're searching! Boy, this must be important if they've got the Yank fighters out to give a hand!"

He watched the squat-nosed, thick-bellied Thunderbolts flash past and swing to the north, and his anger surged up in him as the thin note of his own engine sidled into his brain again, reminding him of their speed.

"Hell's teeth," he roared in a fury. "Look at those boys go! And *we* trudge along with this flaming little two-stroke like a man with a wooden leg – and that broken!"

He put the Walrus into a shallow dive, roared down to the surface of the water, and pulled the machine up again.

"Twenty miles an hour, flat out, wind and tide up her behind," he snorted. "Mother, I'm going to buy myself a paper kite and be a real aviator! A bloody taxi-driver, that's what I am," he said bitterly. "Look at the thing! It looks like a London taxi – an old one!"

Porter was peering through the Perspex window in the square side of the plane, almost as though he were deaf. His solid lack of humour was impervious to Boyle's rages.

"Something in the water down there, Pat," he said quietly.

"Dinghy?" Boyle quietened immediately.

"Nope. Might be a man on his own. In the water. No dinghy."

"Damn!" Boyle felt flattened. His light spirits, which only the speed of the Walrus could damp for long, fell and he began to feel depressed.

He turned the machine slightly so that he came round in a large arc while Porter kept his eye on the object he'd seen.

"Got it?"

"Yes, I've still got it."

"Where is it?"

"Over there." Porter pointed. "Right under the bow there. Port a bit. You're heading right on it now. Don't like the look of it."

"Looks like a man – "

" – floating," Porter added.

"Let's go down and have a look."

The Walrus swept round and down in a shallow glide so that it almost skimmed the wave-tops. Although throttled well back, they shot over the surface of the sea at almost a hundred miles an hour and had barely a second or two in which to identify what they'd seen.

"See it?"

"Once, briefly. Looked like a stiff."

"It's half underneath the surface of the water." Boyle was silent for a while and only the roar of the engine filled the square cabin above the flying-boat hull of the aircraft. "Looks as though those damn dinghies *do* capsize," he ended.

"If they ever *got* into the dinghy."

"Let's have one last look and then we'll get a message through to base. They might like to know. Then we'll find the launch boys and get 'em to pick it up."

six

Leading-aircraftman Tebbitt, wedged into the starboard corner of the tiny bridge of HSL 7525, on look-out with Leading-aircraftman Westover, saw the Walrus coming towards them long before anyone else on board. It was on his side of the bridge and it appeared first as a dot low over the horizon, but in Tebbitt's brain preoccupied as it was with his worries over his wife, it failed to register immediately.

Huddled inside his duffel coat, he was staring into the wind and covering the sea to his right as the launch corkscrewed her way stubbornly north-east. Ahead of him he could see the bow of the boat, sharp and grey, the anchor locked into position slightly forward of the winch, heaving up and round and down in labouring arcs, then up and round and down again, so that the broken sea and the grey sky went down and round and up in the opposite direction in sickening monotony.

One after another the dark waves came at them, rolling under and beyond the launch from one horizon to the other, their tips touched with feathers of white. They came from where the massing clouds curved down to sea-level, from the width of the North Sea, growing more vicious and broken as they ran into the confined spaces where England pressed close to France, down across the wrecks of hundreds of ships whose mastheads marked their graves on the sandbanks of the Channel, whose only tombstone was a green wreck buoy which warned vessels to give their sunken spars a wide berth, whose only requiem was the paragraph concerning their position in *Advice to Pilots*.

The spray rose in little spurts as the waves exploded under the chine and whipped in curving darts across the port side of the fore-deck to rattle on the splinter mats and the wheelhouse windows and so over the bridge. As it fell it coated everything with a layer of salt rime, stiffening the halliards and the heaving-lines that swung from the hand-rail, making the grey decks slippery as the wind-blown drops gathered in larger globules which became streams in the tearing breeze and hurried before it across the deck to congregate in jerking, sidling, quivering puddles by the gun-turrets and the bridge step.

Tebbitt's eyes saw every one of those rolling waves just as they saw the aircraft in the distance, but only about one in ten registered on his brain, for his personal problems pursued him like the hounds of Hell down the dark avenues of his thoughts, never leaving him for a moment.

He was as certain as any man could be that his wife was on the point of leaving him, and had been for longer than he cared to think about.

You great soft oaf, he told himself bitterly, you'd have done better if you'd taken her at her word and let her go the first time she threatened. You'd have done better still if you hadn't been fool enough to marry her – if you'd stuck to your own Westmorland kind…

Tebbitt let his thoughts run riot round the What-Might-Have-Been which for a moment or two cloaked the What-Really-Was in a cloud of pleasant fantasy, then the un-repentant devil in the What-Really-Was soured the What-Might-Have-Been and Tebbitt was back on the bridge of 7525, and the spray was coming over the port side like stinging needles and the sea was the colour of dirty pewter, and he could hear the Flight Sergeant in the wheelhouse talking to Robb.

His thoughts stumbled on in a silent argument with himself as the aircraft went forgotten – or, to be more exact, unmarked in his mind. It wasn't even as though there were any passion in his wife to hold him, he remembered bitterly. Hilda always did seem as cold as a frog. To him, anyway, he thought with burning jealousy.

But Tebbitt was what Flight Sergeant Slingsby derisively called "Well-brought-up" and "All cup-of-tea" – Tebbitt could even then hear the harsh sarcasm as it came from the cheerful, vulgar little Flight Sergeant – and in Tebbitt's well-brought-up circle the men-folk didn't lose their wives except by death. They didn't divorce or run away from each other. They lived dull, contented lives and went to chapel with each other and reared children who would do exactly the same thing. And it was this as much as anything which made Tebbitt hang on to the unrepentant Hilda in the vain belief that she would eventually settle down.

He knew what he ought to do. Wallop her, you great soft-hearted fool, you, he told himself. Wallop her. Hurt her – even if it would never solve the problem. At least show her she couldn't get away with it. Sling her across the room till she ached, and give her what-for until she knew who was the boss.

"That's it, clout her, Tebby," Slingsby had offered as advice once when they'd been trying to discuss it in the forecastle over a mug of tea in a noisy give-and-take which no one but Tebbitt was inclined to take seriously. "Tell her to put her dukes up and give her a fat eye so she can't go out for a fortnight.

"Give everybody what they ask for, I always say, whoever they are. I remember a Jerry we picked up in the Channel during the Battle of Britain – in the days when they were lording it over half Europe. He sat in his dinghy and heiled Hitler a bit and said he wouldn't come on our stinking rotten British boat and insisted we tow the dinghy with him in it back to shore. So he wouldn't taint himself, I suppose. 'OK,' I said, 'we will.' Big-hearted Arthur, that's me. Give folks what they ask for. So we did. We gave him his bloody treat at forty knots. By the time he'd been airborne a bit he was glad to come aboard. That just shows you. Give 'em what they ask for, I say, and you can't go wrong." And he went off into a boisterous reminiscence of the early days of the war, before Tebbitt was in uniform, that amused the forecastle but didn't help Tebbitt at all.

For clouting her wouldn't do much good, he knew in his heart of hearts. She'd have slipped off as fast as she could carry her bag to the station – not to the arms of another man, which was the trouble with most unhappy husbands, but to the subtle charms of that damned city, to the sound of Bow Bells and the sight of the River Thames.

Tebbitt felt frustrated every time he thought about it. He would willingly have smashed in the face of any other man he found interested in Hilda but he was baffled when it came to dealing with a city. He couldn't bash in eight million faces and wreck a million buildings. He couldn't destroy a tradition. Even Goering's whole air force couldn't do that.

He glowered angrily at the thought as he stared sightlessly at the sea and the growing speck of the Walrus. He could imagine her already, sitting in a window seat of the train, in that plaid coat she'd bought with the coupons he'd cadged, the one she always kept for best. And on the rack above her head there'd be the bag he'd given her – the one he'd got from a naval signaller on the base, with her initials painted carefully on it, HT. He'd painted them himself one night on boat watch with black paint he'd found in the after locker. He'd been proud of the job until he caught a rocket from her in her next letter for not remembering her name had become Linda.

She'd be sitting in some corner – his eyes became sad and unhappy as he thought of it – with the light bright on her blonde hair, doubtless talking to some damn Yank about London, about Streatham High Road, or the Ice Rink or the Astoria where she'd liked to dance, or that place she always talked about which made him so insanely jealous, the Rookery – the place where she'd sat after dark on the seats with the boys she constantly remembered.

Tebbitt's mind raced away into a fantasy of his own invention in which Hilda, on arrival at the station, was a different person, ready and willing to be co-operative and loving. It could be done, he tried hard to persuade himself. Money could do it. He'd managed to rouse unwilling affection in her occasionally with presents. Then as his mind ran on, covering the whole of his torment in a few hastening seconds, he wondered unhappily where the hell he was going to get the money from to give her the good time she would demand. His own money would never last out at the pace Hilda liked to spend it. All he had was a pound and a few shillings in his pocket, which might see them through the first day.

His mind writhed with its efforts to see beyond the immediate future and he had completely forgotten the Walrus, in spite of its increasing nearness, by the time Slingsby appeared on the bridge beside him.

"Comfortable, Tebby?" Tebbitt jumped as Slingsby's voice grated in his ear, harsh and hard with twenty years of shouting orders at people like Tebbitt.

"That's right, Flight," Tebbitt said.

"Well, it ain't right," Slingsby bawled. "Get off your bloody knees. Get them great barges of yours down on the deck – both of 'em. You stand like a pregnant WAAF. Now look at that goddam sea till your eyes start looping the loop or I'll put you in the rattle."

He was quivering with his anger and Tebbitt straightened himself up hastily, still thinking, however, even as he did so, about his wife and that train he had to meet, that train he had arranged to meet and had confidently expected to meet – but for the awkward circumstance of an aircraft ditching in the sea in their area of search.

"In case you haven't noticed it," Slingsby went on harshly, "there's an aircraft over there and it's coming over here – fast! And it might be a Jerry coming to blow us to bloody bits like they blew my mate to bits in the Whaleback off Dungeness in '41."

"Er – yes, Flight. I *had* seen it, Flight."

Slingsby exploded. "Well, report it, you fool!"

Tebbitt looked at Slingsby with sad round eyes, the fact that he could have crushed the little man with one swing of his great fist not entering his head.

"Aircraft on the starboard quarter, Flight," he said sullenly, still a little surprised that he hadn't already reported the machine. "It's a Walrus."

"Knox!" Slingsby gave him a final glare and bent to the wireless cabin hatch and shouted – in that rough file-on-an-anvil voice which was the driving force of the boat, the thing which turned the propellers and kept the boat moving through the water, the power to the wireless batteries, the rope's end that stirred the war-weariness out of them all, the goad, the pin-prick and the whip.

They could hear the hum of the Walrus' engine now, and as it approached it seemed to disappear in a flash of light, which stabbed across the sky towards them.

"Knox!" Slingsby bellowed. "On deck! And jump to it! There's a Walrus flashing us."

With Treherne just behind, Knox burst out of the wheelhouse, carrying the Aldis signalling-lamp with him and, shoving Westover to one side, he wedged his lanky frame into a corner of the bridge and took a glance at the aircraft through the telescopic sight. Westover heaved himself on the wireless cabin roof and clung there, his arms round the mast, as the Walrus dissolved again in a series of flashes that stood out sharply against the darkening sky.

"Body" – Knox intoned slowly – "in – water – due – north – of – you – stop – investigate – will – circle – and – mark – for – you."

"Give him the OK," Treherne said. "Due north, Robby," he shouted into the wheelhouse. And he dived inside, as though chasing his own words, as he reached for the parallel rules at the chart table.

The boat heeled over on its side on top of a wave as Robb swung the wheel – over, over, over, in a sickening, hanging motion that sent them all sliding to the starboard side of the bridge. Down below there was a crash of crockery, then the boat's motion changed abruptly from a heaving corkscrew to a solid, thumping crash as it butted head-on into the waves. Tebbitt dully rubbed his chin which he had banged on the searchlight stanchion and wondered if this meant they would soon turn round and head west for home.

"Suppose it's the dinghy, Flight?" he asked Slingsby warily. "Suppose the Walrus goes down and picks 'em up before we get there?"

"Suppose they do!" Slingsby grunted. "Suppose we ram the bastards, that's all. That's what I say. I'm not having any Navy birdcage spoiling *my* pick-ups. Sink the swine and have done."

The keel of the boat was making a steady crunching hiss as it plunged squarely into the rolling water, a solid thump that shook the spars and jarred the nerves. Every time the bow rose to a new wave Tebbitt braced himself forward, then with every sudden drop his heels left the deck and came down again in a jolt that rattled his spine.

Knox finished flashing his message to the aircraft and put down the Aldis lamp as the Walrus roared past overhead and turned towards the north again.

"Looks like we're too late, Chiefy," he said.

"We're never too late," Slingsby said, his eyes squinting against the wind. "Not until we know we're too late. And that'll be two days from now with a gale blowing and no fuel left."

Conscious of being in charge of something Slingsby had never mastered, the wireless operator was unperturbed and pretended not to notice the rebuke. "7526's around here somewhere, Chiefy. They've called her into the search."

"I thought they would." Slingsby scowled. "You sure?"

"I can tell that wireless op. of theirs anywhere. I could tell him in a blast of atmospherics when he's batting it out. He's good and he likes to show off a bit."

Slingsby was staring ahead again. "Where are they?"

"Almost due north of here, Chiefy. Botterill got a bearing on them. They'll be heading south-east."

"And we were heading north-east until that Walrus called us up. It'll be the usual race, with Skinner's engines as the handicap. Keep your ear on that boy in '76 and let us know if you hear anything further. Three times we've been on the point of a pick-up and he's pipped us. Next time I'll sink him with the Oerlikon."

Tebbitt glowered sullenly out of the corner of his eye at the Flight Sergeant's dapper little form as he spoke. To Tebbitt, like Milliken, Slingsby in the two or three weeks he'd been in charge of the launch had taken on the form of some devil incarnate conjured to life by the Air Force high-ups solely to plague Tebbitt. Each was as far removed from the other's ideal as it was possible to be and Tebbitt, with his mind constantly elsewhere, knew he was already in the Flight Sergeant's bad books. Nevertheless, his misery over his wife caused him to carry on the masochistic self-torture with Slingsby in which he'd been indulging with Milliken. Knowing perfectly well what sort of replies he'd get, he persisted in investigating the matter of the launch's return.

"Flight," he said, "think we'll be back home tonight? Or do you think they'll keep us out till morning?"

Slingsby's reply was discouraging. "What's the matter? Can't you sleep without a night light or something?"

Tebbitt ignored the insult and probed further, fully aware of the rage he might rouse. "But they usually *do* recall us after dark, don't they? Not much good searching in the darkness, is it, Flight?" He was still trying to reassure himself that he'd be back at camp in time to meet that early morning train – almost as though by his persistence he could put agreement on to Slingsby's tongue and so help to influence the authorities ashore. He was quite prepared to miss the boat on call-out if necessary the following morning. The only thing he knew he must not miss was that train which would stop at the local station in the early hours on its way to London.

Slingsby's reply to his question was a grunt.

Tebbitt's face was expressionless as he watched the sea, his eyes never still as he searched the valleys of the waves. His uncovered hair was whipped by a wind that blew it the wrong way and his great shoulders were hunched against the cold. He glanced again at Slingsby, who was still staring forward in inscrutable silence.

"If they keep us out all night, Flight," he went on doggedly, in spite of Slingsby's warning silence, "what time will they recall us tomorrow, do you think?"

"Holy suffering St Peter," Slingsby burst out, his red face darkening. "For Christ's sake, put a sock in it! They might keep us out all tomorrow night as well. And all the next day. And everlastingly till the flaming sea dries up, so long as there's a chance. And a good thing, too. That's what we're here for, isn't it? Not to go rushing home at the first opportunity to meet silly bloody wives."

Tebbitt stood in his corner of the bridge in staggered silence
for a moment, for the first time aware that Slingsby knew
why he wanted to get home. He was not looking at the Flight
Sergeant, but still stared out over the waves, his eyes
watering a little at the teasing of the wind. Then Slingsby
dodged into the wheelhouse and Tebbitt caught a glimpse of
Westover looking curiously at him over his shoulder.

"I wish he'd forget the bitch and get on with his job," he
heard Slingsby saying furiously below. "The whole bloody
crew puts years on me. You can easily tell who had this
packet before they posted us to it, Robby. The Old Man was
right when he said the Lad needed someone to look after
him. Chiefy Rollo's left his mark on this tub as clear as if it
was tattooed all up and down the mast. All he ever did was
use his jaw. It was the only part of him that ever worked. I
once took over a boat from him before. That was just the
same. Everybody trying to rat on you at once. The only time
they move is when it's knocking-off time. A good pick-up
would do them all a bit of good."

Tebbitt assumed that the skipper had disappeared into his
cabin below for a moment, for in spite of his rage Slingsby's
voice had a warmth about it that showed only when be was
talking to Robb. They had served overseas together and they
had a confident intimacy of experiences and hardships
shared, of mutual difficulties surmounted.

"Ashore, he can do as he pleases about his blasted wife,"
Slingsby went on, "but at sea he's got something else to do.
He can forget her."

"I don't know that *I* could, with a wife like that," Robb
pointed out with the privilege of long acquaintance, and
Tebbitt, unable to shut out the conversation, had to listen
humiliated as they discussed him. "Could you?"

"I could lay an egg if I tried. I had a wife like that myself,
didn't I? Christ, you remember that, surely? When we went
overseas in 1940, I spent my days, when we weren't being

chased all over the shop by Jerry, sending letters to her so fast they looked like confetti. Mooning over Vera Lynn's songs and all that – you know the stuff – 'Yours in the grey of December' and all that cock – it made your heart bleed at that distance. And when I came back I found she'd been going around with a naval petty officer and I'd had me chips. Rat with a face like an old fender, he was. She said she couldn't stand it on her own for three years. After thirteen years of married life. All me eye and Betty Martin. We arranged a divorce – big-hearted like, that's me, one of God's chosen few – and that was that. All in a day's work."

"I remember, Flight. I'm sorry."

"Sorry? Hell, I'm still laughing about it. I split a gut every time I remember. She'd no sooner got her divorce from me organised, and arranged to marry her sailor, when *he* was posted overseas. And there she was with me, who she'd slung out, back home, and the sailor, who she wanted to marry, posted to the Middle East. Laugh? I thought I'd bust my poop string." But Slingsby's face showed no traces of mirth.

"Think I like chasing Tebbitt?" he went on. "It's my job. Think I like riding that kid – the medical orderly? I got one like him myself, waiting to be called up. He's got guts, that kid."

"You're telling me! You've got him in the galley again, washing up. He looks as gay as an old street-walker, but he's not complained yet."

"He's in the Air Force now. This isn't the Infants' Department. I don't hold with all this kiss-and-be-friends stuff between NCOs and other ranks they're trying to kid us into these days. Oh, sure" – he nodded as Robb opened his mouth to speak – "I know. They're not the same as the recruits we had before the war. They're civilians really. They've got to be wet-nursed. Lots of love and kisses and hoping it finds you as it leaves me at present. Hell" – he glared at Robb – "*you*'re a civilian in for the duration, aren't you? *You* made it – and the same way as this kid's got to make it. With nasty little flight sergeants coming the old acid all the time."

"I was a bit older."

"He'll soon grow old. I'll see that he does." Slingsby scowled through the Perspex window for a while, his eyes angry, then he burst out again. "Hell, I know what's wrong," he said. "It's my fault. I ought to be helping the war effort as an air-raid warden or something, playing darts and pinching lady telephonists' behinds. I'm a reservist, I am. I'd left the Raff and I'd settled down. I was called back. That's what's wrong. I've got ten years too many on my back for this game. Besides, I'm the sergeant and the sergeant's got to be a bastard. You've read *Beau Geste,* haven't you? Now wrap up!"

Tebbitt heard Treherne return to the wheelhouse and Slingsby became silent. Then Treherne put his head through the wheelhouse door and thrust himself up the two steps to the bridge and stood beside Tebbitt. Ahead of them, they could now see the Walrus slowly circling over the water.

The bridge was crowded by this time, everyone staring ahead at the plane. As the launch drew closer the aircraft roared over them, low enough for them to see the pilot pointing ahead and down.

"Keep your eyes skinned," Treherne warned.

"Some poor beggar's had it," Knox said. "Here comes the funeral party."

Slingsby glared at him but said nothing. Then Westover, on the sick bay roof flung out an arm and pointed.

"Something in the water dead ahead, Skipper!" he shouted. "Looks like a stiff."

"Throttle back a bit, Robby," Treherne said into the wheelhouse. "Keep your eye on it, Gus!"

"I've got it, Skipper. Looks like a man, all right."

The Walrus roared overhead again and began to circle once more. Everybody on the bridge had become silent. Then Westover shouted again and his voice was suddenly excited.

"It's not a man, Skipper. If it is, he's had all his clothes blown off."

Slingsby gave a great shout of glee as he stared and did a little jig. "It's a fish," he yelled joyously. "It's a porpoise! Ha, the Navy's made a balls-up of it again!"

He turned towards the Walrus and waved both arms in a wash-out sign as the launch passed the great fish that floated low on the surface of the water in a long valley between two waves, its silver belly facing the sky, the victim of some mine or depth-charge blast, then he held his nose and pulled an imaginary chain.

"Let the Walrus know, Knocker," Treherne said. "OK, Robby, back on your original course. We'll sort out this five minutes' run at the other end."

The boat heeled again as the wireless operator began to flash at the Walrus, then she slowly lifted and began to corkscrew across the surface of the waves once more on her original course.

"We shouldn't be far off now, Skipper," Slingsby said.

"But we've only a little daylight left. How about pushing up the revs a bit?"

"OK" Treherne took the hint and put his head into the wheelhouse. "Push 'em up, Robby."

The twists of the boat were noticeably more vicious as the engines' deep-throated roar grew, and the lurches as she hit the waves were more sickening and more tiring.

Knox, who had had his head near to the wireless cabin hatch, talking to his mate, looked up. "7526's nearer, Flight," he said slyly as he went below again, as though he rejoiced in rubbing Slingsby's wound raw. "Botty says he's slightly east of us now. She's got the legs of us – as usual."

Down in the engine-room of the launch Corporal Skinner was studying the revolution counters. He cast a quick glance at the oil-pressure gauges as the revolution counter needles moved further to the right with the increased speed, then his eyes flickered anxiously to the glass tube on the oil tank on the bulkhead. Dray was singing soundlessly on his toolbox above the deafening roar, his mouth opening and shutting like an actor in a silent film as he beat time with a spanner on the box between his knees. But Corporal Skinner, plugs in his ears, noticed that his eyes were never far from the dials in front of him.

Down there in the stifling heat there was little suggestion of the heave of the sea because the drag of the propellers in the water held the stern steady, so that most of the motion came from the bows. But the howling engines played the same sort of devil down there with the nerves that the jarring deck forward did to the deck crew. The very air seemed to vibrate and, in vibrating, to add to the clamour.

Skinner casually moved aft, screwing down the greasers on the water-pumps and adjusting the sea-cocks to the new speed of the boat. He knew already that the chances of getting back to base in time to dance with and make love to his girl were growing slimmer, though he still hoped to reach the station before it was too late to take her home. It was useless carrying on a search after dark, he knew, and they were invariably recalled when it was hopeless to hang on any longer.

There'd be just time, he decided, to see her back to her billet and crawl into his own bed before that damned Tannoy would be shouting in his ear again across the barrack-room where they slept: "Crew of HSL 7525 report to base immediately. Crew of HSL 7525 report to base immediately."

Skinner scowled and hoped hard they'd make a pick-up quickly – or that 7526 would; he didn't care much which, so long as they could turn west and head for home.

He felt the change of course as the boat swung back to the north-east, though he had no idea of their direction. It was only that he felt the slight tug of the boat's turn – far less noticeable down there than on deck – and he could feel the different motion through the water. Then he saw the revolution counters jump forward a little more and he glanced anxiously round him again and down at the spinning propeller shafts.

He was beginning to wish now he'd changed the faulty piping in the oil-feed. He'd seen clearly that the jubilee clip was cutting into the rubber joint and if it cut too far – . Again he looked round, half expecting to see the spurt of bright hot oil heralding the colossal overheating that would drive the temperature needle clean off the dial, and to hear the shattering vibration of a seize-up, and he was quite relieved when he didn't.

He rested the palm of his hand on the port engine, feeling its vibration run through his arm like the blood through his veins and so through his whole body. It was running well. Damned well, considering, he told himself.

Considering – considering – he glanced quickly at Dray as the little canker of doubt entered his brain – considering the slap-happy job he'd done the previous night. Skinner was a good engineer in spite of his indifference, good enough to know what he ought to have done and to realise the possible disaster that might arise from what he had not done, but he nevertheless attached little blame to himself. He felt only an angry resentment, a bitter sense that someone had played a dirty trick on him. After months of dreary hanging about on rendezvous, after months of monotonous waiting on the grey seas for an emergency call, with the war almost over and the days of urgent excitement past, some fool *would* have to choose that particular day to fall into the drink – and on 7525'S beat, too.

He took his hand from the engine, which was running perfectly alongside him. Then he remembered uneasily that they'd *both* been running perfectly the previous day but there'd *still* been the damage in the oil-feed, a tiny fault caused by vibration, nothing to worry about in itself but something that might cause trouble with high-speed running for long distances. And that was something that had never happened for weeks. Not until today.

The engineer – the undoubted engineer – who lay beneath Skinner's shiftless, casual, indifferent manner stirred uneasily. His conscience was nagging at him with the knowledge of what he had failed to do, prodding him like a tormenting imp with a sharp stick, urging him to do something when he knew it was already too late to do anything. All he could do now was wait for the bang and the stream of bright oil.

Skinner moved aft, where the boat sat low in the water. Beneath his feet he could feel the propellers turning at hundreds of revolutions a minute. The air about him was oven-hot and stank of oil and baked steel but it seemed twice as stifling because of the conscience that was gagging him, the sense of guilt that seemed to suffocate him. Thoughtfully, but almost without being aware of what he did, he lifted the cover of his tool-box and idly toyed through the tools inside, making sure they were all there.

All he could do now was hope and be ready.

More than four hours had elapsed since the Hudson had ditched and its crew had taken to the dinghy, four hours during which the search for them had been inaugurated and launches and aircraft were sweeping the wide wastes of the sea.

To Waltby, sitting in the dinghy and knowing nothing of all this, it was not the waiting that was so wearisome. The hardest thing of all was getting used to doing nothing. Never in all his life had he done nothing satisfactorily. His nervous energy had forced him into activity at all times – in fact, it had been nothing but his nervous energy and a congenital inability to sit still that had thrust him up to his present rank. During those years after joining the Air Force straight from school and after he had completed his apprenticeship, when all the other airmen in the barrack-room had been reading or resting or sitting in the canteen, Waltby had been studying. His efforts had brought him incredibly swiftly to the rank of sergeant and got him a peacetime commission, and eventually a posting to the experimental station at Boscombe Down. There, because he seemed to have acquired more knowledge than most in less time, they had let him specialise until he had become an expert in rocket development

His whole life seemed to have been marked out by the books and the documents he had read. Every new item of knowledge he had acquired – whether from Germany, Japan or America – had been another milestone on the way up. He had still been learning, even in the Hudson when the first sound of a chattering gun had made him hurriedly slam down his book and grab for his briefcase. Hammer-taps on the fuselage heralded the disintegration of Mackay's wireless set and then Waltby had seen the pieces of metal fly upwards, outwards and backwards from the port engine and the sudden flow of oil as it streamed in a black, shining streak across the width of the main plane.

In the first paralysing shock of fear he had thought of a fighter he had once seen diving into the ground out of control and the scream as it plummeted down, straight down; and the sickening thump and the dust and the flying pieces of aluminium as it hit the earth, and he had visualised them all smashed to pulp inside the Hudson as it plunged into the sea – like the pilot he had seen. It was only when he heard Ponsettia firing the turret guns and heard Harding and Mackay coolly discussing their chances as they wrestled with the sloppy controls of the plane that he realised how much braver than he were the young men who went out night after night into the black sky over the Ruhr. They had not lived too long with words and but for them all the words he himself had read or written would have been valueless.

And now, now that they were in the dinghy and the book he had been reading had disappeared into the dark fathoms of the sea with the aircraft, there was nothing to do but sit. His companions seemed to be feeling the same strain of boredom, however, he was relieved to notice. Harding looked paler and Mackay fidgeted constantly. When he wasn't taking a turn with Ponsettia on the handle of the squawk-box generator he was fiddling with the flares, trying to row with one of the glove-like paddles or adjusting the sail.

All their other jobs, the jobs for which hundreds of pounds had been spent to train them, had finished as soon as the aircraft hit the water and carried with it below the surface the controls and the wireless sets and the navigator's charts. The silence was marked, too, after the quivering atmosphere and the swift demands of flying and the smell of oil and petrol. Now there was only the dead slap of the waves and the hiss of the breaking crests.

They had got the mast rigged with difficulty, everyone getting in the others' way in the crowded dinghy, and Mackay getting in the way of the other three with maddening persistence as he tried to do two or three jobs at once.

"Brother," Ponsettia had drawled, "if you can keep this up for as long as we're in the dinghy we sure are going to have a good rest. Take it easy, bud, take it easy."

Mackay had whirled on him, nervous and energetic, eager to get on with something, and hostile as ever as Ponsettia picked up the challenge that he always held out. "Somebody's got to do it," he said furiously. "*You* don't seem very bothered. I suppose you're quite content to sit back and let someone come and find you."

"Mac," Ponsettia said placidly, "sometimes you talk cock."

The growing hostility had been smoothed over by Harding and the three of them had continued with the process of organising their comfort They had unearthed all the gear attached to the dinghy – the hand-bellows, the heaving-line, the flare, the mast and the sail. Waltby had watched them silently, his desolate feeling disappearing slowly. He had been from the first completely at a loss in the dinghy, but the obvious fact that the others knew what they were doing reassured him.

"We ought to try to get the sail up," Harding had said. "At least we might get somewhere then."

Almost before he'd finished speaking Mackay was at work, stepping the telescopic mast.

"Where do you think we are, Canada?" Harding asked as Mackay bent over the aluminium rods.

"God knows," the Canadian answered. "Somewhere due north-west of Antwerp, I guess. And pretty close in, too."

Waltby listened to them weighing up their position, more than ever aware of loneliness and his own lack of ability compared with the naive sureness of these boys who were young enough to be his sons. He desperately wanted to do something useful and intelligent but he seemed only to get in the way. Once he had seen the sour look Mackay gave him as one of the stays for the mast caught in his clothing.

As a desk officer, this was his first real experience of the war. He had been too young for the first war and too important to be risked in the second. And, living and working where he had, even the bombs on London hadn't disturbed him greatly. The bullets which had smashed Mackay's wireless set and stopped the port engine in a spray of hot black oil reaching like wet fingers across the broad wing of the Hudson were the first bullets that had been truly fired in his direction in five years of hostilities. He felt suddenly unable to withstand the hardship into which he had been so unexpectedly flung.

Then, unhappily, he realised that half his depression came from the seasickness which lay on his stomach like a leaden weight, and the throbbing ache in his head where he'd banged it on the escape hatch. To force it from his consciousness, he concentrated again on watching the others.

Mackay and Ponsettia had now succeeded in stepping the mast and were engaged in fitting the sail. While they were both kneeling and Harding was reaching up painfully to assist them, the dinghy gave a particularly violent lurch that flung them all down in a heap again, half covered by the red cotton of the sail, and Waltby had to turn quickly in his seat to be sick over the side. By the time the others had recovered their positions he was sitting up again, quietly wiping his mouth with his frozen fingers as he hadn't been able to get his handkerchief from his sodden pocket in time.

He seemed to shrink back into himself, vaguely ashamed of his weakness, at his inability to cope even with so small a thing as seasickness. Just then all he wanted to do was curl up and try to dissolve into a chilled, shivering sleep until he felt better, but he forced himself to smile weakly as Harding glanced at him, trying hard to pretend there was nothing wrong with him.

They sat back, exhausted by their efforts to rig the sail in the cramped dinghy. Harding lay against the bulbous yellow sides, half leaning against Mackay, his face pale and strained in the grey light reflected from the sea. Lonely and silent, Waltby was still – in spite of his proximity to the others – a being apart from the oneness of the crew, his sparse hair blown over his face, his coat collar up, his hand still clutching the saturated leather briefcase between his knees.

Ponsettia had started again to crank the handle of the squawk box. "Right, here we go, boys," he said. "Never fear, Joe Ponsettia's on the ball. I guess that little WAAF operator with the blonde hair and the squint is picking this up right now. She'd never pass up on a chance like this."

They sat in silence for a while as Ponsettia laboriously turned the generator handle, each of them occupied with his own thoughts. The water was round their thighs in the bottom of the dinghy and splashed over the edge across them from time to time.

Then they tried, ineffectually, to paddle again.

"It was easy enough when we did it in the swimming bath," Mackay choked in a furious voice.

"Brother, when you see a swimming bath as rough as this is let me know. Guess we'd better bale again or we'll be going down with all hands."

"Hell's bells," Harding said suddenly. 'We're a cheerful lot, aren't we? We ought to do something to occupy ourselves. Anyone know any songs?"

"I only know 'Charlotte, the Harlot, the Cowpuncher's Whore'," Ponsettia said, looking up from the bottom of the dinghy as he slopped seawater over the side. "Or, how's about 'Row for the Shore, Boys, Row for the Shore', or 'Round and round went our gallant ship, then she sank to the bottom of the sea, the sea, the sea, then she sank to the bottom of the sea' "?

"If you don't shut up – " Mackay began in a strangled voice.

"Whacko!" Ponsettia grinned. "Mac's threatening me. How's about that Skipper? Let's have a fight. That ought to warm us up."

Harding hurried the quarrel past its climax by deciding they should have a meal. They spread their emergency packs out on their legs and stared at them, their minds busy with the thought of rationing.

"Water-purifying tablets," Ponsettia said. "Say, that's real handy with all this sea round us."

"Biscuits," Harding added. "They're useful."

"And energy tablets," Ponsettia went on, as though he were taking up a chorus. "Just the thing if you feel like swimming home, Mac. A fishing line! Boy, I might have enjoyed that at any other time. Ground bait, too. Say, they do you proud. Cigarettes. Chewing gum. Compass. And what's this? My, now, what a delicate thought – toilet paper!"

As they finished their meagre meal of a biscuit and a concentrated food tablet Harding heaved himself up weakly.

"Mac," he said, "I think I'm going to be sick."

"Hard luck, Skip. These dinghies are bastards in a bit of sea, aren't they?" Mackay's voice had lost all its aggressiveness as he spoke to Harding. "Think it's that whack you gave your tum?"

"I'm sure it is." Harding smiled weakly and lay back against Mackay, his face grey with pain.

"Oh, Christ," he said suddenly. "Here it comes!"

They helped him turn and he puked over the edge of the dinghy.

"Sorry, blokes," he said unhappily, as he sat upright again. "Always was a rotten sailor."

"Sure you won't have my Irving jacket, Skip?" Mackay asked. "Perhaps it's a bit of shock."

"I've got an Irving jacket. Keep yours for yourself"

"*I* haven't banged my guts." There was concern now in Mackay's humourless tones.

"Well, when my guts start to fall out you can wrap your jacket round to hold 'em in."

Ponsettia watched them silently as he cranked the handle of the squawk box. His arm ached and his behind was cold where it touched the thin canvas; and his brain was uneasily dwelling on the time they had already been in the dinghy and what must be going on in the mind of the girl he bad met and fallen in love with so recently. He had a sudden feeling that his life until that moment had been full of insignificant things and that he was being called upon to die before he had experienced any of the important happenings in life, and he felt vaguely resentful.

Waltby was more concerned with the misery in his stomach than with immediate thoughts of rescue. But as he began to feel a little better he also began to have his first doubts about their future safety. He had taken their rescue for granted at first but now, with a shock as great as if one of the freezing waves had sloshed across them, he realised it was in no way assured. The sea was as empty and unencouraging as it had ever been.

For the first time he thought of his wife, who was supposed to be meeting him at the aerodrome where they should by now have landed. She was due to arrive by the early morning train – she would at this moment be mounting it, complete with her books and the inevitable knitting – to spend her first few days with him for months.

He had been looking forward to that meeting, to the family party atmosphere that would inevitably result from the gathering. Now, with a pull at his stomach that was almost as strong as the physical nausea, he realised it would not happen – it might never happen; he might never see his wife again – and he felt in consequence smaller and more desolate on the heaving valleys of the sea.

That the others were also feeling the tremors of unease occurred to him when Harding spoke again.

"Sure no one saw us ditch, Canada?" he asked weakly. "Not unless they've got telescopic eyes," Ponsettia answered.

Waltby saw Mackay scowl at the navigator. "I saw a couple of freighters east of here," he growled, and in a flash of insight Waltby knew he was deliberately lying for the benefit of Harding.

"If you did, bud, they were Jerries," Ponsettia pointed out, unaware of Mackay's attempt to cheer the pilot. "East of here? You bet your sweet life they were Jerries."

"Not damn likely," Mackay grunted. "The only Jerries that come out these days are E-boats."

"Anyway, is there a flare handy in case a kite spots us?" Harding interrupted.

"Yes, Skip. There's one handy." Mackay's voice lost its hardness again as he spoke to Harding, and Waltby realised there was nothing artificial about the note.

"I expect it won't go off," Ponsettia said. "They never will when you want 'em to."

"It'll go off all right." Mackay glowered at him. "Think there's any hope of anybody picking up that signal from the squawk box, Canada?" Harding asked.

"If anybody happens to be flying past within a few yards of us, there might," Ponsettia said. "But then, if they were that close we'd have to duck."

Mackay exploded. "You know those bloody things are all right."

"Sure, they are – if they're working. This one got a hell of a clout from the wing as the dinghy was ejected. The wonder is the dinghy wasn't punctured. Sure, they're all right – *if* they're all right."

"People do pick up the signals."

"But not often."

"For Christ's sake, can't you cheer up?" said Mackay. "We don't want to sit in this damn thing just listening to you weighing up what chances there are against us getting out of the jam."

"Face the facts, I say, bud," the Canadian said placidly. "Still, if you like it that way, OK. How's this? Bags of cheer, boys. I'll bet there's a kite just setting off about now, knowing exactly where we are, with parachute containers containing channel-swimming outfits and midget submarines which he's going to drop right alongside."

"Aren't you going to get sick of cranking that thing, Canada?" Harding asked hurriedly. "I should take it in spasms."

"I'm the champion cranker in all the world," the navigator said.

Waltby watched them, realising that they rarely addressed him, and then only so that he should not feel neglected.

A wave lifted them high above the broken sea and he saw the long miles of empty water. Low across the horizon the grey folds of cloud seemed to huddle more closely together, impenetrable, gloomy and silent.

"Are these things wind-borne or tide-borne?" Mackay asked.

"Stillborn, if you ask me," Ponsettia observed.

"If we aren't far off the coast of Belgium or Holland," Harding pointed out, "we might even blow in."

All four of them looked instinctively to the east, their eyes hard, their faces taut and unsmiling.

"It's getting damn cold." The shock which Harding had suffered was causing the chill to affect him before the others. "A nice warm blanket would be just the job now." He spoke as though the thought of it were sickly-sweet.

"Have my Irving jacket, Skip," Mackay begged. "I don't feel cold. Honest."

"Don't talk cock, Mac. If you don't feel cold you must be dead or something."

"That reminds me…" It was the first time Waltby had spoken for some time, and their eyes all swung round to stare at him. In spite of his rank he felt curiously embarrassed before the frank gaze of these three young men. "That reminds me," he said, "I've something in here I'd quite forgotten about."

He unstrapped the briefcase and produced a silver flask, which he put carefully on the bottom of the dinghy while he strapped up the briefcase again with infuriating preciseness. Only then did he hold up the flask.

"Brandy," he said with the faintest smile. "French brandy."

"Stay me with apples, succour me with grapes." Ponsettia's grin spread. "Brandy!" He stared at the flask. "No wonder you didn't want to let go that case."

They all grinned except Mackay, whose next words seemed to throw a damper over their brief interlude of mirth.

"Why not hang on to that?" he said. "Until we need it?"

"Aw, tell that to the Band of Hope," Ponsettia yelped. "By that time we'll be too weak to taste it. Let's have it now, while we're still strong enough to enjoy it. Let's die happy."

"Mac's right, Canada," Harding said soberly. "Let's save it. We don't know how long we're going to be here." He turned to Waltby. "What do you say, sir?"

"You're the captain of the aircraft."

"Aw, Skip, you can't refuse us now. Not now we've seen it," Ponsettia wailed. "It's like throwing mud in a guy's eye and then borrowing his hanky to rub it in."

"Just a wet, then," Harding agreed. "No more."

Ponsettia groaned aloud. "Just a wet! Talk about temptation!"

They passed the flask round solemnly, everybody watching carefully to see that no one did more than merely moisten his lips. But there was no greed. They were all so anxious not to be accused of grabbing that they barely tasted the precious stuff. But the tiny drop they swallowed sent a warm glow through their chilled bodies.

"OK, sea," Ponsettia said as he handed the flask back to Waltby and ran his tongue over his lips. "I'm ready for you now."

Waltby put the flask back in the brief case, fastening the straps in an old-mannish way that irritated Mackay.

"Jolly useful that, sir," Harding said.

"Do me a favour," Waltby begged. "Drop the 'sir'."

"OK," Harding agreed awkwardly. "What shall we call you?"

"My name's Waltby."

"Hell, you can't say 'Pass the wine, Waltby'," Ponsettia pointed out. "Or 'Just shove over the caviar, Waltby'. Or 'Waltby, how about a bit of breast of seagull?' Not here. What do people call you? I'm Canada. I'm from River Falls. I was going to be a teacher before the war. His name" – he pointed to Harding – "is Rupert, believe it or not. Rupert Edward Lapenotiere Harding. Jees-us! *He* was still a kid at school. That is called Mac. I don't think he ever had a first name. He was a miner or something in some cock-eyed joint in the Midlands. Boy, those Midland towns of yours!" He rolled his eyes.

While he was talking they all watched the air commodore, wondering how he would react to the navigator's suggestion.

"My name's Sydney," he said awkwardly.

"Sydney. Good name," Harding said gallantly. "Very appropriate after the brandy. Wasn't it Sir Philip Sidney who said 'Thy need is greater than mine, chum', or 'After you with the booze, mate', or something?"

Ponsettia was staring at his feet. "First time I've ever called an air commodore 'Syd'," he said thoughtfully. "Syd." He weighed the name on his tongue. "Syd. Say, that sure sounds matey!"

They all laughed and suddenly the ice, the reserve between Waltby and the others, was broken. They were just Syd and Mac and Canada and Skip; They were just four men in a dinghy.

PART TWO

o n e

There were a thousand and one things which could go wrong with any airborne operation – whether it was a bombing raid, the dropping of supplies, the movement of troops, or merely the search for a lost yellow dinghy on the acres of the ocean. It could be a neglected oil-feed pipe, a distracted look-out, a wireless set shattered by a bullet, or even – and more likely – simply the weather.

On the blue-and-green-tinted charts of Flying Officer Howard, the Meteorological Officer, the flowing lines of the isobars crowded tight together in the North Sea area just off the Yorkshire coast, and spread out – like ripples round a dropped stone in a pond that was marked with the word "Low" – so that they touched across Scotland, Ireland, Cornwall and Kent, and bit into the Continent.

Howard adjusted his spectacles and stared hard at the lines. Outside on the balcony his sergeant was squinting through a theodolite at the hydrogen-filled balloon he had just set free. He was watching it rise at a shallow angle towards the underside of the solid grey bank that hung blank and heavy over the land, rise and grow smaller until, as a pinhead, it finally disappeared into the cloud. From its angle and its rate of climb he calculated the height of the cloud and the speed of the wind.

As it vanished he turned, writing on a slip of paper, and put his head into the long meteorological office where Howard sat at the far end behind his desk.

"Cloud's down to fifteen hundred feet now, sir," he pointed out.

Howard nodded. "What's the wind speed?" he asked.

"It's increased to twenty miles an hour, sir," the sergeant said soberly. "That's a pretty big jump in a short time."

At the long bench running down the side of the room, the leading-aircraftman who was plotting the information coming from the central weather office at Dunstable turned round for a moment, watching for Howard's reactions, then he slipped from his stool and disappeared into the next room to tear a new slip of weather information from the teleprinter.

"Got the barometer readings, Sergeant?" Howard asked.

"Yes, sir." The sergeant crossed the room and placed a sheet of paper in front of him. "Barograph's falling steeply," he pointed out. "It's beginning to look a bit dicey now."

Howard made no comment as he studied the charts in front of him, not liking at all what he saw. He was a serious young man with little humour in him – in his job he couldn't afford to treat his information lightly. On him often rested the fate of twenty or more heavy bombers containing anything up to two hundred brave young men. His was the job of giving them weather forecasts that were neither timid nor inaccurate, at a time when their engines might be damaged by flak or their electrical circuits cut to ribbons. No one on the station had to make harder decisions than Howard made – save only the Group Captain and the squadron commanders and the crews themselves. He was immensely proud of this fact and, in consequence, tended to regard his job with a stolid unsmiling seriousness that made him seem older than he was.

At his side was the report from the weather flight aircraft which had just flown in from the North Sea from the direction of Scandinavia, and Howard was trying to fit it into the findings of his own observers and the more general reports which came in from Dunstable.

As he worked he heard the nervous laugh of Squadron Leader Scott, the Administration Officer, in the corridor outside and he winced slightly, remembering the Controller's words as he'd once described it. "Sounds as if he's laying something," he'd said.

Howard sighed, knowing perfectly well he was on the point of receiving a visit. He disliked Scotty, not only for his monumental inefficiency but also because Scotty, with his wings and his last war medals, treated Howard, whose breast was bare of any decoration whatsoever, as little better than a clerk.

The door burst open and Scotty crossed over towards Howard's desk and flopped heavily down in the armchair which stood alongside it – the Meteorological Officer's stay during the long urgent hours of night watches when they waited with one eye on the fog and the low cloud for returning aircraft; his bed on the difficult nights of the big raids and bad weather, where he dozed when he could and tried not to think too much of the gigantic responsibility.

"Hello, Howard," Scotty said as he stretched out. "My God, am I glad to sit down! I'm browned off. I really am. Truly cheesed. You get rushed off your feet in this place more than anywhere I've ever been."

Howard looked up, saying nothing, knowing well that Scotty was *always* rushed off his feet and usually for little cause and for less result. He could see no reason to interrupt his work to show an interest in Scotty's woes. He knew they would be woes. He was right.

"I've lost a file," Scotty began in that eager, energetic voice of his which dissolved immediately into complaints after his first sentence. "Damned office-bashers. Can't trust 'em to look after anything."

Howard looked up again and Scotty went on hurriedly, obviously anxious to talk and grasping at Howard's attention while he had it.

"Bloody files. Desk's littered with 'em. Wish I were still flying. All I do now is sit about and sort out other people's bumph." He flung out a hand in energetic protest, then his little eyes began to peer enquiringly about him so that Howard was irresistibly reminded of a sea lion sniffing for fish.

"Didn't leave it in here when I came this morning, did I?" Scotty asked. "Marked 'Mackay'. I wouldn't like it to be picked up by any of the orderly-room staff. Nosy swine," he went on in his fortitude-under-adversity voice. "Swear they know more about us than we know about *them*."

He sighed noisily. "Found a file on accommodation in the hutted camp on my desk at tea-time that ought to have been in the SWO's hands. Thought I took it in myself but I expect that clot Starr was using it and it got missed."

Howard watched him patiently. "You didn't leave your file here," he pointed out coldly.

"Hell!" Scotty frowned in honest bewilderment. "Can't think where it's gone, old boy. Poor show, whoever lost it. Going to get a strip torn off when I find out. Gen for the Group Captain. That's what it was. Flight Sergeant Mackay's been swiping petrol. And now he's got the chop. In a dinghy in the Channel, I hear."

"I know," Howard said. "That's why I'm producing forecasts every hour."

"Eh? Oh, of course!" Scotty's face wore a hurt look, as though some private information had been filched from him. "Of course. That'll be why Groupy's so edgy today. Practically threw me out of his office. Just when I was trying to get the OK on this damn bus service. And, hell, I *have* to get his decision on *some* things, don't I? We've got to have the bus service. The AOC's coming at the weekend, and he's a holy terror for the comfort of the troops. That's the worst of my job. If Groupy catches a rocket because they haven't got a bus I'll catch a rocket from *him*."

He was appealing to Howard to listen, as he was always appealing for someone – anyone – to listen to his long-winded complaints. Scotty seemed never to have grown up, and his attitude to his troubles was that of a small boy, resentful and despairing at the same time.

"Mackay's up for a commission," he said. "Believe Groupy's rather keen on Mackay. From what I remember of him, he was a surly devil. Looked at me as though I were sticking my nose in when I asked him for further enlightenment to some of the questions on his application."

"Perhaps he thought he'd filled 'em in satisfactorily."

"Well, he jolly well hadn't. I felt one or two of 'em needed further explanation."

Howard glanced over his spectacles at Scotty, and said nothing.

"Somebody has to bring order into the chaos," the Administration Officer went on. "That damned Station Warrant Officer's a wash-out. I'm always having to clobber him. Sly old bastard. Never binds. Just looks at me as though I were telling him how to do his job."

"He's been doing it for nearly ten years now."

"I know. In a rut completely. You'd think he wouldn't require prodding from the Station Admin. Officer. But then I suppose that's what I'm for. That's why everyone likes me so much." Scotty laughed mirthlessly. "Popular Scott, I'm known as – I don't think! Hell," he ended, "I can't help having to chase people." He sagged unhappily in the chair, jaded and inefficient.

Howard rose, collecting papers. "You'll have to excuse me," he said. "They're wanting all this stuff in the Ops. Room. I'm sorry about your lost file."

"Yes. Didn't want to lose that one of all files." Scotty glanced at the papers in Howard's hands. "Well, and how's the weather?"

"A bit grim, I'm afraid."

"Jolly rotten show. Oh, well, you carry on. I ought to be going myself. I ought to go and tear a strip off Starr. I expect he's mislaid the damned thing somewhere."

Howard disappeared, leaving Scotty still sitting in the chair, listlessly looking at a sheet of weather information which must have been pure gibberish to him, and made for the Operations Room. The Group Captain was there, standing by the table with the Controller. The lonely-looking marker in the Channel which represented Harding and his crew was surrounded now by other markers.

Taudevin turned as Howard entered, his face devoid of expression, his curiously still eyes watchful.

"Hello, Howard," he said. "Any relief?"

"I'm afraid not, sir. I'm afraid it's working out just as I feared it would."

"Hm." Taudevin stared at the markers on the plotting table. Howard knew he had fulfilled his function but he remained behind for a while, anxious to see how things were developing.

"You know we've had a message to the effect that they've spotted a body floating?" Taudevin turned to him casually, his face unemotional, his body relaxed, those twisted claws that were his hands thrust deep into his pockets. Outwardly there was no sign of strain but his very presence in the Operations Room belied his calm expression. Howard searched his face for signs of worry that the message might have put there.

"I didn't know that, sir," he said. "I'm sorry."

"Probably not one of the people we're looking for." Taudevin turned away and Howard felt oddly grateful for the crumb of information thrown in his direction. Then the

Group Captain moved towards the plotting table again and the rest of his remarks were addressed to the Controller. "The fighter people are covering that area now," he said, tapping one of the markers. "But it won't be for long. They won't be much good after dark and it seems they'll be grounded tomorrow by the weather. That right, Howard?"

"I'm afraid so, sir."

Taudevin turned away from the plotting table. At the back of his mind he had the thought of the Air Commodore, clear and sharp above the other problems of the search – his wife's brother-in-law and his own good friend and one of the most important people in the war effort.

Group had been on the phone again to find out if anything had been heard. They were clearly beginning to get worried about all those documents Waltby was supposed to be bringing back with him and, while the affair was now beyond Taudevin's sphere of control and in the hands of the Navy and the Air-Sea Rescue people, he still felt it his responsibility to do everything possible to locate the dinghy or at least to prove to himself there were no survivors – if only because Harding was one of his pilots and Mackay and Ponsettia belonged to Harding's crew.

He ran his fingers through his hair, aware of a sudden depression. Then he pulled himself together, brushing aside his gloom. There was no reason to start worrying yet, he thought, as common sense took hold of him again. Anything could have happened. He was trying hard to convince himself they'd get away with it, that Harding and his crew would be saved, while all the time certain that the circumstances were banking up against them.

The door opened and the signals sergeant appeared.

"What is it, Sergeant?" His voice was more nervous and eager than Howard had expected it to be.

"Message come through from the Navy, sir," the sergeant said. "They passed it on to us, knowing we'd be interested. It's from a Walrus in the area of the search."

"Go on, Sergeant." The Group Captain made no attempt to reach for the slip of paper the sergeant held out to him.

"It washes out their last message, sir. The body one. False alarm."

"Ah!" To the Meteorological Officer, Taudevin seemed to let out a sigh of relief as he reached at last for the message form. "Thank you, Sergeant. I'd be glad if you'd pass a message on to the Navy and to Group asking them to let us have any messages between them and the launches and the Walruses. Anything relevant. Helps us to make up the picture."

"I'll do that, sir."

As the sergeant withdrew Taudevin moved again to the map, staring at it as though he could see something fresh on its flat surface. A WAAF nervously reached past him and moved one of the markers, and another one chalked noisily on the blackboard on the wall with a squeaky piece of chalk.

"There's still a chance, thank God," Taudevin said. He glanced through the window at the lowering sky. "Here comes the first of your rain, Howard."

Squadron Leader Scott sat in Howard's office for a while after Howard had disappeared – until the faint patter of rain on the windows stirred him out of the slough of unease in which he was wallowing. He sat up and glanced round, aware of the room being unexpectedly darker, then the slash of rain on the glass, driven by a buffet of wind, drove him to his feet as though it were a whip across his back.

For a while he stood uncertainly, wondering if he ought to try the Station Warrant Officer's department for that lost file of his. He was on the point of setting off for the stairs when he was finally put off by the look he knew he'd see on the old warrior's face if he went in there admitting his own incompetence.

There'd be no words, no recriminations, not even an offer to help, but still that look. And the SWO's looks, after twenty-five years in the Air Force, were things that could crush with ease anyone below a wing commander. The Station Warrant Officer, as Scotty well knew, was probably the most efficient man on the station and ran an office in which nothing was ever lost, either on the desk or in that filing system which clicked away inside his brain.

Scotty shrugged off the small, foolish feeling he could never fail to avoid in front of the SWO and, closing the door of Howard's office behind him, he pranced down the stairs and into the bleak, green-painted corridor that led to the Group Captain's room. Outwardly he gave the impression of cheerful stupid heartiness. Inwardly he was a confusion of subtle strains.

Chiefly, that lost file of his was worrying him to a sickly awareness of failure, and he felt baffled and irritated by the apparent indifference and incompetence of everyone round him.

The Group Captain's office was empty and Scotty turned angrily and set off for the stairs again, knowing he might reasonably expect to find him in the Operations Room. As he began to trudge up the steps he remembered that Taudevin had asked him to visit the Station Sick quarters on his behalf to see the men there who had returned injured from operations, and he made a point of trying in his muddled way to fix a time in his head, a definite hour so he wouldn't forget. After all, he thought in a burst of loyalty, Groupy had plenty on his plate at the moment with this VIP lost over the sea, to say nothing of Harding, Ponsettia and Mackay.

Mackay, Mackay. A restless little movement began again at the back of his mind at the thought of Mackay. He again considered going to the SWO and admitting the loss of the file but he found he had not the courage and he put it off a little longer. There was still plenty of time, he told himself. Obviously the Group Captain was waiting to see just how Harding and his crew had faced up to this dinghy experience before he did anything about it. After all – even Scotty had to admit it to himself in his Air Force slang – it would be jolly tough tit for Mackay to come back to the aerodrome on a stretcher injured or half-dead after a spell in a dinghy at the beginning of winter and find himself on a court martial charge. That was clearly what Taudevin was trying to avoid.

Scotty tried hard to imagine what it would be like to be in a dinghy, but all he could remember was the occasion when he'd ditched his own Bristol Fighter in a shell-hole in France in 1918 and emerged half-drowned from the stinking water it contained.

He was an unimaginative man and his contacts with the flying personnel were only slight in spite of his noisy efforts to be intimate, in spite of his attempts to join in their youthful skylarks to prove that his own fading wings made him one of them. For all his often-unwelcome friendliness, he still had no clear idea of the conditions under which they flew.

He'd often stood and watched the Lancasters take off on operations, to try to catch some of the emotions of the crews. He'd watched the great black machines taxi to the southern extremity of the airfield and, as they swung their snouts to the north, had heard the deep throbbing notes of the engines swell into a brassy blare, like the howling of ten thousand trumpets. He had seen them roll in dark outline along the runway, bouncing into the air as though in slow motion, and had listened to the echoing thunder of the heavens that threw back the clamour of the exhausts as the planes grew smaller and finally disappeared across the unwavering Suffolk fields. Then, flat and vaguely depressed at having learned nothing, he'd turned back towards the truck to the Mess.

He heaved his bulk over the last step on to the second floor and, splaying his feet, set off for the Operations Room.

As he turned the corner from the stairs he bumped into the small figure of a WAAF who had been waiting near the doorway of the Signals Section, and as she turned away with a muttered apology he realised she'd been crying.

He stopped. Scotty was a kind-hearted man, clumsy and singularly unwarlike when it came to tearful women and small children and dogs.

"What's the trouble, m'dear?" He stared at her and she stiffened slightly to attention, her head turned away from him. Scotty felt suddenly for the first time in weeks that he was dealing with something he understood.

"Nothing, sir," the girl said. She was small, very young and pretty, he noticed, and her eyes were moist. He recognised her as one of the Mess clerks.

"Come, come, child," he boomed, so that the girl's eyes flickered from side to side, fearful of the attention he might draw to her. "You're not crying for nothing."

"It's nothing, sir. Really it isn't."

"Come, child," Scotty said with hearty and infuriating persistence. "You must tell me. I'll do what I can to help you. That's what I'm here for."

"I was only waiting to find out something from the Signals Section, sir. That's all."

"Anything I can do?"

"I don't think so, sir." The girl steadfastly refused to look at him.

"Sure?"

"Yes, sir..." The girl paused and Scotty halted as he was about to move away. "Sir, I don't suppose you've heard anything of Mr Harding's crew, sir, have you?" She burst out with the words, as though they'd been released against her will, and turned to stare up at him, suddenly trusting and tearful.

"Well – er – ah..." Scotty stroked his moustache for a moment. "Er – I – Look," he said, "I'm going into Ops. Room now. I'll probably be seeing the Group Captain. I've one or two things to ask him. I'll find out what's happening and let you know when I come downstairs. Er..." Scotty couldn't resist one item of fatherly curiosity. "Who is it you're particularly interested in, hm?"

"Sergeant Ponsettia, sir."

"Your boy friend, hm?"

"Yes, sir, that's right. We're nearly engaged."

"Hm, well, hang about in the corridor below. I'll let you know."

Scotty watched her as she moved towards the stairs. He remembered now seeing her with Ponsettia at station dances and in the local pub. He knew Ponsettia chiefly by his moustache and because he belonged to the same crew as the awkward Mackay who was giving him so much trouble. New Zealander or Canadian or something.

Scotty's heart felt a flood of compassion for the little WAAF as she turned the corner. He cleared his throat noisily, thinking of his own children, blew his nose in a trumpeting sound, and pushed open the door of Operations Room.

Taudevin was there, as he had expected, talking in low tones to the Controller and the Meteorological Officer. Howard looked tired and strained, but the Group Captain was still his normal immaculate, imperturbable self, though one ravaged finger tapped on the table.

In front of them, the markers were clustered tightly round what Scotty knew to be the representation of Harding's dinghy.

The Controller was speaking in his high Welsh voice. "I've been in touch with the Navy at Dover, sir," he was saying. "If it gets no worse, they think the dinghy might ride it out. If it gets a great deal worse, they aren't so sure. I wish we knew where they were."

"What's the temperature, Howard?" Taudevin asked.

"Low, sir. It's cold and raw. Probably frost somewhere on the way. It will be pretty grim out there."

Taudevin thrust his hands into his pockets and began to walk slowly up and down the room. They could hear the chatter of the teleprinter next door, and the whispering of the WAAF plotters by the table in the centre. The WAAF corporal chalking a destination time on the blackboard suddenly made the chalk squeak sharply in the silence, so that the noise cut across the still room, setting Scotty's teeth on edge.

"Could you get a new piece of chalk, Corporal?" the Controller said mildly, and the corporal blushed and moved away from the blackboard.

Outside, Scotty could see the silver finger of a searchlight moving across the damp blue-grey sky, reflecting on the underside of the low cloud, and he remembered it was time the black-outs were up.

Then Taudevin, in his silent pacing, found himself opposite Scotty and he looked up, his pipe still in his mouth. His eyes travelled down Scotty's uniform until they rested on the papers in his hand and Scotty saw the flicker of annoyance in them.

"I'm pretty occupied, Scotty," he pointed out.

"It's not much, sir," Scotty said, shaking himself to life.

"Then I'll deal with it tomorrow." Taudevin turned away.

Scotty opened his mouth to speak. The bus service was really worrying him and he was anxious to get the Group Captain's view on it. He shut his mouth, opened it again, then decided not to say anything. Knowing that the eyes of the Controller and Howard were on him, he fumbled behind him for the door handle, feeling embarrassed and foolish at Taudevin's words. He was glad to get outside.

In the corridor, he stood staring at the closed door for a moment, stroking his moustache, wondering whether he ought to try once more and chance Taudevin's annoyance. He knew the Group Captain invariably gave way when he insisted, but somehow, at that moment, Scotty had the feeling he might burst out into one of the violent angers he sometimes roused in him.

He turned on his heel and pranced towards the stairs, suddenly noticing how much darker it appeared to be than when he had climbed up them.

As he stopped thoughtfully on the bottom step he became aware of the little WAAF who had spoken to him outside the Signals Office, looking up at him out of the shadows, white-faced and frightened.

"Oh, ah…" Scotty searched for words. He had clean forgotten to enquire about Ponsettia and the others of Harding's crew.

"Did you find out, sir?" she asked breathlessly.

"Er…" Scotty put a plump hand on her shoulder, rather like a friendly uncle. "Yes, m'dear," he said. "Er – they're going to be all right."

"Have they got them, sir? Have they found them?"

"Well, they know where they are, m'dear," Scotty said, uneasily remembering the words of Howard and Taudevin and Jones. "They've not got them yet, exactly, but it's only a matter of time."

"Are they going to, sir? They're going to be all right, aren't they?"

"All right?" Scotty searched for words that would not commit him and failed to find any. "Of course they're going to be all right, child," he said in desperation. "Just you wait and see. They'll all be back here and in bed before you know where you are. It's just a matter of time. That's all."

She smiled shyly at him, and Scotty waved a hand in a kindly dismissal. "Now run along and don't worry any more. He'll be on the telephone to the Waafery before you know where you are."

"Thank you, sir." The little WAAF, her face suddenly gay, saluted him smartly and Scotty, a little startled to be saluted without his hat, nodded and watched her as she turned and disappeared down the corridor alongside the Station Warrant Officer's room.

Uncomfortably aware that he'd deliberately misled her, he tried to soothe his conscience by persuading himself he'd told her nothing definite. But he *had* told her Ponsettia was coming back, he remembered, and he knew very well that Ponsettia's chances of coming back were slightly less than even by this time, and he wondered how he would face her in the Mess if Ponsettia didn't come back.

As Scotty turned towards his own room he found himself hoping that the weather was growing no worse.

t w o

Scotty's uneasy foreboding about the weather was well founded.

The slate-coloured seas were higher now and greyer, and with a weighty deadness about them that was ominous. Down the valleys of the waves the foam was streaked into bars and there was a fierceness about the lurch and roll of the dinghy in the fret of the wind that flung them against each other and made them grab for handholds as they slid in sickening plunges into the steep folds where the seas towered high above them, seeming to blot out the light, sloshing water over them with a nerve-shattering suddenness that took their breath away.

And, intruding into all the other sounds – the flat splash of the water under the dinghy and the hiss of the breaking crest – came a new noise, the moan of the rising wind whipping the splintered surface from the sea in spits of spray, slicing off the tips like a knife and carrying them in icy darts from one peak to the next in line. Above them, the solid immovable sky lay like a grey pall on their hopes of rescue.

"Tell me if I'm wrong," Ponsettia said suddenly, "but is this goddam wind rising?"

Waltby and Mackay looked round them at the grey lifting water, now growing darker as evening approached. Harding was asleep, lolling against Mackay, pale and young-looking and strained.

"I've been staring at this damn sea ever since we ditched," Ponsettia went on gravely, "and I've been noticing that the waves seem just a bit higher than they did. And I notice that the crests are whipped away just a bit smarter by the wind than they were at first."

They stared over the relentless waves, all of them aware of the tomb-like coldness of the sea and the frostiness of the air around them.

"Where are we now?" Mackay asked, his small eyes sharp and glittering and unwearied by the cold and the motion and the lack of hope.

"Same as before. Close in to Holland, I guess," Ponsettia said. "Just north of the Scheldt and Walcheren. Only now we're closer in."

"They can't be far away," Mackay muttered half to himself. "The bastards must be somewhere about. They *must* be searching."

" 'Patient, ever patient, and joy shall be thy share', my old grandma used to say," Ponsettia observed solemnly. "My grandpop used to put it differently. He used to say 'Sit up, chin up, and dry up'."

Mackay glowered at him, nursing his cut hand, white and puffed now, the gash black with dried blood beyond the knot of the tie. His fingers were stiff and dead looking, and the raw pain in the wound put an edge on his temper. "I haven't time to be patient," he said bitterly, thinking of those plans of his gathering dust, fading more with every day and every hour, in danger of being lost in the tangle of so many other lost hopes. "I'm older than you, chum. When the war's over all the blokes who've dodged the column will be there getting the pick of everything. I haven't the time to go on waiting."

His voice rose a little as he finished and Ponsettia's words, when he next spoke, had lost the sharpness of sarcasm.

"All the same, it don't do any of us any good for you to sit there worrying, bud. Cheer up."

Watching the growing tension between them, Waltby began to realise just what it had meant when he had heard on the wireless the dry phrase, "One of our aircraft is missing." He'd heard it often, but had never seen beyond it to the tensions it might hide, the furious anger, the impatience, the fears.

"How long is it since we ditched?" Mackay asked. He glanced at Harding for a moment, but the pilot's eyes were closed, and he found himself appealing to Waltby. Rank, that intangible thing he had always despised, that cause of so many of his grouses, that right to make decisions and give orders, that right which was denied him now because there was someone superior in rank present – it was always cropping up, as indestructible as the Service itself. All his Air Force life Mackay had been kicking against rank, like a restless horse under an ill-fitting saddle, but now he instinctively turned towards it for advice and encouragement.

It came as a shock to Waltby to hear himself appealed to. Over the years, he had got out of the habit of making decisions and giving orders except where they affected his experiments and research. He had almost thought he had forgotten the trick. But with Mackay staring at him, a puzzled anger in his eyes, he suddenly sat more upright.

"Eight hours or so, I imagine," he said.

"Could a Sunderland get down to us?"

"Perhaps, if they found us."

Mackay had been staring round the sky almost from the first moment they had climbed into the dinghy but gradually, although his eyes were sharp still, a listlessness had crept over his movements – as it had over all of them. They had been baling, throwing the water out of the well of the dinghy with tired sweeps of their arms, but without Harding to goad them on they had slowed down and stopped, and Waltby, to his own surprise, found it was he who was thinking of their danger if they ceased baling or allowed the blood to stop circulating in their bodies to combat the iciness of the water round their legs.

Even as he considered it, Ponsettia put his thoughts into words. "If I could just move my foot about," he said, "I wouldn't mind so much. I've had pins and needles in my behind now for an hour or more and I can't get rid of it. I can manage an inch or two but that isn't kinda enough."

He looked across at Waltby with sombre eyes, then down into the tangle of legs between them.

With every roll and bob of the dinghy the grey-yellow puddle in which they sat slopped from one side to the other, flooding round their thighs, carrying with it Mackay's helmet and the empty tobacco tin Ponsettia had found in his pocket and used for baling. For the first time, Waltby saw in the icy puddle a potential danger that was as great as capsizing.

"Let's work our arms," he suggested, sitting up, alert and with new strength. "Let's do exercises or something. It's time we tried again." And he began to flap his arms backwards and forwards round himself as well as he could within the confined limits allowed to him

Ponsettia looked up under his eyebrows without moving his head, listlessly and with a wealth of weariness. Then he seemed to gain interest from Waltby's clumsy actions and he sat up himself.

"I'll show you a better one," he said. He leaned across the dinghy to grab hold of Waltby's hands, and they began to work their arms backwards and forwards, vigorously, as though they were using a two-handed saw.

"Just the job to work up an appetite," Ponsettia panted. "Boy, am I looking forward to my energy tablet!"

"You next, Mackay," Waltby said and, as Ponsettia released his hands, he reached across to Mackay. The wireless operator stared at his outstretched arms sourly, almost disbelievingly, and kept his hands where they were.

"Don't be a stupid clot, Mac," Ponsettia said angrily.

"Give Syd a couple of laps round the side of the dinghy."

"Oh, what's the use? Waste of time!"

"Get hold of my hands," Waltby snapped. "And stop arguing, for a change."

Mackay glared at him for a moment, then unwillingly he joined hands and they worked their arms together until their muscles ached. They sat back, tired but warmer, then a wave slashed across the dinghy, drenching them again.

"Showers thrown in," Ponsettia said. "All we want now is a lady masseur."

"I told you it was a waste of time," Mackay growled.

Ponsettia glanced at him, then turned to Waltby again. "How about a go at baling, Syd? Water's rising again."

Waltby took the flying helmet from him and they bent to work, laboriously emptying the dinghy, Ponsettia using the tobacco tin. Mackay threw water out with his good hand.

Waltby was watching the sail as he worked. "I think," he said, "that instead of trying to sail somewhere we ought to try to tack a bit if we can. I mean, we're miles from home, and we can't do a lot of good trying to get there. With this wind, we're only being carried further and further south – that is, nearer to Occupied Belgium or Holland. We can't paddle because it's too rough, so wouldn't it be better if we used the sail to tack, and tried to stay as near the ditching position as we could? Then, if they have any idea at all where we are, at least we'll be there when they come to find us."

"The Skipper didn't suggest that," Mackay said immediately he'd finished.

"The Skipper probably didn't know much about sailing," Ponsettia pointed out.

"I reckon he'd have said if he wanted to tack," Mackay insisted stubbornly.

"Aw, Jesus, man, he probably never even thought of it. Dry up and try to be helpful."

Mackay thought for a second, obviously troubled by his loyalty to Harding, then "How do you tack?' he asked quickly.

Recalling scraps of sailing lore from his youth, Waltby showed him how to use the lines attached to the sail and immediately, as he was told what to do, Mackay became eager to co-operate again, forgetting Waltby's rank and his own hostility. As Waltby finished talking he saw Ponsettia staring at the sleeping form of Harding.

"What do you reckon we ought to do about the driver?" the Canadian asked.

"We've done all we can do." Mackay, who had been toying with the guy ropes attached to the sail with an obvious pleasure at having a task to perform, turned and interrupted, brusquely, jealously.

"Think we ought to have a squint at his bread-basket?" Ponsettia went on, ignoring the wireless operator.

"I don't think so," Waltby said. "At least he's as warm as he's likely to be at the moment. Let's leave him. If he's sleeping he couldn't be doing better for shock."

Ponsettia nodded. "OK, Syd," he said. "You're the boss." He seemed to have accepted Waltby as being in command of their frail craft now that Harding was asleep, and they sat silently for a while, Mackay occasionally adjusting the sail, Ponsettia grinding the handle of the squawk box.

Waltby watched them both with interest. Ponsettia was staring at the surface of the sea, his thoughts apparently far away. He seemed placid, easy-going, prepared to accept in the same mood whatever came, in direct contrast to Mackay's over-anxious desire to get on with something, to help themselves despite their obvious inability to change their circumstances.

"How long do you reckon it'll take 'em to find us?" – Mackay said, baling awkwardly with his uninjured hand.

He had clearly been trying to work out their chances of rescue.

"Well, bud," Ponsettia said cheerfully, staring over the sea still, "say we're forty miles from Blighty and say that a wave covers two yards. That's a bit on the small side, but let's take that for example – "

"What the hell are you getting at?"

"I'm answering your question." Ponsettia's eyes opened wide and his face was innocent. "Let's see, then. That's eight hundred and eighty waves to every mile. That's eight hundred and eighty times forty. That's thirty-five thousand two hundred waves between us and the UK. Now every wave is, say, four yards up and four yards down. That's eight yards. That's" – he worked the number out in his head with his navigator's swift arithmetic – "two hundred and eighty-one thousand, six hundred yards between us and England. Might be a yard out one way or the other. Say," – his voice rose indignantly – "that means those jokers in the Air-Sea Rescue launches have got to go nearly two hundred miles to get here. Hell, that's a long way, man!"

"You stupid clot!" Mackay spoke the words with hatred. "Those jokers have gotta go up and down every goddamned wave, haven't they?" Ponsettia grinned. "I reckon I've made a conservative estimate. It'll take 'em from now till Doomsday to get us, I guess."

Waltby looked at Mackay's angry face. "Shut up, Canada," he said quickly, finding the Canadian's light spirits as jading as Mackay's heavy lack of humour. "Don't make it any worse."

They sat in silence again, listening to the slap and smack of the water under the dinghy and the soft hiss as it fell across their legs when they slid down into the troughs between the waves.

"Christ, I hate the bloody sea," Mackay said suddenly. Waltby watched him, his mouth sour with the taste of his sickness, his lips cracked and painful with the brine on them. His eyelids were stiff with salt now and felt brittle as he blinked, and he was numb with cold. But with the responsibility of command on him again he had thrust away his weariness and felt far better than when they had first ditched.

Ponsettia was staring over the side of the dinghy as he slopped water steadily over the inflated walls with the old tobacco tin. He seemed to find some absorbing thought that protected him from the cold and from Mackay's sullen resentment, and kept him cheerful in spite of the wretchedness of their position.

"They say the sea's full of plankton," he said suddenly. "Fishes live on it – even whales. They say that's what makes the water phosporous at night."

"Who the hell cares what it's full of?" Mackay said furiously. "All I wish is that it was full of Air-Sea Rescue launches." He stared round him. "Where the hell are they?" he demanded. "They've had time to get here. Plenty of time. The lazy bastards aren't trying. That's what."

For a while Ponsettia watched him as he stared along the horizon and studied the sky, obviously itching to get on with something, bored by the inactivity.

"What do you normally do with your spare time, Mac?" he asked unexpectedly.

"What the hell's that got to do with anything?"

"Just something running round my mind. What do you do with it?"

"I never have any."

"Go on, don't give me that. What do you do with your off-duty nights?"

"Pictures. Beer. Dance. Girls. That sort of thing, I suppose. Anything to pass the time till I'm demobbed."

"Thought so."

"What's wrong with it, anyway?" Mackay was aggressive immediately.

"Nothing, brother. Nothing at all. Lots of people do. And I'll bet every goddam one of 'em would behave like you're doing now if they suddenly found they had to pass a long time without pictures, beer and girls. Give us a rest, bud."

Mackay gave him a furious look.

"Just watch that gull there, Mac," Ponsettia went on cheerfully. "See him? Floating. There, see him? Up he comes again." He pointed across the water to where a solitary gull bobbed up on the crest of a wave and disappeared again. "He's not getting all het up about nothing, is he?"

"That bastard can fly away. *I* can't," Mackay snapped. "He's got nothing to get het up about."

"One up to you there, Mac."

While they were arguing Waltby had been listening to them with only half his attention on their words. The other part of his brain was focused on something just beyond the slap and splash of water.

"Listen!" he said suddenly. "Shut up, you two, and listen."

The argument stopped short, cut off immediately as they cocked their heads. Faintly they could hear a light high-pitched drone.

"An aircraft!" Mackay shouted the word, half jumping up. "An aircraft! A Walrus, by the sound of it!"

"Take it easy, bud," Ponsettia yelped, cranking the generator handle. "You can't reach it from here and we don't want capsizing. Where's your dinghy drill?" His voice was cracked with excitement.

"The flare, the flare, where's the flare?" Waltby was pawing round the dinghy frantically.

"Here, give it here. I know how it works." Mackay snatched it from him and began to wrestle with the tape.

"Hold it a minute, Mac," Ponsettia said quickly. "Let's see the aircraft first."

The excitement swelled, catching at them all as their desperate eyes swept the sky, stopping the breath in their throats as they tried to talk.

"There it is!" Mackay pointed, his arm flung out in a vigorous gesture. "Over there. Low down. See it? It's a hell of a long way away!" He struggled with the flare for a while, his head down, his face twisted with fury. "This bloody flare! My fingers are too cold."

Waltby could see the moving speck over the southern horizon.

"Over here, we're over here!" Mackay lifted his head and began to yell over his shoulder in the direction of the aircraft, his eyes blazing with excitement, his fingers still struggling with the release tape of the flare. "Oh, Christ!" he yelped in an agony of disappointment. "I can't get hold of it."

"It's a Walrus. They're searching for us," Ponsettia yelled, his surface calmness suddenly cracking and showing the frantic excitement beneath. "Get that son-of-a-bitch flare going, can't you?"

"He's about ten miles away," Waltby said desperately, keeping his eye on the moving speck. "Hurry, for God's sake, or he'll miss us!"

"Oh, the bastard! The bastard!" Mackay was sobbing the words. "It won't come. I can hardly feel the flaming thing, my fingers are so cold." He thrust the flare at Ponsettia. "Here, Canada, you try!"

"He's going now," Waltby interrupted flatly. "We're too late, I'm afraid."

"He's turning away." Holding the useless flare in his hands, Ponsettia was staring after the Walrus, his eyes hard, his face dead and expressionless. "He's heading south now."

Mackay started to shout, the veins standing out on his neck with the effort, his voice cracking with the strain. "Here! Here! We're here!"

"No good, Mac," Ponsettia said heavily. "He can't hear you, bud."

Mackay choked to silence and stared at Ponsettia for a moment, then he grabbed the handle of the generator and started to crank desperately.

"No wonder he didn't spot us," he shouted.' 'Why weren't you turning this thing? You Yanks are all alike."

"I *was* turning the goddam thing till you passed me the flare." Ponsettia's eyes lit up with anger. "And don't call me a Yank. The squawk box must be busted or the Walrus would have heard. She must have caught a bang when we ditched and a valve's burnt out. You're the wireless operator. You ought to know."

"All right, cut it out, you two," Waltby said sharply. "Quarrelling won't help. It was nobody's fault."

"I said these things were no goddam good," Ponsettia muttered.

"He was too far away," Waltby said as calmly as his voice would allow. "He might never have seen us, anyway."

Mackay stopped cranking and sat limply. "I'll bet the careless swine wasn't listening out," he said with a cold fury, his eyes glistening with tears. "They're all the same. *They* don't care. *They're* warm."

They flopped back against the sides of the dinghy, dumb with misery, exhausted by their excitement and wretched at the anti-climax. The incident seemed to have happened so quickly that it took on a quality of unreality and Waltby found himself half-imagining there never had been an aircraft.

Then they realised that Harding was still motionless. During all the excitement he had not stirred.

Ponsettia was peering hard at him now, his face close to the pilot's, listening to his breathing. Then he sat back and looked at the others.

"I guess the Skipper's passed out," he said.

three

As the Walrus turned to the south, above the driving infinity of water and just too far away to see the small blob of the dinghy on the darkening seas, Boyle, the pilot, was whistling slowly between his teeth in a way that made Petty Officer Porter crouch lower over his wireless set, his ears stopped by his earphones. The thought of four men in a dinghy, half-frozen, perhaps afraid or injured, certainly anxious, had driven the songs from Boyle's lips and he had conducted his part of the search largely in silence. But his nature being what it was, he was unable to be depressed for long and his light spirits eventually emerged unconsciously in the excruciating tooth-whistle that set Petty Officer Porter's teeth on edge.

The Walrus chugged heavily along, helped by the tail wind until its speed reached a phenomenal figure. Boyle stopped whistling.

"One last leg south," he said. "Then we turn home. Sort the course out, Ted."

Petty Officer Porter, bent over the wireless set, turned clumsily. "I always feel a bit chokker when I'm just setting off for home," he admitted with a weighty unhappiness. "When I think that in about an hour or so I shall have my feet up in front of the Mess stove with a pint of dark, I always remember there'll still be some poor bloke sitting in a dinghy with a wet seat and feeling as much like death as he can get."

"Might not have made the dinghy," Boyle pointed out, ceasing his whistle.

"We've heard nothing," Porter agreed. "And they've got squawk boxes in all those dinghies these days."

"There's not much more we can do now, anyway." Boyle held the Walrus steady on its new course. "With this wind blowing they ought to be south of here, if anything. Tide's setting south, too. In any case, it'll be dark before we touch down, and we've reached our limit."

"Besides" – he flipped a piece of paper, a slip from Porter's message pad – "there's this bad weather report. They don't send these things for fun. It's addressed to us personally and to the launch boys, not to all units at sea, so there must be something nasty coming this way. If we don't turn for home very soon we'll be down in the drink ourselves."

In the east, where the land lay, the night was rising like a grey fog from the surface of the Channel, creeping slowly upwards until it would eventually envelop the whole of the sky and slide down again towards the west. The sea below them was more turbulent than before as they reached the broken water of the Narrow Seas. The clouds were edging closer to them and the wind was strong enough to buffet the aeroplane.

"Compass course 270, turning in five minutes exact," Porter said. "I'll give you the word when to bring her on to it."

"Roger-dodger!" Boyle began to hum quietly and it was perhaps symbolic that his song was Irish and sad. Inevitably, he kept thinking of the men for whom they had been searching. Boyle was a happy soul but, like most Irishmen, he was easily moved to anger or sadness.

He stared out of the starboard window of the Walrus, feeling more than ever, in the square little cabin, like a taxi-driver looking for a fare. In front of him the stub float-nose of the machine quivered in the vibration of the engine and the hammering of the wind. Inside, the shadows were deeper and more opaque, and the light in the windows had taken on a bluish tinge. Porter had switched on the little orange light over his chart table. Once, for a second or two, drops of rain beat against the Walrus, to be driven into rivulets along the flat top of the hull up against the Perspex wind-screen. On the glass itself the rain divided, as though it were parted hair, some going to port and some to starboard.

Although what he was seeing registered sharply enough on Boyle's brain his thoughts were far away. He was thinking, oddly enough, of his home at that moment, and not about the grey surface of the sea, curiously flattened by their height; nor the lines of shadow made by the waves; nor the flecks of white which were the crests; nor even about the black blob which swam unexpectedly into his field of vision...

"Ted," he said abruptly, sitting bolt upright out of his comfortable crouch. "Something down there. Could be a dinghy. I'm going down."

They were both leaning forward now and craning to see out of the window as Boyle dropped his starboard wing and came round and down in a sharp spiral.

"It *is* a dinghy! By God, it is! It's a dinghy!"

The Walrus flew low over the yellow rubber raft and they saw an arm wave back at them, frantically. Then Porter spoke in a flat, disappointed voice.

"Only one man in it," he said. "I thought there were supposed to be four."

"This is only a *one-man* dinghy!" Boyle stared out of the window in bewilderment. "This is a fighter boy. This isn't who we're looking for."

"One of the Thunderbolts must have ditched."

Boyle grinned. "Sometimes," he said, "I think a Walrus isn't a bad kite to be flying, after all. Let's go and fish him out and gloat over him."

"He might have seen something of the Hudson crew." Porter reached for the Morse key instinctively, still staring through the window.

"Might have," Boyle agreed. "Better let 'em know at base."

"It's going to be too dark soon for anyone to do any good," Porter growled. "*Whoever* comes, they'll get here too late to spot him."

Boyle was peering hard through the Perspex glass now, down at the small grey-yellow dot below them on which a man lay, waving stiffly with one hand. The heave of the sea was rolling him wretchedly.

"Ted," Boyle said, "this bod's been winged. He's injured or something."

"Think we'd better go down and pick him up?"

"I think we better had. At least we can help the poor blighter."

"Think we'll get off again?" Porter looked anxiously at Boyle, unhappily aware that the warm fire he'd been thinking of was now in sudden danger of not materialising.

"Should think so." Boyle started to whistle again and his tune now was not so sad.

"How about petrol?"

"Just do it, I reckon. In any case, we can't leave the poor bastard there with something bust. We'd better try. Even if we stick, at least it'll be warmer in here than on the dinghy. With that sea running and a busted wing, he might be over the side before he can be picked up. Besides, it's almost dark and he might be suffering from shock. It's hardly the weather to spend a night in a dinghy."

"Right! I'll let 'em know at base," Porter said gloomily, beginning to pound the Morse key. "Just in case we can't get unstuck again."

The Walrus hit the water with a sheeting, gushing splash that sent the spray whirling across the Perspex, temporarily blinding them, then she leapt to the next wave with a bounce that set all their equipment rattling and caused Porter to bang his head against his wireless set, before she finally settled safely, like some great gull floating on the surface of the water.

"Done it," Boyle said breathlessly. "Thought the wings were coming off for a minute, though. Rougher than I thought." He glanced round. "Where's the dinghy?"

"Ahead, slightly to starboard."

Boyle revved the engine and as the propeller bit into the air, pushing them forward, the Walrus slid up a wave, lurched over the top and skidded sideways down the following slope.

"Dead on target," Boyle said. "Hold tight, Ted. Do you ever get seasick?"

"If I'd thought I'd been in danger of going to sea I'd have joined the Air Force." Porter, big and clumsy as he struggled to the forward hatch along the fuselage of the plane, which seemed to be standing first on its nose and then on its tail in the towering seas, halted and looked round at Boyle. "Seems to be blowing a hell of a lot harder down here, Pat. These waves are big."

The dinghy ahead of them came into view again as they were lifted on the crest of a wave. Porter, with his head out of the forward hatch in the nose of the Walrus, heard the faint cry that came down-wind to them.

"*Hilfe! Hilfe, bitte!*"

"Christ," he yelled. "It's a Jerry!"

"I'd have let the swine drown if I'd known," Boyle growled with an unconvincing show of disgust. "Can you get a line to him?"

"I'll have a go."

Its rudder swinging port and starboard as Boyle tried to head into wind towards the bobbing dinghy, its motor screaming a high-pitched note, the Walrus beat clumsily up the waves as they approached, so that Porter, with the wind drumming in the wires of the wings over his head, was drenched by the water sheeting over the bows every time they plunged into the valleys of the sea.

As they swept up to the dinghy he threw a line to its occupant, who managed to catch it awkwardly with his left hand, then the dinghy had swept behind them and underneath the wing so that the folded amphibious wheels caught the German a crack on the head.

"Hold it, for God's sake!" Porter yelled.

The German had managed to wrap the line round his wrist with a quick twist of his arm, but the jerk as he reached the limit of the line almost yanked him overboard. He sprawled awkwardly half over the side until he managed also with the same hand to grasp a rope on the dinghy and wriggle back to safety.

Porter began to haul on the rope and the dinghy came nearer to the bow of the aircraft, but with his one sound arm the German could not manoeuvre it beneath the low wing of the machine, and the heaving sea kept swinging him up against the underside of the wheel in sickening jolts.

"*Ich kann es nicht aushalten!*" he yelled despairingly.

"Pat," Porter shouted, "I can't get to him here. I'll have to yank him through the after-hatch."

He began to pay out the line again so that the dinghy drifted astern from underneath the wing until it bumped against the flat hull of the Walrus alongside the hatch aft of the main plane. The German, seeing them move ahead of him again and obviously under the impression they were about to cast him adrift once more, began to call out in an agony of fear.

"All right, all right, you sausage-eating bastard," Porter panted furiously. "No bloody panico. I'm coming."

He made the line fast round the bollard and struggled back inside the plane, saturated from the spray, and pushed past Boyle to the after-hatch.

The German's face was a mixture of apprehension and surprise as Porter appeared beside him.

"Serve you right if I left you where you are," Porter snarled as the water slashed across him.

The German was shouting in a high-pitched, excited voice, making taut, vague gestures with the hand that held the ropes. Boyle, to hold his machine into wind and to avoid being swung broadside on to the waves, kept his engine running and the Walrus was still making headway through the water, up and over waves that seemed enormous now they were down to sea-level. And every time they lurched over the crest the dinghy was bounced up against the fuselage so that the German, in danger of being thrown out, screamed a rigmarole of words they couldn't understand.

"Tell him to turn off the tap, for God's sake," Boyle begged from inside the cabin.

"Oh, come here, you ugly swine." Porter leaned over the side, grabbed the German by the collar as the dinghy swung alongside, and heaved with all his strength. As the dinghy bounced away again the German was yanked across the fuselage and he gave a sudden scream, partly with pain as he banged his injured arm and partly with fear as he thought he was about to fall into the sea. Then he and Porter were sprawled inside the machine, panting in a spreading pool of water.

The German was still holding on to the line which Porter had thrown and which now went through the hatch and along the outside of the machine to the forward bollard. One end of it was wrapped tightly round his wrist with the line attached to his dinghy, which was also dangling outside, holding his arm rigidly up into the open hatch.

"For God's sake" – Boyle's frantic voice brought Porter hurriedly to a sitting position – "tell the silly fool to let go that line. The dinghy's standing on its end. It'll jam up under the elevators soon. It'll get wrapped round something in a minute."

For a second or two Porter pawed over the German, trying to make out which of the two lines he was holding belonged to the dinghy, then he wrenched them both from his hand with a savage, imperious gesture that had urgency in it rather than cruelty. It brought a new yelp of pain from the German, then they both flopped back again on the deck, and the dinghy bobbed clear and vanished quickly astern.

While Porter was still getting his breath back the German sat up, lifting himself with one arm.

"*Danke! Danke! Gott sei Dank.*"

"Oh, *heil* bloody *Hitler!*" Porter snarled the only words of German he knew. "Now dry up."

Boyle turned in his seat. "I wonder if this merchant saw anything of the other dinghy?" he said. "Let's ask him. If he did, we'll chance a last look and then go home."

The two of them glowered at the German in the dim interior of the Walrus, while the light outside grew steadily less and the vicious sea changed from grey to black. The German sat staring at them, his eyes wide and fearful, young, small and pathetic – like a damp, half-drowned puppy, so that they felt neither hatred nor anger.

"*Achtung,* you bastard," Boyle said without emotion. "You see any other dinghy, no?"

The German shook his head. "No English," he said "No speak English."

"Dinghy. *Comme* – oh hell, what's German for 'like yours'? *Wie – wo ist die Dinghy?*"

The German pointed aft and started to gabble excitedly.

"He thinks you're talking about *his* dinghy," Porter said disgustedly.

Boyle pointed hard at the German, stuck out his fore-fingers like guns and made a mime of firing. Then he raised his eyebrows and said: "*Wer?* Who did it? Who got you?"

"Bomber. Hudson." The German was lying back, his face pale and strained.

"Hudson?" Porter grinned, still sitting on the floor. "Hear that? That's the one we're looking for, Pat. Where was it?"

"Hudson?" Boyle shaped his hand into an aeroplane flying. "*Wo? Wo ist die Hudson?*"

The German patted his chest, shrugged his shoulders expressively, then flourished a hand to describe an aircraft diving into the sea. "*Kaputt*," he said. "*Verschwunden. Im Wasser.*" He pointed. "*Nördlich. Gegen Norden.*"

"This is the johnny who shot 'em down, I'll bet," Boyle said. "They must have got in a poop at him, too, and sent *him* down."

"What's his name?"

Boyle pointed to the German. "*Wie?*" he asked.

"Hax. Rudolf Hax."

"Well, that was easy. Let's ask him which direction the Hudson took. It might help."

This was more difficult than they had imagined, however and after a tiring five minutes Boyle sat back.

"I think he's half-baked," he said peevishly to Porter.

"*Bitte?*" The German's eyebrows rose.

"Not you. I'm not talking to you."

The German smiled. "*Ja*. Yes. Yes." He grinned and Boyle glared at him furiously.

"Better fix him as best we can," he said to Porter. "Shove his flipper in his jacket or something for now. Then we'll get off. You can fix it properly when we're airborne. We'll go back northwards and we might spot something."

He waited until Porter sat the German upright and tucked the broken arm into his jacket.

"OK?" he called out. "Right! We're off. Let's not waste time. We haven't all that much petrol. Sort him out after we're unstuck."

Porter nodded and Boyle opened the throttle as the machine poised on top of a wave. The Walrus slid at speed down into the valley, then screamed up the next wave as though it were a living thing clawing up the solid side of the sea. Then she was airborne, poised for a moment as though hovering, before the engine spluttered.

The sudden lack of power caused the aeroplane to drop sharply. She bounced awkwardly and lop-sidedly on the crest of the next wave, and the engine spluttered again.

"Hold tight, Ted!" Boyle yelled.

Ahead of him a huge wave reared, dark and green and menacing, its crest curling over already. Then the Walrus dug its nose into it and water poured madly over the bow and across the Perspex. Boyle was flung forward and Porter and the German slid along the deck until they crashed in a yelling tangle of arms and legs behind Boyle's seat The engine spluttered once more, then died completely, and they heard in the silence the water dripping off the wings on to the fuselage in swift little hammer-taps.

"God blast the man who invented these thrice-damned tripe-machines to everlasting awful bloody Hell."

Boyle tore out the oaths painfully, slowly. Then he sat back and stared at Porter and the yelling German sprawling on the deck behind him.

"That's flaming well torn it," he said to Porter. "Better get busy on your buzzer, Ted, and get our position away. The launches aren't far away. It's still not too dark for them to pick us up."

As Porter crouched at the wireless set Boyle tried the starter, but the engine was as dead as if it had never been warm above their heads. Boyle glared at it, all the hatred he had in him for the slow-flying old machine welling up inside him. Then the German, lying behind his seat, hauled himself upright one-handedly.

"*Bitte, bitte*," he said, indicating his injured arm.

"You shut your row," Boyle said in a fury. "Sure, but for you we'd have been half-way home now. You keep out of the way for a moment until we get our breath back."

The German didn't understand him but he could see the threat in Boyle's bright blue eyes and he sank back.

"Are you through, Ted?" Boyle asked, and Porter, his head low over the transmitter, nodded. The crackle of Morse filled the cabin, then Porter finished off with a flourish and sat up, staring at his message pad.

"A launch'll be directed towards us immediately," he said.

"We last saw 'em about ten miles west of here," Boyle said. "With this sea they'll be here in about an hour. Just in time before it's too dark. Oh, well" – his good humour reasserted itself – "at least we can tell 'em where the Hudson ditched. And that's more about it than they'll have heard all day."

f o u r

Across the width of the bridge from where Flight Sergeant Slingsby stood at the wheel, his mind revolving bitterly round Skinner and the engines of HSL 7525, beyond the spot where Tebbitt and Westover huddled and where the mast drummed under the roaring wind, the wireless cabin lay – stuffy, lurching like the rest of the boat, and noisy with the sound of Morse. In there, Leading-aircraftman Knox and Aircraftman Botterill, their headsets over their ears, sat huddled over the receiver, waiting for any instructions that might advance the search. About them were pads of paper and message forms clipped to the side of the cabin in bundles, signal pads and pencils, novelettes and – fastened to the bulkheads with strips of sticking plaster from the first-aid kits – the inevitable nudes.

Knox, with the two-handed split mind of the wireless operator, was twiddling the dial of the receiver with one hand while he thumbed through the pages of a novelette with the other.

"7526 is still around," he announced. "How about getting a spot on him, Botty, with the direction-finder?"

Botterill silently reached up with his right hand to the handle of the direction finder and began to turn it slowly, his eyes on the calibrated ring, watching the duel between the two boats with the aid of wireless.

"South-east of us now," he said after a while. "And close. It's a toss-up which of us finds 'em first."

"7526 for a bet," Knox said gloomily. "The only thing 7525 could ever pick up would be a cold in the head – "

"Hold it!" Botterill suddenly bent over his message pad and his pencil began to move rapidly. "It's us. Plain language," he jerked out of the corner of his mouth.

Knox leaned over his shoulder and began to read what he wrote down. "*Proceed – immediately – to – assistance – of damaged – Walrus.* Chiefy's going to be pleased when he sees that," he said. He watched as Botterill wrote down the bearings and made a wry face. "That's south of here," he went on. "Away from the area of search. How sweetly thoughtful of 'em to do that. It leaves everything wide open for 7526 to make the pick-up." His pursed expression of sarcastic affection changed to gloom again. "Hell, the balloon's going to go up when Slingo sees that!"

The two of them stared at each other, both busy with the same thoughts on Slingsby's fury, then Botterill shrugged, his expression martyred.

"Take over. I'll let the Skipper have it if I can dodge Chiefy," he said, picking up the message slip and taking off his headphones. "They must be leaving 7526 here or they'd send *her* on this job. She's nearer and faster. Poor old 7525 – doing the dirty jobs again. That's what comes of having a kid for a Skipper and a dud fitter. Loxton wouldn't have this lark with 7526." His shoulders humped with melodramatic woe. "This blasted boat's got a jinx on it."

He threw down his pencil and stumbled noisily down the swaying steps from the wireless cabin into the sick bay, throwing a momentary glance of compassion at the huddled figure of Milliken on the steps by the after-door, then he dived into the well behind the forecastle and shouted up the ladder into the wheelhouse.

"Skipper!" he said. "Change of course. Walrus in the drink by the sound of it."

When Botterill shouted his message to Treherne, Slingsby, his square, stubby little fists gripping the wheel, was brooding on the value of all the mechanical aids to searching they possessed and just how little help they seemed to be in bad weather.

The first Air-Sea Rescue launch, he remembered, was nothing more than a converted naval boat manned by former Royal Navy personnel. Communication had been chiefly by shouting and rescue was largely a catch-as-catch-can affair without rubber dinghies or Mae Wests. The aircraft had been Bristol Fighters, seaplanes which looked like flying birdcages, or even dirigibles, and the knowledge and experience of the men engaged on the job was largely nil.

Through the years since the nineteen-twenties the service had developed until now there were even great ships able to establish a marine-craft section of the Air Force or an Air-Sea Rescue base anywhere in the world at any time. To Flight Sergeant Slingsby, who could still remember the days before Hubert Scott-Paine and Aircraftman Shaw, once Lawrence of Arabia, had produced the first RAF boat, way back before the Schneider Trophy races had developed Air-Sea Rescue, it still seemed incredible they had come so far and yet, paradoxically, had made so little headway.

Here they were, he thought bitterly, buffeting their way slowly north into the oncoming seas, with all the aids of radar, wireless, radio-direction-finding beams, wireless telephony, spotting aircraft, and launches with vast engines and patent logs which operated through the hull instead of on the end of a long line trailed like a mackerel spinner astern – and the result was exactly the same as it always had been, given the same conditions of bad weather and low cloud: nothing.

Visibility was rapidly falling to nil now, and with no visibility not even the radar, radio and spotting planes could help them to find one small round yellow dinghy on the wastes of grey water that flung HSL 7525 about like a cockleshell for all her sixty tons.

For three hours now they had been operating what was known as a square search. Arriving on the spot where the dinghy was believed to be bobbing, they had steamed north for half a mile, then turned west and steamed a similar distance. Then they had steamed south for a mile, west for a mile and north again for a mile and a half, and so on, the distances lengthening with every other leg of their course, so that their track, plotted on the chart, appeared like a square spiral as they covered an area several miles wide round the spot on the ocean where the Hudson was supposed to have ditched. Then they had moved south and repeated the procedure.

Every time they had steamed north, with the fore-deck streaming and the spray curving and slashing against the spinners on the wheelhouse windows, the boat had thudded and smashed in short, jolting dives into the crests of solid steel with the motion of a tank crossing rough country, the waves striking heavy blows under her bows that made her tremble. Slingsby, on the wheel, watched the sharp prow rise high above the level of the sea, so that ahead of him there was only grey cloud dropping swiftly away. Then, as the boat balanced on the foamy crest before its next plunge, the sky steadied itself and began to climb again with rapidly increasing speed, until it gave place to the stormy horizon again, and all the width of the sea whirled upwards in front of him until the sky and the clouds had disappeared, and the boat smashed into the next curling green wave which hissed across the deck and beat with heavy fists against the wheelhouse and the splinter mats. Slingsby could see the great black numbers of their wireless call-sign painted on the fore-deck quivering, like the foremast and the stays and the locked anchor and the cowls, with the whip of the boat as she hit the water.

Every time they turned east or west the motion changed, so that the diving stopped and the rolling became enormous, and Tebbitt and Westover wedged themselves more tightly into the corners of the bridge, their eyes screwed up against the wind. And Milliken, just inside the sick bay door, hung on for dear life and prayed – not now that he might die, but that in this awful world of crashing and heaving that strained his legs and arms with the effort of holding himself upright and his nerves and brain with the constant noise, he might be allowed to live to set his feet on solid earth just once more.

And then, turning south, the motion changed yet again to another one, a hideous sickening corkscrew as the boat, with the waves striking her on the quarter or the stern, tried to turn round in her own length so that Milliken's heart lifted to his throat and he was certain she was out of control. Every time her racing screws were heaved clear of the water by the wave thrusting forward under her stern, the vibration started the mast rattling and the crockery forward clinking, and set Milliken's teeth chattering together as the whole boat developed a ghastly shudder.

Across the splintered water as they worked, Slingsby could see the waving topmast of HSL 7526, performing her own square search a mile or so to the south-east. And every time the boats, by some trick of the sea, were hoisted simultaneously to the top of a wave, Slingsby caught an infuriating glimpse of the other boat, hazy with distance but there – most definitely there. Jealous of 7526's faster engines – which were due not only to her more diligent fitter but, as he well realised in spite of his chivvying of Skinner, to that freakish fact which could make two of the same type of boat or engine as different in power and temperament as chalk and cheese – he cursed the luck which had posted him to this bitch of a boat with its boy of a Skipper and its indifferent crew of sea-lawyers, the heritage of that jaw-breaking old dodger, Flight Sergeant Rollo, whom he had known and disliked through all his years of service.

His angry thoughts grew, stirred by the tiring, depressing monotony of the wild weather that made the slashes of spray across the windscreen into a whip across his temper.

Then rain, grey rain, came and went in squalls, like dirty cotton wool moving towards them from the horizon, sweeping the sea, deadening the waves a little in a distinct whisper they could hear above the engines, smoothing out the sharp iron crests into curves with the weight of it. It came, iron-dark and ugly, blotting out the horizon and blurring the distance, like a view seen through sick eyes, so that below deck everything dripped with condensation and above deck they had to don oilskins. Duffel coats smelt musty and saturated, and Treherne or Robb, coming into the wheelhouse for a glance at the chart, dribbled water in streams to the slimy floor.

As it cleared again, Botterill's shout brought Treherne from the bridge giving instructions to change course away from the search, and Slingsby's quiff quivered with his rage and his knuckles grew white as he gripped the wheel.

His jealous anger didn't last long, however. As he savagely swung the wheel and 7526 began to slide away astern to the north-east of them, his disappointment and rage dwindled with the consideration of the new job in front of them. Disappointment and dispensability were merely part of a day's work. He had been putting up with them, or causing someone else to put up with them, with one boat or another for twenty years. Rescue work had never altered, not even when the war came – not even when he had seen the Whaleback containing his lifelong friend attacked by a Messerschmidt off Dungeness and blown up in a flare of orange flame and flying splinters of wood from which they rescued one dazed survivor who had dived overboard just in time. Not even through Dunkirk and Dieppe and D-Day, nor the hundred incidents like the nightmare of trying to hack a trapped air gunner from the turret of a Flying Fortress as it wallowed half under the surface of the sea and finally slid out of sight with the gunner shouting a farewell until the water sloshed up to his neck and gurgled in his throat.

Disappointment was as natural to Slingsby as eating or sleeping, after dozens of fruitless searches and wasted nights, after the deadening depressions that had accompanied every one of all the floating empty dinghies they'd found or the scraps of torn charred wreckage which spoke of an agony of suffering by men who had not lived to see rescue. Where Milliken felt only fear, Slingsby consciously felt nothing – only the need to keep the boat going. Somewhere in their vicinity there were four men in a dinghy, swamped with water, cold and wet and wretched, and it was his life – not merely his duty – to rescue them if they were still alive.

Alongside him in the chilly, unheated wheelhouse Treherne was huddled over the chart, watching their position, his body wedged against the chart table so that he could retain his position and still have his arms free to use the parallel rules. On the other side, Corporal Robb watched the dial of the Chernikeeff log, which measured their speed, and the distance they travelled through the water...

It was growing dusk when Tebbitt first saw the Walrus on the horizon.

He had been listening to the conversation of the Flight Sergeant, the Skipper and Corporal Robb in the wheelhouse, trying to glean one item of information that might reassure him in this new turn of events.

Treherne, trying hard with frozen fingers to hold his parallel rules steady on the chart as the boat corkscrewed in the following sea, was speaking.

"I suppose 7526 got the job of staying on the search," he said, "because she's faster than we are."

"Ought not to be," Slingsby growled over his shoulder. "Sister ship. Built the same time. Better fitter, that's all."

"There are good fitters and bad fitters, eh?" Treherne said. "And we've got a bad one?"

"I wouldn't say that," Slingsby replied. "Skinner can do the job all right. All his interest's inside his trousers, that's all."

"Oh!"

On the bridge, Tebbitt could hear the note in the Skipper's voice, the awareness that he had missed something he ought to have checked, then the boat smashed into another wave and Tebbitt ducked to avoid the spray that lashed over the bridge into his face. As he raised his head again unhappy resentment flooded over him.

He glanced to the other wing of the bridge where Westover huddled, diminutive, wizened, clad in the tremendous sheepskin coat he invariably wore at sea over his white submarine jersey – whatever the weather and even in summer when the others were walking about the decks without shirts. His face was green and miserable.

But the spray had missed Westover and Tebbitt gave him a sour look, as though even the weather were helping to make his life more miserable and uncomfortable. His resentment began to feel for a reason for its own existence, probing until it settled on Gus Westover's affluence and normal state of wealth.

Gus had spent all his life as a stable boy or a jockey. He was reputed to have won and lost thousands on the Continent before the war and to have a small fortune tucked away in Australia, the result of accumulated winnings he had never collected. Only a malicious fate had sent Gus, who hated the sea, via the balloon barrage and an enforced transfer when women had been called up to balloon tending, into Air-Sea Rescue and the boats with the most spiteful motion of them all. His off-duty position always was and always had been, as long as Tebbitt had known him, as far towards the relative stability of the bilges as he could get – underneath one of the sick bay bunks and among the spare ammunition for the point-fives, the Mae Wests, the old oilskins and the pigeons.

Tebbitt thought of the bulge of the wallet in Westover's back pocket with bitter annoyance, for Gus, the most thriftless of people, through the mysterious sources of racing men had information which enabled him whenever he was ashore to place bets that never left him short of money. What he called his sinking fund of twenty pounds was never allowed to leave his back pocket in case that one great tip which would make his fortune for all time should ever come his way.

Doubtless Gus, who was a generous soul, would be good for a loan, Tebbitt decided, his mind still on Hilda's visit, unless he'd had a run of bad luck and there was nothing left beyond the sinking fund. Gus would never have let that go on anything but a bet, even if its addition to the coffers of the Allied Nations could have staved off an inevitable defeat and a lifetime of slavery.

If he was in the money – Tebbitt's face still wore its melancholy stare but his brain was working hurriedly beyond it. Twenty pounds was more than enough to keep even Hilda satisfied for a week. Twenty pounds. He heaved his bulk to one side, uneasily conscious of the evil in his thoughts as he considered means of acquiring the money somehow – anyhow. Then as a wave lifted them high above the surface of the sea they saw the Walrus ahead of them, together with the boat which was towing her, sharp and black against the sky.

Hastily, aware of its closeness and Slingsby's presence just below him, he put his head into the wheelhouse. "Walrus in sight, Skipper," he reported. "On the starboard bow. She's already in tow. Somebody's beaten us to it."

Robb and Treherne came out of the wheelhouse together, staring across the sea through binoculars.

"A Navy launch's got her, Skipper," Robb said. "Don't suppose they'll want us now. Navy plane and Navy boat. The Air Force won't be able to get a look in."

He turned to Tebbitt, still huddled in the corner of the bridge, as Treherne re-entered the wheelhouse. "Well, you've made it this time, Tebby," he said softly. "But only just. Looks as though you'll get your wish. If we take the survivors back you'll be on the nest with your wife tomorrow and Gus will be putting his sinking fund on a winner."

Westover interrupted gloomily. "Like hell I will," he said. "I put it on Touralay last Wednesday and she fell at the first fence." He peered ahead for a while as Robb disappeared again into the wheelhouse, then went on heavily to Tebbitt. "That's what comes of betting on jumpers," he said. "I shoulda stuck to the Flat like I usually do. Twenty quid down the drain just because a horse couldn't pick its feet up. I shoulda known better. If horses were meant to jump they'd have legs like kangaroos."

Tebbitt didn't answer. He was still staring out over the starboard bow at the Walrus and the naval launch in front of it. There'd be no borrowing from Gus now, he realised in dumb misery, and there was no one else in the crew from whom he could hope to borrow enough to keep Hilda even for a day...

As 7525 drew alongside the naval launch, only a few yards of dark, white-flecked water between them, the other boat's loud-hailer was switched on and they heard over the slap of the waves the naval skipper testing it by whistling into the microphone.

Milliken emerged unsteadily from the sick bay, one hand gripping a handrail, suspecting he might be needed at last and wondering what complicated manoeuvre was about to be enacted before him. Ever since the boat had first put to sea he had been at a complete loss to understand half of what was going on around him, and it was of little comfort to him that everybody else on board didn't suffer from the same lack of knowledge.

"Now what do they want?" Tebbitt was complaining noisily alongside him, conjuring up woes like a magic incantation to make more certain his return to base. "If they're going to send us off somewhere on one of *their* errands I'm going to see the Skipper. We'll never get home on time and I've got permission to meet that train."

"Take over my tow, please." The naval launch's loud-hailer boomed unexpectedly. "I have an injured man on board. I must hurry him back to base."

Tebbitt swore bitterly and Milliken heard Slingsby's voice from the wheelhouse, sharp and furious as he uttered one solitary expletive, and Robb muttering in a rage he didn't understand, then he heard their own loud-hailer answering in Treherne's voice.

"Can't I relieve you of the survivors? Save you changing the tow."

"Sorry. Better not move the injured man. You take the tow. If you'll come closer, we'll pass a line to you."

"Bastards!" Slingsby spoke feelingly. "The Navy doesn't like us using their sea, that's the trouble."

"Always the same." Milliken turned as he realised Knox, the wireless operator, stood alongside him, his long body swaying to the heave of the deck, his eyes angry as he studied the naval vessel across the narrow strip of water. "They resent us having faster boats. In the early days, they even used to pick up survivors and then take great pleasure in calling us out to look for them so they could swank they'd beaten us to it."

7525 was edging closer to the naval launch now and the Walrus, bobbing astern of them both, seemed huge in the half-light of dusk. Tebbitt and Westover had left the bridge and stood on the after-deck holding the lifelines while Robb balanced miraculously as he waited on the fore-deck for a heaving line to be thrown.

Suddenly, to Milliken, darkness seemed to be upon them and the grey misty shape of the Walrus to turn to shadow. The sky had changed from the gloomy grey of a wintry afternoon to the blue-black of dusk. While he was still wondering at the change he saw a heaving-line from the naval launch coil round one of the stays that held up 7525's mast. Robb, bulky in a Mae West, ran aft with it to Westover and Tebbitt and they hauled in the heavy tow-rope attached to the Walrus. As they came past Milliken, staggering and falling under the wet hemp rope across the uneven, cramped deck, he dodged hurriedly back inside the sick bay door out of the way, until he saw them performing miracles of balance on the stern where they took a turn with the rope round one of the after-cleats.

Slingsby appeared on the deck on his way aft, balancing wide-legged against the roll of the boat, his head lifted like an old hound's as he sniffed the wind. Milliken glanced quickly at him and bobbed back again into the sick bay. Instinct told him the Flight Sergeant wasn't a man to bump into at that moment, any more than the cursing Robb had been. He classed them together inevitably in his dislike, one coarse and garrulous and vulgar, the other big and strong and confident with his cultured voice and smooth sarcasm.

"You get back on the bridge, Tebbitt," Slingsby was saying in the group by the stern. "You'll go and get your fat head fast, or something soft."

Milliken saw Tebbitt's big figure stumble back to the bridge, insulted and sick at heart in his private misery, and the group on the after-deck huddled round the gun and the Carley float dissolved into semi-darkness as they worked, merging into the deck and the sea and the shadowy shape heaving upwards at the end of the tow-rope. Then Slingsby returned to the wheelhouse and Robb emerged from the shadows and stood on the after-deck near the sick bay door, huge against the light, disreputable, and, to the wretched Milliken, superbly and irritatingly sure of himself.

"OK, Skipper!" he shouted to the bridge. "She's made fast."

"We have secured the tow," the loud-hailer boomed out immediately. "Good luck."

"Good-bye, you selfish sods," Robb added quietly.

"Them and their stinking sea." Milliken could hear Slingsby's voice coming loudly from the bridge. "Think because they've got Nelson they own the show. Nelson! What's wrong with Jimmy Slingsby?"

The naval launch's bow rose as her engines blared out and she began to draw away from 7525, which was wallowing with idling engines on the ink-blue seas. Milliken watched the other boat diving and plunging, her bows under the dark waves which rolled off her deck in splinters of foam, until she merged with the twilight. He was conscious of a sour feeling of anti-climax. For a moment he'd hoped there was work for him and his eagerness had beaten down his nausea.

When he turned round he was surprised to realise it was quite dark. The Walrus was already little more than a dim shape in the distance, merging with the iron crests of the waves, and on 7525 the ventilators, the Carley float, the water casks, the ropes coiled on the deck, were losing their identity in the dark outline of the hull which was all that stood out against the sea.

The conference in the wheelhouse as the boat got under way again was a bitter one. Tebbitt, listening on the bridge, could hear every word.

"This means that 7526 will make the pick-up in the morning," Slingsby was saying. "Those medal-hungry swine will be there to do the job while we act as wet-nurse to a Walrus."

There were sour looks all over the ship. In the wireless cabin, Knox was laying the law down to Botterill.

"They should have let us take the survivors home," he was saying, indignant for his rights. "That's what we're here for, isn't it? That's why we've got those flaming great engines that make the forecastle so uncomfortable when we've got to sleep in it. Speed – that's what we're built for, isn't it? Of course it is. But the Navy knows better. *They* use us as tugs and snatch the kudos for themselves." He sighed noisily. "Ah, well, they were always the same."

Milliken, sitting disconsolately again on the steps of the sick bay, dog-tired now and shivering with the cold and the shock of seasickness, thought gloomily of the work he might have done had the injured man been transferred. He had boarded the boat with the heroic intention of tending the sick and wounded and all he had managed to do so far was to cower on the uncomfortable steps through most of twelve weary hours, not knowing where his bag of bandages and slings had gone to, torn with bouts of seasickness which left him weak and ill, and in fear of the terrible Flight Sergeant.

Gus Westover, sitting half-frozen in the Carley float on Slingsby's orders, watching the shadowy shape of the Walrus bowing and bobbing astern of them, swinging swiftly up the waves as 7525 slid down the other side, was convinced he was going to die of pneumonia. The Walrus whipping over the water reminded him gloomily of that dead cert of his that had fallen at the first fence and lost him his precious twenty pounds.

In the engine-room Corporal Skinner stood between the two thundering monsters that gave the boat motion, watching Dray still singing soundlessly below the metallic howl that filled the air, and anxiously placed a hand against the starboard engine. Then he stepped back and lifted the bilge boards and stared below. The black scum down there seemed no deeper and no more oily than usual, and he examined the botched-up pipe minutely for traces of the thin hot oil that might be forced through it. He found nothing, and the oil-pressure gauge seemed normal enough.

There was less movement now in the stern of the boat as it was held steady in the racing sea by the weight of the tow-rope and the tug of the aircraft, but the engines were straining and Skinner glanced round him again, cautiously, taking in all the danger points, then he went to his toolbox and examined it carefully once more for his spares.

He squinted again at the pressure gauges and the revolution counters, wondering if he dare ask the Skipper to reduce speed a little, then climbing slowly on to the after-deck he stood and watched the wake for a while, aware of the increasing strength of the wind and the increasing height of the waves. He stared aft again for a second, balancing against the lurch of the boat, then he went to the stern and nudged Westover, squatting uncomfortably in the Carley float, one eye on the towrope.

"That Walrus's flying," he said earnestly. "You watch. Every time she hits the top of a wave, she takes off."

Westover peered through the blue-black darkness, the wind pushing and nibbling at his hair. In the distance, almost indistinguishable against the starless sky, they could see the vague shape of the Walrus heaving and rolling as she was dragged over the waves.

"She's all right," he said cautiously.

"She's taking off I tell you," Skinner persisted breathlessly. "And every time she hits the sea again she ships a lot of water, I'll bet. Better tell the Skipper to reduce speed, hadn't you?"

"She's all right," Westover said irritably. "She *looks* all right."

"Ah, she might *look* all right, but it's dark and you can't see, can you?" Skinner's words were full of the threat of disaster.

Westover stared at the Walrus again, nagged by uncertainty. "You sure?"

" 'Course I'm sure. What's the matter with your eyes?" Skinner's voice had a thin edge of insistence that made Westover nervous and fully aware that it was his responsibility to report any odd behaviour on the part of the aircraft.

"Oh, hell!" Westover heaved himself out of the Carley float and stumbled across the deck towards the wheelhouse.

"She's taking off Skipper!" Skinner felt easier as he heard him shout. "Every time she hits the top of a wave." Then he felt the check as the revolutions fell – as though the boat were an animal that had shortened its racing stride.

On the bridge, Treherne stared backwards, trying to distinguish the seaplane in the darkness, but all he could see was the same shadow Westover had seven, and the faintly phosphorescent glow from the wake that threw the stern of the boat into sharp relief.

"Keep her at that, Flight," he said into the wheelhouse. Then he straightened up again and stared round him, watchful of the rising wind and the deeper lurching of the boat.

His mind was rapidly ticking off on a mental list the things he should have done, and he came to the end of it with a feeling of satisfied certainty that there was nothing he had forgotten. He had worked out their position carefully when they had spotted the Walrus and had marked it on the chart with a neat cross. But he knew perfectly well that as soon as he had left the wheelhouse for the bridge Slingsby had glanced at the charts and quietly checked his course and position, and it was because of this knowledge that he dwelt longer on the things he knew he must not forget.

Treherne had got used to Slingsby in the few weeks he had been aboard the boat. In his own first few days, when he was fresh from the skippers' course at Corsewell, he had made a couple of bad navigational blunders chiefly due to nervousness and through trying to concentrate on half a dozen things at once. Nothing had been said to him, however, and in his humiliation he, too, had said nothing. But he knew that Slingsby had been watching him ever since. Indeed, he had learned that Slingsby had actually replaced Flight Sergeant Rollo because the CO had known Treherne needed someone to keep a discreet eye on him until he found his feet.

It hadn't taken Treherne long to find out that Slingsby had been called into the CO's office ashore after their first few trips together. The CO's "How do you get on with Mr Treherne?" would be only an invitation for Slingsby's discreet comments. But as nothing had been said to Treherne by the CO, he guessed that so far, in spite of his early errors, Slingsby had not found him wanting.

Considering it all, Treherne felt no resentment. He had grown to trust Slingsby and his judgement in the few weeks he had known him. There was a lot he wasn't sure about still – for instance, he had an uncomfortable feeling that he ought not to have let Skinner go so soon the previous evening – but as far as the deck crew were concerned he knew he had little to worry about with Slingsby and Robb in charge.

As his mind moved he heard the sharp rap of Knox's pencil at the window of the wireless cabin behind him. "Weather report, Skipper!" The wireless operator's voice came through the tiny hatch, small and dwindled. "Gale blowing up, they say."

He pushed the message through to Treherne, who fingered it thoughtfully, then stared aft again at the dark shape of the Walrus behind them against the sky. The sound of the wind buffeting his cheeks and ears and eyes reminded him of his lack of experience as it seemed to grow; swelling with the thump and crash of the seas on the bow of the boat and the nerve-racking howl of the engines.

five

The wind that slapped and hammered at the side of Tebbitt's face came directly from the north, seeming to grow stronger with each wild gust that rattled the mast and set the stays drumming. He was still thinking gloomily of Hilda, knowing that she would arrive while he had no money and consequently no bribes to keep her there. But as he considered it longer he realised that at least the launch was heading home and in the direction of the train he must meet, and he began for the first time to bless the chance which had brought the Walrus down into the sea on their beat.

Astern, the dim shape of the aircraft still clung to them, bobbing and bouncing behind, sometimes high above them as it balanced on the crest of a wave, sometimes apparently miles below and out of sight against the darkness of the sea. The rain was slanting thinly down in spitting angry squalls, gurgling somewhere in the scuppers and beating against Tebbitt's right cheek with a paralysing iciness, gathering into drops that were whipped by the wind off the end of his chin. The folds of his duffel coat were stiff and damp and heavy on his shoulders as the material soaked in the rain and the spray which curled like bullets over the starboard bow and round in a wide sweep to slash across the wheelhouse windows and lose itself in the tumultuous air above the bridge.

Stolidly, Tebbitt was aware that the Skipper was worried – by the number of times he appeared on the bridge, glanced round, then disappeared below again. In his unimaginative way and with his mind clouded with his own troubles, he knew the boat was making its way through the water with difficulty, hampered by the growing weather and the weight of the Walrus at its stern.

The wheelhouse was dark except for the faint, reflected glow of the orange light that fell across the charts, but Tebbitt could hear the muttering in there.

"The wind's increasing, Skipper," Slingsby was saying. "And that damn Walrus is airborne too much. She's pulling the stern round all the time. It's hard to hold her on course."

"Think we ought to get 7526 to give us a hand?" Treherne asked. "She could probably get a line on the Walrus and help to hold her square."

"She might if she's got a crew of acrobats." Slingsby's voice came dry and sarcastic, but still somehow respectful. "Besides, we don't want that medal-chasing bunch hanging about. Time enough if Skinner's engines pack up. We'd never hear the last of it if we asked that lot for help."

There was silence for a while, then Tebbitt heard the rattle of Knox's pencil on the wireless-cabin window. He reached down, took the message form and passed it to Treherne as he appeared in the wheelhouse doorway.

"Thanks, Tebbitt," Treherne said, and disappeared below again to read it by the faint light over the chart table.

"Gale warning again, Flight." His voice came slowly a moment later. "It'll be blowing like Old Harry by daylight tomorrow. How about the Walrus now?"

"Hang on to her as long as you can, Skipper. Cast her off when the weather grows too bad. At least she'll be that much nearer home than she is now."

"Skipper!" It was Corporal Robb's voice, this time. "I think the Chernikeeff log's packed up."

Tebbitt resisted the temptation to glance just inside the door at the dial of the log which showed its regular flash with every fifteen feet they travelled.

"That's handy," Slingsby said without rancour. "That makes it a proper caper. That complicates matters just that little bit more to make things interesting. What's happening?"

"It's reading zero. I think the spinner must have carried away or got fouled up."

"Tebbitt!" Treherne's voice rose. "Get Skinner. Tell him the log's packed in. Robby'll take over up there."

Tebbitt felt his way cautiously along the two-foot-wide catwalk by the sick bay to the after-deck, all that was between him and the dark sea alongside, knelt on the unsteady deck, one hand on the lifeline to stop himself sliding away with the lurch of the boat, and bawled down through the engine-room hatch.

"Skinner! The log's packed in!"

Twice he shouted, without reply, so he climbed down the iron ladder into the engine-room, dazzled and blinking in the deckhead lights. There, out of the wind, the heat took his breath away and the vibration and the noise set his tired nerves on edge. The engines, hot with several hours' steaming, threw off their heat like an open oven door.

Skinner was sitting on the edge of the small bench aft, while Dray crouched on his tool-box, still singing his soundless song in his world of shrieking noise. Tebbitt carefully picked his way aft on the greasy, quivering floorboards and put his mouth to Skinner's ear.

"Log's packed in. You're wanted in the wheelhouse."

Skinner replied with an angry single-syllable oath. He was loath to leave the engine-room just then. Normally willing enough to leave the dial-watching to Dray, he had crouched the whole of the engine-running time on his tool-box or the work-bench in the aftermost part of the engine-room, his eyes on the quivering needles, the turning of the shafts down in the bilges of the boat, and the level of the water under the after-floorboards where it was deepest, his fingers busy with the greasers on the water-pumps and the sea-cocks, or stroking the port engine.

He glanced round anxiously as he set his foot on the ladder, then he hoisted himself up on deck and, blinded by the darkness after the lights of the engine-room, made his way forward chiefly by touch. Tebbitt followed him, feeling a twinge of uneasiness at the knowledge that their only means of measuring speed and distance had become useless. A broken log meant inaccurate navigation and the boat might have to put in somewhere other than its home base, which would disorganise his arrangements for meeting Hilda.

As they reached the bridge Slingsby's voice came harshly from the wheelhouse, driving away his worries immediately with its more urgent anger. "How many more times," the Flight Sergeant demanded, "have I to tell you people not to use the deck unnecessarily at night? Use a bit of common. If you go overboard nobody's going to see you. Go through the sick bay."

They said nothing and Skinner sullenly made his way into the wheelhouse, while Tebbitt took his place in the corner of the bridge again, straining his anxious ears for scraps of conversation.

"The log's gone, Skinner," Treherne said. "Can you put it right?"

"Probably," Skinner said warily. "It might only be fouled up with seaweed – or, on the other hand, it might be that the impeller's been carried away with this cross-tide. It's pretty strong round here, I think, and that sometimes does happen."

"Can you put it right?"

"If it's not carried away, I can. Are you going to stop the engines?"

Treherne glanced at the Flight Sergeant.

"No need to, Skipper," Slingsby said immediately. "Besides, we've that damn Walrus hanging on to us."

Skinner disappeared and Tebbitt heard the sick bay door slam and Skinner's feet on the engine-room ladder. He was beginning to feel a little sick with anxiety and worry again.

How long he stared out across the swaying blackness of the night, drenched with spray and the occasional spatters of rain, listening to the slap of the water and the creak of the mast, and the crash every time the boat bounced sickeningly on to a wave, he didn't know. Busy as he was with his own worries, his mind was not receptive to what was going on around him and it was almost with a start of surprise that he heard Skinner in the wheelhouse again. At first he thought he had returned to report the repair of the log, then he realised the fitter's voice was raised in a bleat of despair.

"Skipper, the water-pumps have packed up! Both of 'em!"

"Water-pumps?" The voice was Slingsby's, hard and suspicious out of the semi-darkness. Tebbitt could just make out his shadowy figure against the pale orange glow that came through the doorway.

"Yes, Flight."

"Both of 'em?" Slingsby sounded incredulous.

"Yes, Flight. Flight, the engines are overheating. There's no water coming through."

"Shut down." Treherne's voice was flat and cold, and as angry as Slingsby's but in a different way.

The noise of the engines ceased immediately, and as the way went off the boat the bow fell and she began to wallow, dead and heavy, in the sickening seas.

"Tebbitt!" Slingsby put his head through the doorway. "Get aft and stand by to give Gus a hand. There's probably going to be some fun with this Walrus. She'll probably try to board us. Robby, go and keep an eye on 'em."

"Aye, aye, Flight."

"How is it both the water-pumps have packed up together, Skinner?" Treherne stared at Skinner in the pale light of the wheelhouse. The fitter's face, black in the shadows, and picked out by the orange light, was strained and he seemed on the verge of tears.

"Skipper, it's this cross-tide against the turn of the screws. It's sheared away the water-pump keys. It was the cross-tide that stopped the log."

"What have you got to do, then?"

"Dismantle the pumps, Skipper, and fit new keys."

"How long will that take you?"

"Can't say. More than an hour or so, I should think, with the roll that's on her."

"As long as that?"

"Yes, Skip. I've got to make new keys."

Treherne turned away and Skinner was making thankfully for the companionway when Slingsby stopped him, his voice low-pitched and suddenly deadly.

"Haven't you got any spare keys?"

"No, Flight. I shall have to make 'em."

"We had the keys shear off once before in a cross-tide on one of my boats. That's normal enough. But the fitter had made spare keys. He had 'em ready in his kit. Haven't you?"

"No, Flight."

"Why not?" Slingsby's question came back at Skinner like a pistol-shot.

"Well, Flight, it's like this – "

"Go on, Skinner," Treherne interrupted coldly. "Let's hear it."

"Well, Skip, I've been pretty busy for a bit with that oil feed – "

"That started two days ago. You were supposed to have fixed it last night. What about the week before that? We had no running troubles then."

162

"No, Skipper, but the auxiliaries have been giving a bit of trouble."

"First I've heard of it."

"Well – er – I didn't want to worry you."

"It's part of my job. If the auxiliaries were giving trouble it should have been on the report sheet. Go on, what about before that?"

"Well – er – well, Skipper, it's pretty busy down there with only two of us."

"All the other boats have only two fitters."

"Yes, but – "

"Skinner" – Treherne spoke slowly – 'I don't know you very well. This is my first boat and I've still a lot to learn. But I'm beginning to realise you're the Grand Master of Blow-You-Jack-I'm-All-Right. How long did you take to fix that oil-feed last night?"

"It took me about three hours, Skipper." Skinner was beginning to look desperate now. Slingsby stood in the background, saying nothing, watching Treherne with a look of complete approval on his face.

"I don't believe you, Skinner," Treherne said. "Judging by the time you came to me and asked to leave it couldn't have taken you that long. How long *did* it take you? – ten minutes?"

"No, Skipper, honest – "

Treherne suddenly seemed to weary of the argument. "Go on, Skinner. Get down in that engine-room and get those new keys made. I'll sort you out when we get back – *if* we get back."

Skinner disappeared thankfully and Treherne turned towards the chart table. Like the others, he was beginning now to feel the strain of the violent motion of the boat. He was hungry – he had had nothing more than soup and sandwiches for over twenty-four hours – and every lurch and jar slapped at his hollow stomach, making him aware of its emptiness.

"Flight," he said, "I'm beginning to see through Mr Skinner. Let's get a message off, then we'll go and have a look at that Walrus."

As they walked wide-legged through the sick bay Treherne put his head into the wireless cabin. "Knox," he said, "give me a message form. It's an emergency. Get it off as fast as you can. Then one of you get up on the bridge and keep a look-out until one of the hands comes back from aft."

He hurriedly scrawled out his message for assistance, pushed the message pad back, and followed Slingsby through the sick bay doors.

Milliken watched them, his eyes wide and a little frightened. The sudden silence after the thunder of the engines, Skinner's hurried scramble through the sick bay to the wheelhouse, then the appearance aft of Tebbitt and Robb and finally the Skipper and Slingsby, made him worried and uneasy. The emergency message and, above all, the dead wallowing of the boat left him with a sense of impending disaster.

After the fashion of her kind, 7525 was slewing round a little, now that the way was off her, and the waves were already beginning to roll her sickeningly port and starboard again, so that the bulkhead against which Milliken leaned was one moment beneath him and he was almost flat against it, and the next was above him and flinging him away across the sick bay. Over all, he could hear the thin spatter of rain and the groan of timbers.

On the after-deck, hanging on for dear life to the safety-lines, to the Oerlikon and the Carley float, to anything within reach, Westover, Tebbitt and Robb felt rather than saw Treherne and Slingsby approach, crabwise across the rolling deck.

"Out the way, Tebbitt," Slingsby said demoralisingly. "Shift your great carcase and let the dog see the rabbit."

The boat was lying now at an angle of forty-five degrees across the waves and the stern rose mountainously, then fell with a twisting motion that was half a roll and half a pitch, and the water rose above them, black and ugly, sensed rather than seen against the darkness of the night. Every wave that slapped the chine sent the spray outwards, upwards and round in a swift curve across the deck, so that it beat against the five huddled figures staring out towards the Walrus.

"Let's hope she'll not fill with water," Treherne said. "If she slides sideways into a wave, she's had it. Better get that axe out and lay it handy in the sick bay, Robby, in case we need it to cut the tow."

"So long as she doesn't sink or ride up on us we're all right," Slingsby pointed out. He was hanging on with both hands to the jackstaff on the stern of the boat, where the lifelines met, oblivious of the water that slapped upwards at him. "Christ, if she rides up on us it's going to be the biggest bloody uproar since Ma caught her behind in the mangle."

"Skipper." Westover spoke haltingly. "I think she's beginning to stream out against the wind. She's a bit to port of us now. I think she's riding bow to wind."

"By God, I think you're right," Slingsby said. "And so long as she keeps bow to wind, she's safe. She'll ride. We're laughing. We're right as a clock."

"And, Flight," Westover went on, a little more certain of himself, "I think she's beginning to pull the stern round, too. If you look, we're facing more up to wind than we were a minute ago."

They glanced over the side at the hissing waves that hurried past, more along the length of the boat now and hitting her less on the beam.

"You're right, Gus. She's blown back the length of the tow-rope," Slingsby said slowly. "That's what's happened.

Skipper, this damned boat's going to ride bow to wind for the first time in her life."

Corporal Skinner, wedged against the bulkhead aft of the engines, over the bench and the vice that was fitted there, sweated over a small piece of monel metal with a file, sawing away on it to shape it into a tiny key that would fit into the shaft inside the water-pump. Bitter anger surged over him at the thought that he had watched the faulty oil-feed all this time and, by an ironic twist, the engines had stopped from an entirely different cause.

As he sawed furiously he rubbed his thumb against the metal; it started to bleed and he flung down the file with a curse and sucked his thumb.

"Pick it up, Skinner." He turned and found Slingsby standing alongside him. "Pick it up and get on with it."

"It's bleeding, Flight."

"Do it good. Just the ticket. I'd like to see you bleed slowly to death, Mr Flaming Skinner. Get on with it. If you'd done your job this wouldn't be necessary. This caper's all your pigeon. We're going to have to bob to the Navy or somebody for help now because of you. Get on with it. Pick it up."

Skinner picked up the file sullenly. The bleeding was only slight and he had thrown down the file chiefly because he was hot and sweating and angry.

"I'll just strip off, Flight," he said. "It's a bit hot in here."

"We haven't time for stripping off, Mr Skinner," Slingsby said in a flat voice. "File away. I'll be watching you for a bit. I want to see you sweat yourself to death. I'll read the burial service, in fact, as they shove you over the side and I'll be the first to shout 'Hallelujah' when you sink. And if you come up again I'll bloody well push you down again with the boat-hook."

Skinner's eyes were held for a moment by Slingsby's own flinty look, then he again began to file, perspiration

streaming down his face in the oven heat of the engine-room
As he realised he had on his best jacket, the one he'd worn so
that he could get away to his date more quickly, he stopped
again.

"I've got my best tunic on, Flight," he bleated.

"Good! Nothing like a drop of dirty oil for a best tunic,
Skinner. You won't be able to rub it up against a WAAF in a
corner on a dark night now. You'll be able to wash it, like I
do. Get – on – with – it."

Skinner wanted to weep with mortification, humiliation
and fury, but Slingsby seemed to lose interest and turned to
where Dray was wrestling to dismantle the water-pump,
surrounded by shining spanners.

"How's it going, son?"

"All right, Flight. It's coming off."

"How long's it going to take?"

"*Christ* knows, Flight. All night at this rate."

"Mr Corporal Skinner suggested about an hour."

"He'll be lucky." Dray shot Skinner a sour look and bent
over the water-pump again. Then the boat pitched
unexpectedly and one of his spanners slid into the bilges and
Skinner hit his head against the bulkhead and swore bitterly.

Surreptitiously Skinner slipped off his jacket and laid it
across one of the auxiliary engines, hoping it wouldn't get
too oily and bent again to the filing. The motion of the boat
was a pitch and toss now that made the job difficult as it kept
throwing him backwards away from the bench, and half the
time he found himself missing the piece of metal and
swinging only at the empty air. And the heat and the smell of
hot steel and petrol fumes were overpowering. He stared
down at the vice on the small littered bench, black-greasy
with oil, missed his stroke again and, jabbing his thumb once
more, felt ready to sit down and howl.

It was an hour later when the men on the heaving deck first heard the sound of another launch. Above the bash of the waves the sound of the engines came faintly at first, growing deeper as the other boat drew nearer. Then a searchlight stabbed at the sea and swept round in a wide arc.

Treherne grabbed the signalling lamp and flashed it briefly in the direction of the searchlight, which immediately swung about and fastened on them for a second before the lifting sea sent the boat and the beam high into the air and round in a roll. Jerkily it picked them out once more, lost them, and found them again.

As it lit up the tips of the waves the water shone green and brilliant and transparent, and they could see the turbulent sea between them, and the white racing crests.

Gradually the other boat drew closer, its searchlight swinging on and off them as she heaved in the swell, then they heard her loud-hailer.

"Ahoy, there, Twenty-five! Broken down *again*?"

"Loxton!" Slingsby swore bitterly. "That's 7526. God, this is going to be wonderful!"

The other boat slowly came abeam of them, twenty feet away, the water between the plunging vessels lit by the searchlight and covered with flying steam from 7526's exhausts. The spray, whipped off the wave-crests, sped away like flung jewels as the light caught it.

"My word, Twenty-five" – they could hear the triumph even in the boom of the other boat's loud-hailer – "you do have a time with yourselves. What do you want us to do for you *this* time?"

Slingsby's leathery face was hard and set. Treherne stared expressionlessly across at the shadowy form of the other boat behind the light.

"Take over my tow, please," he said calmly into the microphone of the loud-hailer. "My engines are unserviceable."

"Sure! And we'll come back for *you* in the morning if you like."

"Ha, ha!" Slingsby said quietly. "Very funny. Laugh? Shall I ever stop?"

Treherne deliberately refused to join in the banter. "If you'll come a bit closer," he said, "we'll send you a line across."

Robb, down near the stern, was calmly fastening a heaving-line to the eye of the tow-rope and coiling it carefully in his hands. Tebbitt was coiling another on the foredeck.

7526's engines roared as she went astern, then she edged closer and Tebbitt, clinging to a handrail, threw his line one-handedly. But the wind caught it and whipped it away astern, making it splash in a diamond-flurry of spray into the brightly-lit water.

"The silly stupid fool," Slingsby hissed to himself and Milliken, standing by the sick bay door, sensed the hatred that seemed to flicker between the two boats like lightning.

"Oh, hard lines!" Even in the harshness of the loud-hailer they could hear the smug, sarcastic tones of Loxton as Tebbitt hauled in his heaving-line. "Hurry up and get that line out. I don't want it round my props. Er..." The speaker paused and they heard a distinct chuckle. "Flight Sergeant Rollo says if you'll hang on a moment he'll see that we send a line across properly."

"Rollo!" Slingsby's face was an angry red in the reflected light. "Get it across, Robby!" he shouted. "And for Christ's sake don't miss," he added under his breath.

Robb's arm swung back and round as he balanced on the rolling deck without holding, and his heaving-line uncoiled and fell across the deck of 7526, where it was immediately grabbed by a deckhand.

"Haul her in!" Loxton shouted. "Let go, Twenty-five."

Robb and the two deckhands aft laboured on the frightful deck to release the heavy eye of the towline.

"Look slippy!" Loxton shouted.

"Shut your great jaw," Slingsby muttered. "We know what we're doing."

Then the towrope splashed into the water astern of them and they saw in the searchlight's beam the ruffle on the water as it was pulled through the broken waves to 7526.

"I'll come back for you in the morning," Loxton's sarcastic voice went on. "I'll make a note of where you are, in case you're not sure. Like a chart check?"

"I know where I am, thank you," Treherne snapped into the microphone. "But you might warn the Navy that we're here. If this weather worsens we might need help."

"I'll come myself" Loxton said cheerfully. "Have a good night. You'll get a medal for this."

"Take your blasted medal and shove it up your jumper," Robb panted.

They heard the roar of 7526's engines and saw the white foam that was flung up as her screws began to turn, then she slowly slid ahead, moving away to port, the steam from her exhausts blowing away astern.

The loud-hailer sounded again as she disappeared, and this time Loxton's voice was serious, all the banter gone.

"Hold tight, Twenty-five. I'll pass on your message. Good luck."

The engines roared out louder as the throttles were opened and 7526 disappeared into the darkness, only the white foam of her wake visible. Treherne and Slingsby on the bridge of 7525 watched the shadowy shape of the Walrus move forward and then swing away after 7526 to port.

"Bastards," Slingsby said feelingly and without a trace of gratitude.

The wind grew steadily worse. Relieved of the drag of the Walrus on her stern, 7525 swung round to her normal broached-to position and her motion increased until her starboard side went below water at the climax of her rolls and it became impossible even for the experienced hands to rest normally on a bunk. They had to stand, hugging a ladder, or jam themselves in corners in the sick bay, the wheelhouse, or the forecastle; or sit on the floor, their feet against the bulkhead, wedging themselves into position.

In the engine-room, Corporal Skinner laboured savagely, the perspiration running down his nose and dripping on to his file. With every roll of the boat he felt his feet slipping and had to keep wedging himself more tightly against the bench with his aching thighs. His head throbbed with the heat and the motion, his thumb was sore and his best trousers were stained with grease. He was muttering to himself all the time.

Dray sat on his toolbox with the unscrewed log with its damaged impeller, and the parts of the fresh-water pumps, spread on the deck in front of him. He had long since repaired the faulty oil-pipe on Skinner's breathless instructions. His round, moon face was expressionless as he watched Skinner labouring in the corner by the bulkhead, his shirt dark and soiled with sweat in the middle of his back.

He had been watching Skinner for a long time now, wondering which was the safest way to inform him that his best jacket had slipped from the top of the auxiliary engine and dropped into a pool of oil in the bilges.

In the chilly forecastle where Flight Sergeant Slingsby sat on a bunk, drinking out of a tin of self-heating soup, his knees up against the edge of the table to hold himself rigid in his seat, the oilskins on the bulkhead swung in great wild arcs. The maddening cla-clank of empty soup tins in the box on the floor came every few seconds and the bread knife still slid backwards and forwards among the crumbs on the table with the empty tin mug, clicking every time it hit the raised edge. The place was damp and streaming with condensation, like everywhere else on the boat, with a dull film over the polished top of the table, and in the cold light of the deckhead lamps was cheerless and dim.

Rain and water flung by the waves to the cabin tops found its way through inevitably and dripped steadily to form puddles on the sick bay bunks and floor, trickling backwards and forwards and quivering with every wave that hit the helpless boat. Milliken had gone beyond sickness now. He was bruised from head to foot where he had been slammed by the motion of the boat against bulkheads or doors every time he stood on his feet. He sat on the deck of the sick bay, oblivious of the puddle that wet the seat of his trousers and, every now and again, as he listened to the satanic symphony of the sea, the terrifying thought occurred to him that only thin planks of wood stood between him and its fury.

Everyone except Slingsby had long since passed the stage of talking and performed what duties they had to perform with a heavy weariness. The silence of the sick bay, which seemed to exclude the crash of the water and the drum of the rain and the wind, was beginning to get on Milliken's nerves a little. Opposite him, he could see the feet of Gus Westover, in his usual place behind and beneath the bunk among the spare ammunition, the Mae Wests and the wretched pigeons, rolling with every movement of the boat in lifeless fashion. Every time Tebbitt appeared his face was longer and his complaint louder. "Two o'clock," he announced bitterly. "Only an hour to get home. We'll never do it."

Milliken was impervious at last to Tebbitt's sorrow for, though his legs ached with bracing himself against the steps, he dared not relax even for sympathy. Once, when they had first started to protest, he had eased them for a while, only for the next lurch of the boat to send him sliding on his back across the wet floor to the bunk at the other side.

He could still hear the cheep of Morse in the wireless cabin and every dot and every dash seemed to split open his aching head. He was back at the state of mind when he wished to die and when nothing short of violent hard work would have made him wish to live. The axe Robb had produced winked dully at him in the light, its blade dark with grease.

He lay sprawled on the floor, hanging on with hands and feet and knees, always in danger of sliding across the deck again, his bagful of bandages and splints and slings moving backwards and forwards beside him, bumping softly first on the starboard side, then on the port side. And Milliken, in his misery, was indifferent to its fate.

Only Robb, eating his colossal sandwiches with a voracity and an obvious enjoyment that made Milliken in his misery detest him, and the boisterous, bounding little Flight Sergeant seemed undisturbed. Slingsby had visited the engine-room with monotonous regularity until Skinner, in one of the periods when Slingsby was on the bridge, had burst out: "That little swine wants examining! He's persecuting me!"

Throughout the rolling Slingsby had been all over the boat at once, down in the engine-room, in the wireless cabin listening in with Knox and Botterill to the progress of 7526, highly delighted at their difficulties with the tow, asking the wretched Milliken how to set a fractured arm or treat a cracked skull, arguing boats with Robb in the forecastle over the self-heating soup and the corned-beef sandwiches, and finally in the sick bay again, helping Milliken to his unsteady legs and sending him reeling to the ghastly confines of the galley to help Tebbitt clear up the mess there where the cupboard doors had burst open and pots and pans had exploded in glorious confusion to the floor with the knives that were scattered from the upturned drawer. The crockery had fallen from the fiddles above the sink and their only attempt at tea-making had come near to scalding Tebbitt as the lurch of the boat had wrenched the kettle from the stove, breaking the cord with which he had tied it on.

Jammed in the narrow galley with Milliken, Tebbitt had mopped up most of the water and picked up the broken crockery that slithered and rolled noisily back and forth, with a dull misery born of the knowledge that his wife was gone from his life for ever. Vaguely, he still had hopes of searching for her, or even that she had waited for him at the station. But he knew that neither could be the case and that he would never see her again.

"She's gone now," he announced wearily to Milliken. "I've had it. She'll be in London before morning."

"And a damn good job, too," Milliken said sourly, his face screwed up and his mouth pursed with the dislike of his job and the smell of paraffin, his frayed nerves rubbed raw by Tebbitt's chant. " 'Cos *I'm* jolly well sick of her."

He had the malicious satisfaction of seeing the startled Tebbitt's eyebrows shoot up almost out of sight before he bent over the powdered crockery with the brush and shovel again.

The long hours trudged wearily through a nightmare of noise and movement. No one could sleep or even rest with the seas yelping down on them like a pack of hounds, and the cold seeping up through the hull and the bilge boards and biting through sodden clothes.

Then Botterill brought a message to Slingsby in the forecastle. "Gale warning, Flight. Everybody recalled."

"That'll be nice. Especially as we've got to stay here."

"And there's this one, too. Came straight through after the other one."

Slingsby glanced up sharply and took the proffered slip of paper.

"What's this?" he demanded. "*Engine serviceability permitting, request early morning inshore search of Belgian coast in area Becq-le-Plage – Zeemucke.* Hell, they don't intend to let us get away with anything. *Engine serviceability permitting.* Nice of them to grant us that. Perhaps they'd like us to row the bastard." He squinted at the paper again and read on. "*Dinghy possibly in this area. VVIP in aircraft crew. Request launch crew do utmost – repeat utmost – to effect rescue.* Hm. England expects that every blasted man this day will do his duty. I know. I've heard it all before. And Sunday tomorrow, too. Come on, Robby. Let's tell the Lad."

He went off, trailing Corporal Robb, towards the Skipper's cabin and the next moment the noise of the three of them climbing the wheelhouse ladder was followed by the rattle of the charts on the chart table.

"Schouwen Bank. Wandelaar. North Hinder. West Hinder. Oostekerke." Milliken and Tebbitt, silent in the sodden galley, alert for news, their feet crunching the broken crockery, heard Slingsby hesitantly reading the names of the charted Belgian light vessels and small villages, making them sound like South Yorkshire mining towns in his north country accents. Milliken could almost see his square, spatulate finger moving slowly across the orange-tinted chart. "Zeebrugge. Mariendaele. Oudenberg. Wuyndelen. Here we are. Becq-le-Plage. Zeemucke. Nice big sandbank in the way, Skipper. It runs all down here on and off from Brown Ridge and Ostende Bank. We'd have to go in parallel with the shore and be a sitting duck for shore guns. I know the place. There's a hell of a tide-race inshore of that bank. Christ, will I be glad to see the Shipwash and the Sunk Lights again and know we're only a mile or two from England, home and beauty!"

Their voices died away to a murmur and Milliken found himself dropping off to sleep on his feet from sheer exhaustion. Then Robb brushed past him into the forecastle and picked up his sandwich again slowly, with an air of sober weariness.

"Engines permitting," he said. "God, what a hope!"

Milliken had hardly returned to his place in the sick bay when he was startled out of his half-doze by Robb's shout and the sound of running feet and Tebbitt's great boots clumping to the deck as he leapt for the door. Milliken sat up, convinced that his nightmare voyage was going to be brought to an abrupt end by drowning, and he leapt after Tebbitt for the door only for an unexpected swing of the boat to fling him into the doorpost with a smash that knocked him silly.

Later, clinging dazedly to the lifeline on the after-deck, he watched the violent moment of excitement round the mast where the rolling had caused one of the stays that held it upright to snap and set it heeling dangerously, groaning in its socket. Westover, Tebbitt and the Flight Sergeant were holding on to it as it threatened to go over the side with every roll and carry away their wireless aerial and their sole means of communicating with the shore. Slingsby, lost in the scramble, was cursing steadily in an unbroken flow which, in spite of the tenseness of the moment, shocked Milliken by its carefully thought out balance and the very absence of panic in its obscenity.

"God damn Rollo to hell," he ended in a snarl. "If he'd used his flaming tallow on these instead of his jaw there'd be nothing much wrong."

For a moment Tebbitt was magnificent as he reached above the smaller figures of Slingsby and Westover and held the mast mostly by the strength of his own great forearms while Robb got a heaving-line round it and lashed it to the handrail by the cabin top. There followed a panting huddle on the bridge, all four of them occasionally lurching in a knot of cursing humanity across the deck and back again, while Robb secured another line round the mast and made that fast too, before Milliken returned to the sick bay, trembling and afraid of the violence of the night-black seas and firmly convinced that nothing – not even if it should mean the defeat of the Allied Armies in Europe – would ever get him to set foot on a high-speed launch again if he should ever reach home.

He had just sat down, wedged in position by his heels and his straining muscles and frozen by the wind blowing down the bridge companionway, when Slingsby lurched into the sick bay. His immaculate uniform was soaked with spray and rain but the quiff on his forehead was still quivering in its place.

"You – Billycan – " He pointed an accusing finger at Milliken. "On the bridge, smartly! At the double! You're doing bridge look-out!"

"Bridge look-out?" Milliken climbed unsteadily to his feet. "What's that?"

"Keeping your silly little eyes open. That's all. You know how to do that, don't you? Like this." Slingsby blinked his own two bright eyes sharply at Milliken. "My boys need a rest and that mast needs someone handy. You've had it easy, sitting there like Lord Muck all day, wearing your behind out." – Easy! Milliken almost laughed in his face. – "Report anything you see. That's all. Go on now. Off! Away!"

Milliken staggered to the doorway.

"Not that way, you benighted bloody fool!" Slingsby shouted. "Through the galley." – Milliken thought with a retching nausea of the paraffin fumes. – "You'll go and fall in the drink. We've enough to bother about without fetching you out. If you go in, you stay in. Medical orderlies are two-a-penny, anyway."

By the time he'd fallen into the galley well and stumbled up the swaying ladder to the wheelhouse and the bridge and got more than a lungful of those dreaded paraffin fumes, Milliken was glad to get his head into the fresh air. Robb dressed him in an oilskin and helped him outside where the lurch of the boat immediately slung him against the starboard side of the bridge, so that he lost his footing and sat down heavily.

He had slid across to the other side of the bridge and halfway back again before Robb got him on to his feet and clamped his hands to the handrail.

"You look like Captain Bligh," he said as he fastened the sou'wester on. "How do you feel, doc?"

Milliken's humiliated soul by this time detested Robb for his smooth mockery and apparently unlimited capacity for food when he ought to have been seasick. His calm infuriated him for its kinship in its smugness with Slingsby's angry egoism, and Milliken's reply was a fretful snap.

"Like death," he said.

"Good! That's grand." Robb chuckled in the darkness. "If you'd like to sit just inside the wheelhouse you can watch the mast from there. I'll stand your look-out."

Milliken had the grace to feel ashamed of himself and he decided for the first time that day that Robb already did enough. "Thanks," he said, thinking also of those galley fumes coming up from just below the wheelhouse. "I can lean here. That is," he added wryly, "unless the Flight Sergeant's coming up. He's not keen on people leaning."

"Don't worry about Chiefy, doc. He doesn't bite."

"He's a bit of a terror, though, isn't he?" Milliken said with a nervous but more friendly laugh.

"Terror? Chiefy? Not he. Don't kid yourself. Listen to him now."

Milliken put his head inside the wheelhouse and Slingsby's voice floated up to him from the forecastle with the paraffin fumes.

"If we find this lousy VIP, all the newspapers will be full of how hard it was for him, after being used to a plush-lined office, to spend a night on the ocean. But there won't be any mention of Mrs Slingsby's lad, Jimmy, having to miss his breakfast and dinner two days running to get him home. And when the war's over he – being one of God's chosen few – will get knighted and earn a thousand a year, which is a lot of potatoes, whichever way you look at it. And we'll be door openers and night watchmen. That's what we'll be. And *I've* got a lousy figure for a commissionaire."

Robb laughed and Milliken felt better.

"The big shots won't admit us," Slingsby's voice went on, ebullient and fierce, as though he were enjoying his complaint with all the energy that he put into everything he did. "The Navy don't like us using their sea, but we've pulled a few thousand men out of the drink in our time and put 'em back in flying. And only the Yanks have a good word to say for us. The *Navy* won't thank us and that's a fact."

Milliken could just imagine the sour-smelling forecastle, perhaps with someone listening to Slingsby with one arm round the forward-hatch ladder, trying to saw a slice off the crumbling loaf without cutting his arm off as he swung backwards and forwards to the motion of the boat.

"We can't march," Slingsby ground on heartily. "They say we're sloppy. No duty-free fags like the Navy. When we sleep aboard, the place gets as stale as an old dog's basket. It's a lousy life. Nobody loves us. It's boring and cold and miserable. But" – his voice rose to a challenging shout – "did you ever hear of anyone ratting on us and wanting to go back to a shore job?"

Milliken suddenly got a lungful of paraffin fumes and hastily withdrew his head as the boat lurched sharply again. Below there was the sound of crockery crashing and an oath.

"Don't take too much notice of Chiefy's purges," Robb advised. "You know why he does it, don't you?" Milliken shook his head. "Why do you think Donald Duck makes so much noise? No one would ever notice him otherwise. No one ever notices little blokes and Chiefy's got too much about him to put up with that.

"You know who holds this boat together?" he resumed casually. "Not the rivets and the nails. It's Chiefy. He's not exactly out of the top drawer, if you like, but the best don't always come out of the top drawer. After all, a better man than me said that the sailors weren't gentlemen and the gentlemen weren't sailors. Make no mistake about it, these old flight sergeants are the backbone of this game. You watch him handle this boat if there's trouble and then you'll know."

Milliken began to see where the link lay between Robb and the vulgar little Flight Sergeant. It came from mutual respect and admiration and he suddenly began to see them both differently. He realised there was a wisdom and skill behind Robb's mockery as there was behind Slingsby's garrulous obscenity that was beyond his own experience and comprehension and years.

As he was pondering it, braced with all his nerves and strength on the bridge while the boat did its slow hanging rolls on to its beam ends, all its timbers creaking, they heard the faint sound of firing, dim over the crash of the weather, and Robb was out of the wheelhouse in a flash, his boots thumping on the steps.

In the distance, sharp against the blackness of the night, they saw the streaking fireflies of tracer bullets sweeping in slow curves over the sea. Then he heard the broken hum of engines.

"Skipper!" Robb called and Treherne joined them on the bridge. A moment later Slingsby arrived alongside them.

"I heard launches," he said. "More than one by the sound of 'em." There was no hint now of the fierce grouse in his voice.

The four of them stared silently over the swinging bow and across the black mountains of the waves.

"Due east of us," Slingsby pointed out, listening hard like an old setter.

"They're not Air-Sea Rescue launches," Treherne declared.

"Bet your life they're not, Skipper," Slingsby agreed. "We're right in *E*-boat alley here."

"Could they be Navy boats?"

"Yes. But not *our* navy. Not here. We're too close inshore and Jerry's got too many bases in this area. Our boys wouldn't be firing there without somebody firing back. They're testing guns. They're on their way out."

"Will they run into us, Flight?" Treherne asked quietly.

"Not this trip, I reckon, Skipper," Slingsby answered. "They probably will on their way in. Hell, fancy that lot coming out on a night like this! Hope to God they're not around if Skinner gets his engines going again and we find ourselves inshore at first light with nowhere to manoeuvre at Becq-le-bloody-Plage."

Milliken, forgotten at the back of the bridge, his heart fluttering with excitement at their tense figures, leaned forward. "Is it the enemy?" he whispered.

"Enemy?" Slingsby barked. "No, son. This is the enemy. This all around us. This waste of bloody wet water. It's been a sailor's enemy ever since I was a kid and long before. Those bastards are only an incidental unpleasantness."

"There they go again!" Robb nodded and they saw the arcs of tracer, and heard the faint sound of guns above the noise of the sea.

"And again. They're testing guns, all right."

"If they come this way," Slingsby said slowly, "let me have one blast at 'em with the Oerlikon, Skipper. Just one at the swine."

"I'd rather they didn't see us," Treherne replied. "It'd be hard lines on us if they did. How do you scuttle these damn things, Flight?"

"Lift the floorboards and get Tebbitt to stamp twice – hard – in the bilges," Robb offered and they all laughed, breaking the tension,

They glanced round and saw a row of heads against the sick bay roof where Westover, Tebbitt and one of the wireless operators stared in the direction of the firing.

"All right, you bunch of heroes!" Slingsby roared in his harsh nasal deck voice, and Milliken felt godlike to stand beside it and hear it directed at someone other than himself. "Get back into your holes. They've not found us yet!"

s i x

"Firing!" Mackay sat up sharply in the dinghy and reached with his injured hand for the flare. "They'll not miss us this time."

"Hold it, Mac, you fool." Ponsettia leaned quickly over and grabbed his arm. "Let's have a look first. They might be Jerries. We're pretty close in."

Waltby stared over his right shoulder in the direction of the red tracer bullets that curved in a low trajectory across the dark sky not far away, and suddenly they could hear the sound of engines. They had all three been dozing fitfully, their heads nodding, Mackay holding Harding upright with his arm round him, when the sudden chatter of machine-guns had broken into their sleep.

"How do you know they're Jerries?" Mackay hissed.

"Who the hell else would it be just here, man?" Ponsettia snorted his words coming in a hoarse whisper because it suddenly seemed that for their own safety they must all lower their voices. "We must have drifted south faster than we thought. We must be somewhere off the mouth of the Scheldt."

"There they go again!" Waltby flung out his right arm, his left arm still resting on the brief case between his legs. The firing was further in front of him now and he noticed he didn't have to crane his head round so far. Either the boat that carried the guns was moving fast or the dinghy was spinning slowly. The beat of engines came in swelling crescendos, as though the waves interposed a barrier of water between them and the sound from time to time.

"Pretty, ain't they?" Ponsettia said grimly. "They're testing guns. They'll be *E*-boats."

"You sure?" Mackay, still unconvinced, sat with his hand clutching the flare.

"Haven't we been trying to drop heavies on their pens for months? Our boys wouldn't be firing little bursts like that round here. And if our boys were firing at all here somebody would be firing back at them, you bet your sweet life. They're *E*-boats going for a dab at the cross-Channel supplies – the sea's lousy with cargo ships just now."

They sat silent for a while, peering over the water, their heads rolling wearily on their shoulders as the dinghy slewed and slid away off the crests of the waves. Then they saw the curves of red tracer again, further away from them this time, and heard the faint rattle of guns once more.

"Hell!" Ponsettia stared in the direction of the firing for a moment, and they waited for him to speak again. "See where they are? They're *west* of us. *West,* man! If this goddam wind's still blowing from the north as it has been all the time, they're *west* of us. Give us that compass, Mac!"

They fished in Harding's pocket and crouched over the minute sliver of luminous metal "That's right," Ponsettia said. "Over here's north. They're west of us."

The other two stared at him for a moment, wondering what he was getting at.

"Don't you see?" he went on emphatically, as though trying to hammer his thoughts into their brains. "They're heading *south*. That means they must be on their way *out* – of course they must at this time of the night."

"Go on, man," Mackay barked impatiently. "What the hell are you getting at?"

"Listen, those sons-of-bitches are outside of us. We're nearer the Belgian coast than they are. Unless the wind or the tide or whatever it is that's propelling us changes, by daylight we'll have been blown right inshore. Just ready to be picked up by the bastards when they sneak home."

"Right where the shore batteries can see us."

"That'll put paid to any rescue. Hell, what stinking luck!"

The thought of capture as the end to their ordeal damped their spirits and they all huddled against the sides of the dinghy in silence, baling slowly and instinctively with their hands, the flying helmet, anything they could find. Mackay worked still holding on to Harding, throwing water over the others more often than out of the dinghy.

The waves broke across them now in freezing spits that sloshed, phosphorescent and oddly ghostly, in the bottom of the dinghy, numbing in their iciness so that their cramped legs no longer had feeling in them. Around them, the slow pagan roll of the sea seemed endless and ageless and supremely indifferent to their misery. They had lost all sense of time and, occasionally, as though it were caught by a smack from the gusty wind, the dinghy skidded and whirled round in a sickening movement that destroyed all notion of direction.

Once, as it lurched violently over a steep crest, Waltby was certain it was about to capsize and a yelp of fear escaped him. "Holy Jesus," Ponsettia muttered, while Mackay sat still, clinging to Harding, solid, immovable, unutterably resentful about the whole thing. They regained their places uneasily from the heap into which they had been slung, all of them troubled by thoughts of capsizing, and used the heaving-line to tie themselves to each other so that in the darkness no one could fall or be thrown overboard without the others being aware of it. But Waltby knew very well that if such a thing happened now, no one would ever be able to summon sufficient strength to pull a man back.

They were exhausted with the effort of keeping upright through the violent movements that constantly threatened to throw them out, and Waltby felt dazed with hunger and cold, stupefied by the ice in the wind which seemed to cut his cheeks into raw strips like the blade of a knife.

The rhythmic surge of the sea caused his unhappiness to swell round him in suffocating folds that stifled the hope in him. His lips were swollen and cracked where the water slicing across them had dried to brine on his face, and he found it painful to speak. His throat was raw with salt and his stomach was still painfully tremulous after the water he had swallowed when the aircraft ditched. All he felt he wanted just then was a long drink of ginger beer, the pop of his childhood days.

The dinghy still seemed round and firm and solid, and the darkness, a threat in itself had paradoxically taken away some of the savagery from the sea. The waves were only shadows which they sensed from the rocking of the dinghy and from the sloshing thump as a crest broke close by, sending a cascade of water across their legs and chests. Above them the sky was an intolerable blackness.

Only once, during an incredible momentary break in the driven cloud, they saw the flare of a narrow cold moon, sharp and frosty and clear, swinging gracefully above their heads, lighting the sea. But it served only to accentuate their loneliness and smallness as for a brief second it touched the wave-tips with silver points before it disappeared.

The wind seemed stronger as well as colder, and the wet smell of the sea more powerful, a travesty of the smell that Waltby had experienced on cool evenings spent on the coast with his wife. He thought of her with an anguished longing for a moment. He had given her too little time. Often he had thought his was a selfish life and had said so, but she had reassured him he was wrong.

She would be on the train still, he suspected, probably even preparing to descend at that moment, expecting him to meet her at the station with her sister and Taudevin. He wondered how she would receive the news that he was missing. Never in the whole course of the war had she had cause for worry and he wondered how she would take it now. With an agonising desire to protect her, he hoped she wouldn't find out.

The dinghy gave a twist and the splash of water in his lap startled him out of his thoughts.

"Are we all awake?" he enquired.

"I am, Syd," Ponsettia answered immediately.

"Harding's still unconscious," Mackay said, almost as though he held Waltby responsible.

"I think we'd better give him some more of the brandy," Waltby said. "Is he warm?"

"He feels all right," Mackay said unwillingly. "I don't know."

Unfastening the brief case with deliberate care in the darkness, Waltby took out the flask and they forced a little of the brandy between Harding's lips. He moaned softly and moved his head so that some of the liquor ran down his chin.

"Rub his hands and feet, Mac," Waltby said, putting away the flask, and Mackay bent to the task immediately.

Waltby felt at the brief case for a moment. "There's one thing I'd better settle now," he said, "before it's too late. None of us knows what's going to happen to us. It's cold and this sea's rising. Whatever happens to me, this brief case must go over the side if any enemy vessel attempts to pick us up. Shove anything you can into it to make it sink more quickly. Anything."

He felt them looking at him.

"All right?"

"All right, Syd."

"All right, Mac?"

"Why not shove it over now?" Mackay growled. "After all, but for that damned thing we shouldn't have been flying

187

the Hudson and we shouldn't be here and the Skipper wouldn't be unconscious."

Waltby knew he was staring in the direction of the unseen brief case, which lay where it had been all the time, between Waltby's legs. It seemed to symbolise all the distrust Mackay clearly felt for the non-combatant members of the Air Force. Briefcases and trouser-seats shiny from sitting on smooth chairs – Waltby knew just how Mackay's mind was working. His own had once worked that way on a visit to New Delhi from the North-West Frontier when he was still a sergeant. Pink gins in the Mess. Spotless uniforms and smooth hair unruffled by flying helmets, and hands untouched by grease. Middle-class types, he had thought. Manufacturers' sons. Temporary gentlemen.

"Sling it in the drink," Mackay said again.

"Dry up, Mac," Ponsettia said harshly.

"If we should be picked up by our own people" – Waltby affected not to hear the resentment in Mackay's tones – "it must be passed over to them at once without fail. And make it clear that it's important and urgent."

"Don't know why we can't sling it in the drink instead," Mackay said again. "It's brought nothing but bloody bad luck. The war's almost over. What the hell do we want Jerry's documents for?"

"Listen to me, Mac." Waltby kept his anger under control with difficulty. He was feeling in no mood to be patient with the intractable Mackay. "I've not reminded you up to now that I'm an air commodore. Now I'm giving you an order about this brief case. All right?"

"All right – sir!" Mackay's tone was defiant and sneering but Waltby knew he would do as he was told.

"Right! Now let's shut up about the brief case. It's time we had some exercises."

For a while they sawed their arms backwards and forwards, working life into frozen limbs, or rubbing and slapping Harding. Then, when they had finished, they sat back again and slumped against the dinghy walls.

"How about a sing-song?" Waltby suggested.

"Christ!" The voice was Mackay's and it was full of derision. Waltby took no notice.

"Come on, let's sing," he said. "What do you say, Canada?"

"OK by me, Syd. What'll we have?"

"How about 'God save The King' for a start?"

"OK, get busy."

They sang in the darkness, their voices puny in the wilderness and reedy against the bluster of the wind.

"Funny," Ponsettia said after a while. "It does cheer you up, I guess. Strikes me we ought to sing sea shanties or 'For Those in Peril on the Sea'."

They sang "Shenandoah" and "Blow the Man Down", but they found that their voices stuck in their throats and died slowly to nothing as they became aware of Mackay sitting there opposite them, in disapproving, despising silence. Ponsettia had a pleasant light voice and he obviously enjoyed singing, but even he faded away to muteness. Mackay was oddly more of an influence as he sat brooding unseen in the darkness than he had been all day when they could see his sullenness and the chip on his shoulder.

They sat without speaking for a while, then Ponsettia stirred.

"You guys know what?" he said.

"What?" Waltby lifted his head wearily.

"I guess I'd like to do a little praying. The singing didn't go so well so I'd kinda like to pray. I was always a lousy choir boy when I was a kid." He was speaking quickly as though he were a little embarrassed. "My mom used to lay into me because I wouldn't go to practice but just now I sorta guess a prayer wouldn't come amiss. 'Specially as it's Sunday by this time. Mind?"

"Not at all. Good idea," Waltby said. Mackay sat in silence.

"Thanks. Well, here goes. I guess I'm not much of a hand at this."

Waltby had expected Ponsettia's prayer to strike an odd note, particularly as he himself wasn't a churchgoing man. But there was so much obvious sincerity in the little Canadian's words and they seemed so much at variance with his light-hearted character that Waltby couldn't help but be impressed.

"I guess this goes for the lot of us," Ponsettia said in the darkness. "Almighty God, we have no hope here but in Thee. We are four men alone and in need of Thy help. We put our trust in Thee that, in Thy great mercy, Thou wilt not forget us and wilt give us strength to endure till Thou shalt bring us safe back to land." He paused. "I guess that's all, fellers."

"Amen," Waltby said, and he heard Mackay's unexpected, mumbled "Amen" alongside him.

He felt vaguely reassured and better as they settled into silence again, and he started to think that he ought to go to church when he got back – to give thanks for rescue or something of the sort. He was still thinking about it, yet knowing all the time he never would, when he drifted off into sleep.

Waltby awoke with a start, suddenly horrified that they might have been found by an enemy vessel before the precious brief case could be thrown overboard and, for a moment, he was caught in a feeling of panic once more. Then, as he became aware of where he was, he lay blinking slowly in the darkness, the icy drowsiness over him gradually dispersing and being replaced by a sharp determination not to sleep again.

As he recovered his wits completely he began to feel that something was wrong. The long sweeping motion of the dinghy seemed to have changed and he could feel a shorter rhythmic movement with it, too, that puzzled him at first. Then he realised it was Mackay rubbing Harding's hands. Waltby listened for a while as he continued to work, slowly and steadily chafing away at the pilot's hands, stopping every now and then to bale with the binocular case. Ponsettia was fitfully asleep, his hand still on the crank handle of the squawk box.

There was a method about Mackay's movements, a routine to his actions that suggested he had never rested from the time the others had fallen asleep after Ponsettia's prayer.

After a while, however, he stopped the rubbing and sat motionless for a minute or two, then Waltby realised he was moving his right arm slowly from where he'd put it round Harding after dark and had begun to wriggle carefully out of his fur-lined flying jacket. Gradually, in spite of the cut hand which was clumsy to use, he got the jacket off and began to ease it round Harding's shoulders, trying to lift the younger man in an attempt to slide the warm folds between him and the side of the dinghy. But Harding appeared to be heavier than he had imagined and he slowly eased his legs up, apparently to get a better purchase on the other's body.

Quietly, so unexpectedly that it made Mackay jump, Waltby leaned forward and spoke. "Let me help you."

Mackay whipped round in a quick, guilty movement, but Waltby reached across him, got his arm under Harding's shoulders and lifted him gently, and Mackay was able to slip the flying jacket down behind him and fold it across his chest.

"Better fasten it if you can," Waltby said gently and purposefully, with an air of authority of which Mackay had imagined him incapable.

Mackay fastened the jacket and lay back exhausted. The thanks he felt would not come to his stubborn tongue.

For a while he lay among the tangled bodies in the dinghy. With each lurch Harding rolled gently against him, and at the pressure of the slack body he felt an anxiety that made him forget the throbbing pain in his hand.

For himself, he felt no fear – only the desire to get out of the dinghy and on with the job of finishing the war and going home to the demands of his own plans. In his rough youth in the back streets he had never had room for fear. There had been so much to conquer, and violence and ugliness were so much a part of the struggle, that he felt no awe at the nearness of death, which came not infrequently among his friends or their families. For coal mining took its toll every year and every month in injuries and death and disease.

But for Harding, the only person he had ever contrived to love, he felt a very real terror.

"Think he'll die?" he blurted out to Waltby, his voice still vaguely accusing.

"I don't know, son," the older man said, his voice steady and unemotional.

"Think he'll be all right?"

"I hope so."

A wave of anger swept over Mackay that Waltby, with his rank and the brass on his hat, could be so indifferent to it all. Then it occurred to him that at least Waltby was sharing the same chances as the rest of them.

"What's the odds on being rescued?" he asked. "I mean, *you* ought to know. You're an air commodore. You ought to know better than me. I'm only aircrew. I'm here to be shot at. But you're in a position to know all about it from the top."

"Lad," Waltby said wearily, "I don't know half as much as you. My job ever since I joined the Air Force has been to deal with stresses and strains. With revolutions per minute and aerodynamics. I'm an engineer."

Mackay almost snorted. "Some people have an easy war."

"Perhaps they do," Waltby agreed. "But it's probably easier sometimes to go out and do the fighting than to sit back and watch when others don't come back."

"That's easy to say."

"Yes, it is. And it's often said. And for a lot of people it doesn't mean much. But there are a lot of people, too, who *do* mean it. There are a lot of pen pushers who'd be glad to be fighting. People are too quick to shout the odds that they're afraid."

"Aren't they?"

Waltby smiled to himself at the other's naivety. He was tired – far too cold and exhausted to argue but he persisted. Mackay seemed to need the encouragement of a quarrel to keep him going.

"Son," he said, "there are a lot of people they won't let fly because, from a medical point of view, they'd be anything but a help to a healthy man like yourself. They'd get in your way and let you down. You like this lad, your skipper, don't you?" he went on after a pause.

"Yes, I do." Mackay sounded defiant. "I've never met anyone like him in my life before. He's a toff. A real toff. Not one of these temporary toffs."

"I'm pleased you do feel that way – it means you're a human being after all." Waltby spoke with a trace of sarcasm. "Try to feel the same compassion towards others, too."

"He made *me* feel I was a human being," Mackay went on accusingly.

"He wouldn't be getting your affection if he hadn't."

"Ah, it's all right to talk," Mackay said with a sudden burst of anger that cheered Waltby a little with its new found energy. "You regular officers. You go into the Service for something to do. Not because you've got to earn your living. I've seen 'em all – at Sandhurst and Dartmouth and Cranwell."

Waltby felt like a grandfather as he replied. "Haven't you heard of scholarships?" he asked. "The Service these days is too technical for the wealthy to get to the top unless they've got skill as well. If it's of any interest to you," he went on a little angrily, "I joined the Air Force straight from school as an apprentice. I was crazy about flying but I never thought of flying myself. I thought that was only for the wealthy – the people *you're* talking about – and I'm not wealthy. But I thought I'd be near aeroplanes and that was good enough. When I discovered I *could* become a pilot, too, quite easily, it was too late and I never did become one." He paused before he went on, wondering if his words were having any effect.

"By that time I was interested only in making engines go round. As a result it took me twice as long to get a commission. I did it by studying and night school. I'm still a young man to be an Air Commodore in my line. And if it will help you at all, my father was a railway porter and still would be if he hadn't retired."

Mackay felt vaguely uncomfortable and didn't quite know what to say. He could hear the slop and splash of the waves and the pummelling of the wind every time they were lifted out of the troughs of the sea, then a sudden shower of rain stopped them thinking about themselves as they tried without success to catch it in their clothes.

Waltby started to bale again and it was only as he bent his hand to the water that he realised that Mackay's feet were bare.

He lifted his head sharply, staring in the darkness at the other.

"What's happened to your flying boots?" he asked.

"The Skipper's got 'em on. I thought he needed 'em more than me. He'd only got shoes on."

"How do you feel?"

"I'm all right. I don't feel the cold much."

Waltby knew he was lying. "Can't you put *his* shoes and socks on?"

"Too small. They're in the bottom of the dinghy somewhere. They'll do to bale with."

Waltby said nothing. There seemed to be absolutely nothing he could say. He knew well Mackay's desire to live, to be rescued – it was obvious from the energetic way he tried to perform what few duties he had, from the way he snatched things from the others to do them more quickly. Yet here he was taking a chance on dying of the cold for the sake of Harding.

It dawned on Waltby that Mackay was not quite so independent as he had thought. He needed affection and interest, someone to break through the wall of cynical resentment he had built round himself – as Harding by force of circumstance had done. Mackay had withstood everyone else; Harding, for the simple reason that they flew together and risked their lives together, had broken through the barrier. Mackay wasn't half so tough as he seemed, and that chip on his shoulder was one of unsureness, a defence against his own loneliness. Waltby suddenly felt a flood of warmth and comradeship towards the hard-faced, unsmiling Midlander.

"I think you'll do, Mac," he said. "You'll do."

"It's nothing," Mackay said sourly, giving nothing away in the shape of friendship. "He'd do the same for me if it came to a pinch."

"How's the hand, Mac?" Waltby asked irrelevantly.

"All right," Mackay lied. Waves of pain were shooting up his arm and had been ever since he had cut it. With every slash of salt water across the open wound, with every jolt of the dinghy, he had suffered agonies. He sounded a little surprised at Waltby's question, however, and a little less hostile.

Suddenly he had begun to find that nothing much mattered any more. So long as he and Harding got through all this alive it didn't matter greatly that Waltby belonged to the class he hated so much, the brass hats and the office-wallopers. And in any case it seemed that Waltby didn't actually belong to them. Mackay even began to wonder after what Waltby had said if there were in all honesty such a class in the Air Force.

"Why is it you think so much of Harding?" Waltby asked gently.

"Oh, it's nothing! It's just the way he is. The things he does. The way he speaks to a bloke."

He felt no embarrassment at his anxiety for the pilot's safety. All he had ever felt for Harding was a warm glow of affection, admiration and probably even love, but he found it hard to put it into words. There was no sentiment beyond the hardness in Mackay's nature, only awkwardness that amounted to rudeness, and his words did not – could not – show what was behind his feeling.

He had been in Harding's crew ever since he had started flying and had a series of memories that left out even Ponsettia. Ponsettia had joined them to take the place of a navigator whom they'd brought back dead on the charred floor of a Lancaster. A great hole had been torn in the nose by the flak shell that had killed the bomb-aimer. The rest of the crew had been wounded, and Harding and Mackay had struggled with the controls in the teeth of the wind roaring through the hole.

There had been autumn take-offs with the slipstream whirling into the air the leaves and the chaff in the fields and the inevitable sheet of newspaper, and winter landings with the blue mist of cold across the ground. They had shovelled snow together from the runways and watched anxiously when the ice had formed on their wings as they'd struggled over the Alps to Italy. They had flown from Malta and the dust-laden desert together, their lives growing daily closer with every danger shared. Other flying personnel had come and gone but only he and Harding were left of the original crew.

They had gone through a whole tour of operations together and started on another after their rest period – never allowing the fact that one used the Officers' Mess and the other the Sergeants' Mess to hold them apart. They had become one being in their experiences. Harding was the first cultured, well-educated individual Mackay had ever known intimately, and between them had sprung up over the months a strong affection that was in no way marred by Mackay's knowledge that they could never be equals.

Until he was posted to Harding's crew he had imagined that what he had always known as the upper classes were snobs with no time for such as himself, people who ground the faces of the poor, swindled them, forced them to live in rotten houses for high rents, and victimised them at every opportunity. Harding had shocked him at first by his lack of knowledge of the places where Mackay had lived, even angered him. But gradually the other's natural, youthful good nature and complete lack of affectation had won him over. It was no dramatic action that had accomplished it, no life saving, no going through fire and water together that had brought it about. It had happened slowly and without Mackay's being aware of it. But Harding so obviously liked him, and trusted him, so obviously wanted to be friendly, that Mackay had lost all his hatred and now felt only warm, flattered friendship.

"Don't ask me what it's all about," he said lamely. "I couldn't tell you. I only know he could have gone about with other blokes but he stuck to me. His dad's got estates as big as our town. I'm just an ordinary bloke. I've got a little fruit and vegetable store. That what I am. A fruiterer. I started when I was sixteen in the mines, but I left and started carting buttons and elastic for birds' bloomers round in a suitcase. Then, eventually, I started up with my shop and that's what I am. That's why I want to get this lousy war finished," he said savagely. He suddenly started to talk as though Waltby, having prised a chink in the gates he kept so tightly closed, had let loose a flood.

"I want to get back to it. I was just beginning to make the thing pay when Hitler started this lot. I've got an old bloke running it for me now, but he doesn't care," he said bitterly. "All he wants to do is shut the flaming thing up and go home. It's not the same when it's not your own."

"Besides," he went on after a pause, "*he'd* never worked down the mines and he didn't care. *I* had and I'm not going back to them – not even if they shove the wages heavens-high as they're talking of doing. I want to see the sky above my head, and the sunshine.

"I might have shut the place up when I was called up," he continued, "but it felt like committing suicide to think of it. I swore I'd keep it going whatever happened. And I have, by Christ! It's been hard enough, God knows. I've worked some sticky leaves to get home and sort out the mess – when I shouldn't have. I've – I've – I've put in for a commission," he said unexpectedly, as though a little startled by his own effrontery. "Think I'll get it?"

"Don't see why not," Waltby said. "Why? Thought you didn't like the commissioned ranks?"

"Well" – Mackay's voice faded a little – "other people are getting 'em. Didn't see why *I* shouldn't. Something for nothing. More pay. Why shouldn't I? When you look round at *some* of 'em who've got 'em..."

He was unable to say he needed the money and, above all, that he wanted to be nearer to Harding than the Sergeants' Mess would permit.

He paused, clearing his throat, then he blurted out again. "I've had it, though," he said. "I pinched a jerrycan of petrol the night before we left. MT petrol, it was. It fell off a truck near dispersal and I found it in a ditch. I've got an old bus – I bought it off a bloke to get home quickly to my shop when I wanted and it's been useful – and I swung the petrol into the back of it and left it there. I was going to use it to get home some time when I needed to. I thought I'd keep it in the village. I know a bloke there who'd look after it for me. It'll be there for me when I get back. I'm going to get some survivors' leave out of this" – Waltby noticed he obviously still felt a real, vitalising belief that he was going to escape, a belief that was rapidly beginning to die in Waltby – "and I'll nip off and sort out that old fool who's ruining my shop. I've kept it going this long and I'm not going to let him run it down now – not now the war's almost over." He thought for a while. "Hope to God nobody's found the stuff," he concluded. "I'd catch it in the neck sure as eggs. That's what I'm scared of."

"I suppose it's a bit soft to tell an Air Commodore I've pinched some petrol," he went on in a puzzled fashion. "But there you are. If you don't like it, you can lump it. I'd better get rid of it, I suppose, if we get back. Safest."

He paused. "Only, you see," he went on, "I've *got* to keep the business going. I've got to. I can't let it slide now. I've got to get back and sort it out. That's why I want the flaming war to end. Hell, I never had a chance in my life as a kid. Then I made this one off my own bat. I don't want to lose it again now just because of a lot of bloody Nazzies."

He halted again for a moment, then went on gloomily. "The Skipper always swore he'd come and get his groceries from me," he concluded. "Even if he had to bicycle all the way from Gloucestershire, where he lived."

"He will, Mac!" Waltby was startled to hear Ponsettia answer out of the darkness, his voice gentle and bereft of sarcasm. "So help me, he will, bud. Those jokers in those goddam *E*-boats aren't going to stop the Skipper fetching his spuds and cabbages from you. Not if I can help it. Just give us a chance and let those bastard *E*-boats be somewhere else at daybreak. That's all."

PART THREE

It was raining steadily when Group Captain Taudevin left the Officers' mess and made his way towards Headquarters – slanting down in long slender spears that hissed and whispered about his feet and ruffled the wet surface of the road. It spoke to him in a sibilant murmuring above the wind that set the trees at the other side of the building roaring and rushing with sound.

He was tired. It had been a long day for him. He had been to a conference at Group Headquarters and on his return had made his usual call at Station Sick Quarters, not certain whether Scotty would remember to make the round of the wards as requested. Sure enough it had slipped Scotty's memory, but even in the silent building darkened for the night he had found a symbol of Scotty's inefficiency in the shape of a small, pretty WAAF enquiring about the health of Sergeant Ponsettia, Harding's navigator.

Standing in the shadows by the entrance, the smell of antiseptics and sterile cleanliness sharp in his nostrils, Taudevin had watched her as she waited outside the door of the Sick Quarters office where the medical orderly on duty had been engaged in sticking a "No Smoking" notice to the wall with strips of sticking plaster from a tin prominently labelled "Not for sticking notices".

"I tell you," the medical orderly was saying impatiently, as though repeating something he had said half a dozen times already, "that there's no Sergeant Ponsettia in here. And as far as I can make out he's in no other sick bay either. We've been looking for him ever since you came the first time and we'd have been informed for sure if someone had got him. If it's anything to you, you started a proper old uproar coming in here and saying he'd been found. We've been searching all over Suffolk for him." The medical orderly clicked his tongue disapprovingly.

"But the Squadron Leader Admin. definitely told me it was only a matter of time before he was back." The girl's voice was thin and unhappy.

"It might be, but he's not back yet. Not here, he isn't. From what I've heard from Operations Room, nothing's been heard of 'em yet. I'm sorry, kid, but there you are." The medical orderly turned with an air of finality, tore off a strip of plaster and stuck down the last corner of his notice.

"But Squadron Leader Scott said definitely they knew where they were," the girl insisted wretchedly.

"Squadron Leader Scott talks out of the top of his head sometimes," the medical orderly said loftily.

The little WAAF turned away, obviously on the verge of tears, and the medical orderly, struck by compassion, called out after her. "Listen, ducks, I'll tell you what: if he's brought in here tonight, and you don't mind being wakened up, I'll send one of the WAAF medical orderlies round to your billet to let you know. Let's have your billet number and the position of your bed."

"Of course I don't mind being wakened up." The girl was sniffing slightly as she wrote down the required instructions on a sick-report form. "I wouldn't have bothered you at all, only the Squadron Leader Admin. said they'd be back any time." She was repeating her words as though the very repetition could put right her unhappiness. "I've rung the Sergeants' Mess and he's not there."

"I keep telling you" – the medical orderly's voice had a ragged edge of irritation – "Ops. Room says nothing's been heard of 'em yet. I rang up some time ago. *We* want to know, you know, same as you. We're keeping beds ready, and water bottles and the whole bag of tricks. The MO's on tap and everything. Have no fear, kid, if they find him they'll be bound to bring him in here, if only for a check-up. Keep your chin up," he finished as she turned away again.

Taudevin, standing in the shadows of the waiting room, opened the door for the girl and she crept past, too obsessed with her anxiety to notice who he was. Then, as he closed the door quietly after her, she saw the rings on his sleeve and her eyes widened with a sudden start of horror.

"That Scott!" the medical orderly was saying to an unseen companion in the dispensary as Taudevin silently crossed the waiting-room. "Tells 'em anything to get rid of 'em. Crikey, nothing's been heard of that lot since yesterday morning. For all we know, they're down among the fishes. Perhaps it's as well, too. There's a court martial waiting for one of 'em, I've been told. Pinching petrol."

Taudevin, on his way up the stairs, paused again. So Scotty hadn't been able to keep his own counsel after all! In spite of everything Taudevin had said about secrecy he hadn't been able to keep his mouth shut. Taudevin was frowning as he mounted the rest of the steps...

Now, remembering the incident, he walked across to the office building where his car was parked, his hands deep in his pockets, his shoulders hunched, his hat jammed down over his eyes.

The camp was silent in the black-out. Over by the hangars, where there was usually the gleam of red lamps against the sky and the glow from the chance-light at the end of the flarepath, there was nothing tonight but darkness, and no sign of a star through the low, folding clouds. There were no searchlights on the move in the distance either, as there normally were, lighting up the roadway with their reflected glare.

What buildings he could see loomed in bulky shadows above him, their black sides picked out here and there by the dim blue lights in the barrack-rooms. In one of them, late as it was, he could hear an argument taking place – obviously some roisterer who had taken advantage of the absence of flying to get himself drunk.

Taudevin glanced up in the direction of the disturbance but his mind was still busy with his thoughts. One half of his brain was struggling with what he was going to tell Waltby's wife, the other half was wondering what he could do about Scotty.

Obviously Scotty couldn't be allowed to go on as he was doing. They couldn't go on for ever picking up the bricks he let fall. He'd have to go eventually. The time would inevitably arrive when he would make the most ghastly bloomer imaginable that no amount of effort could cover up. But Taudevin shrank from the job of personally getting rid of him. Scotty was rather a pathetic individual, with his slang and his prancing walk and his pilot officer's moustache and that unhappy air of failure that brooded over him. After all, Scotty's only crime was that he was too old for his job – not too old by any means in years but too old in manner. He'd lost his vigour and clarity of thought – if indeed he'd ever had any – far too soon. He was nothing more now than an old woman, and it was only his old-womanish manner that had caused him to mislead Ponsettia's little WAAF. He'd obviously only been trying to comfort her and no more. But – Taudevin's mouth set hard – he'd still no right to buoy the child up with false hope when there was precious little.

Taudevin turned into headquarters and went to his office, in case any messages had been left for him since his return. On his desk was the usual pile of papers left for him by Scotty, business that Scotty should have handled on his own. On the top was the copy of an order for the Officers' Mess, typed out, signed and left for Taudevin's approval.

In accordance with King's Regulations and Air Council Instructions, officers are reminded that Dress Regulations state that flying boots will not be worn in the Mess except by crews returning from operations and then only...

Taudevin read the document through carefully then slowly drew a pencil through the first half of it. Trust Scotty to make it as legal as he could and drag in airmanship and loyalty and all his other little tin gods. His own name and rank underneath the order were sufficient to make it stick, without invoking King's Regulations and Air Council Instructions.

Beneath the order there was a batch of applications for commissions and it startled Taudevin to realise that one of them concerned Mackay, Harding's wireless operator. Apparently Mackay had been passed fit by everyone concerned – the Medical Officer, his squadron commander – and the paper required only Taudevin's signature to make the commission certain. He studied it for a while, trying to read into the replies to the printed questions some of the angry thwarted character of Harding's operator; then he began to put the applications on one side, his mind still on the fringe of that search across the dark sea and the storm that was now upon them, the gale that would make useless all their work unless the dinghy were found quickly.

He glanced at the window. The rain was rattling in gusty blasts against the panes now.

Taudevin thoughtfully laid the sheets down, then he noticed another one on his desk, half-hidden by all the other matter – a carbon copy of a charge sheet from the Station Warrant Officer's department, obviously made out by the Station Police and passed along by someone for Taudevin's information. Suddenly suspicious, he picked it up and glanced at the name on it then he slammed it down on his desk.

"Damn Scotty," he said aloud.

He lit a cigarette and stood looking at the charge sheet on his desk for a while, then he picked it up again and studied it more closely. Obviously the Station Warrant Officer, a far wiser man than Scotty realised, had spotted the name on the sheet and decided Taudevin would want to know about it. Taudevin silently thanked God that the old SWO, with his leathery face and his iron lungs and sarcasm, had more intelligence than Scotty had ever credited him with.

He slipped the charge sheet into a drawer and went out and up the stairs towards the Operations Room. The Controller was still there and Taudevin was pleased to see Howard, the Meteorological Officer, with him too, tired-looking and pale but obviously still working. He had not suggested to either of them that they should stay on duty, but he felt relieved and pleased that both had done so willingly.

Neither of them spoke as he entered, and he crossed the room in silence to stare at the map. The marker for Harding's dinghy was still there, further south and almost touching the Belgian coast – but the other markers, representing the rescuers, had been moved away. They were all of them off the board now, except for two, one off the English coast near Felixstowe, the other off the Belgian coast north-west of Antwerp.

Jones, the Controller, moved to his side.

"One of the launches has broken down, sir." He tapped the map with his pointer and his manner told Taudevin there was fresh news. "She's about here. Nothing serious in itself, I gather. If she's serviceable by morning they're going to call her into the search again. That is, providing the weather makes it possible for them to operate. I gather it must be pretty grim by now."

"The Navy at Dover report heavy rain and wind up to forty-five miles an hour and still rising," Howard put in.

Taudevin struck a match as he listened, the matchbox held awkwardly in those raw talons of his. His eyes did not move from the plotting table.

"This German prisoner the naval launch brought in – " the Controller continued – "you'd get the message about him. It was passed on to you at Group HQ." Taudevin nodded. "The naval people have questioned him closely and from the position he gave they've worked out from their tide and wind tables that if the dinghy is afloat at all it can only be in this area here by Becq-le-Plage and Zeemucke. About there." He tapped with his pointer.

"As close in as that?" Taudevin raised his eyebrows as he put his matches away, his eyes on the tip of Jones' pointer.

"As close in as that," Jones repeated soberly. Taudevin was aware of Howard's face, watching the two of them closely. The sergeant plotter had stopped working and was listening, motionless, with all his attention on them as Jones continued. "The Navy says they'll be right on the beach by mid-morning."

"It's a devil of a place for a launch to go. I wonder if we ought to ask them to – right under the shore batteries."

"They'll go in if they're told to. The weather we're getting now might be on their side if they can only spot the dinghy. It will make visibility difficult from the shore. Pity it also makes air cover difficult."

Taudevin said nothing. He was thinking of his own cold spell in a dinghy and the awful sense of being forgotten by the rest of the war.

Jones waited for a while for him to make some remark, then he went on.

"If only we could have kept the fighters flying a little longer, sir, we might have found them. As it is, with this weather blowing up and due to reach them any minute their chances are growing shorter all the time, I'm afraid."

"If they can hold out until daylight there's still a chance," Taudevin said, his mouth hard. "We'll get everything that can fly off the ground over there at first light, unless there's thick fog or heavy rain. I'll ring up Group myself and suggest it if they haven't laid it on already. One or two of those Mosquito pilots would be willing to have a go, I'm sure. If only the dinghy doesn't capsize," he ended slowly.

He studied the operations board for a while. The space opposite Harding's name and the number of his aircraft was still blank, but while his name remained there seemed to be hope.

He straightened up, shrugging off his depression.

"I must go down to the station," he said sharply. "My wife's down there. I expect she's finished off the night porters' tea by now. She usually does. She's getting pretty well known now, meeting odd wives as she does at all hours. I'll find her in the night porters' room as usual, I suppose." He glanced up at the others and suddenly his eyes looked haggard. "I've got the job of telling Waltby's wife," he said.

The train was just pulling into the station as Taudevin left his car and walked on to the platform. He found his wife quickly in the dim lights of the station, as he had expected just coming out of the night porters' room where there was the only fire available.

She jumped as he took her arm, then she turned and smiled up at him, her face shadowed in the feeble lights. Their ears were full of the hiss of steam and the roar of the engine as the dimly lit carriages slid to a stop, doors half-open, the porters shouting the name of the station.

"Before Eve arrives," Taudevin said quickly above the noise. "Sydney's missing. The aircraft disappeared during the day and nothing's been heard of it since. You'll have to help me."

His wife flashed a quick look of fear at him. It was a look he'd seen before during the war on many occasions – fear not for herself but for other people or for him.

"They've been searching all day," he went on. "Everything that will float or fly. Nothing's been heard. But we're still hoping."

His wife stared at him silently for a while, moving a little closer to him as she turned her attention to the carriages once more.

The train had come to a stop now, sighing noisily like a tired animal, and people were descending – a few airmen and sailors with late passes, clutching bags, hurrying towards the exit with their tickets to be the first for lifts or late taxis. The station seemed a mass of movement for a moment, all in one direction. Then they saw Waltby's wife in her old-fashioned green hat, one of the last to descend from a first-class carriage crammed as usual with third-class passengers, stuffing her knitting into a bag and hefting a suitcase from the rack.

A tall, handsome, hard-faced blonde woman in a plaid coat was standing in the doorway of the carriage. As Taudevin watched her she stepped down and accepted a suitcase from an American sergeant who was standing behind her – one of the green naval suitcases, Taudevin noticed – with the letters HT painted on it in a clumsy attempt at artistry.

"He's not here, Carl," she was saying. "The big soft clot. I knew he wouldn't make it. He's too slow to catch a cold."

Eve Waltby had to push past her towards Taudevin and his wife as she stood irritably tapping her foot. Taudevin took the bag and stood in silence as the sisters kissed.

"Hello, Chris," Eve Waltby said at last. Then her expression of pleasure changed quickly. "Sydney? Where is he? I thought he was going to be here to meet me. He said he would. I expect those precious statistics of his are holding him up again, are they?"

Taudevin's wife flashed her look at Taudevin again and Eve Waltby saw it and looked up too.

"What is it, Chris?" she asked quietly. "Has something happened?"

Taudevin suddenly found he could not look at her. He was staring over her head, his eyes on the hard-faced blonde woman with the naval suitcase. The American sergeant had returned to his compartment and the woman was standing alone on the platform, still tapping her foot.

"I'm afraid Sydney's missing, Eve," he said slowly, drawing his breath in deeply. "The aircraft he was returning in from the Continent disappeared during the day and nothing's been heard of it since."

Eve Waltby continued to watch him, saying nothing. Taudevin was still staring over her head. The train must have been late arriving, for the porters had already finished slamming in the mail bags and were moving along the platform, pushing the doors to. One of them touched the blonde woman on the arm as he passed, and she shrugged his hand off angrily.

"They've been searching all day," Taudevin went on, aware that he was repeating to Waltby's wife the exact words he had used to his own wife. "Everything that will float or fly. Nothing's been heard yet, but we're still trying and we're still hoping. We believe he's in a dinghy."

Eve Waltby's expression showed no fear – not even the quick darting glance his own wife had shown. She had trained herself well to calmness over the years she had been married to Waltby. She had forced it on herself to soothe her husband's nervous brilliance and quieten him when he got too irritably tired over some job that couldn't be left.

"In a dinghy?" she said. "It's terrible weather for that."

"Yes, I'm afraid it is, Eve," Taudevin said, aware of the inadequacy of his words. "But those dinghies are pretty foolproof you know. We're hoping to pick them up at first light."

As he spoke he knew he was indulging in the same false optimism that had caused Scotty to distress Ponsettia's little WAAF with unfounded hope, and he suddenly sympathised with the older man.

"Well – " Eve Waltby seemed to clutch at her courage as though it had been in danger of suddenly running away from her. Her voice was stronger and firmer than normal " – I suppose this is no place to do our worrying. Shall we get on?"

Taudevin's wife took her arm to guide her through the dark station to the exit and Taudevin turned to follow. As he moved away he heard the guard's whistle blow, and he saw the blonde woman in the plaid coat climb back into the train. The American sergeant, standing in the corridor now, offered her a cigarette and they stood leaning on the handrail, saying nothing as he lit it for her.

Taudevin heard the first deep, stomachic puff from the engine and the slam of the carriage door, then, as he followed his wife and Eve Waltby, he caught sight of the dimly lit windows of the train starting to move forward.

By morning the rain lay heavily over the land, making the outlines of the hangars dim and silvery in the grey daylight. The straight tall poplars outside the main gate of the aerodrome were flinging their bare spars in a frenzy as the wind lashed at them across the wide fields, and the ensign rippled straight and hard from the top of the flagstaff which drummed in the beating of the weather.

Sick with disappointment, Taudevin stood at his streaming window and stared out, his vision blurred by the raindrops which hammered occasionally at the glass, breaking up the view across the wide entrance to the aerodrome as though it were a picture that had shivered suddenly to a thousand fragments. The sentry by the gate huddled inside his box and the canvas cover on the lorry just passing him fluttered and whipped in the rising gale.

From the hangars, Taudevin knew, the tethered Lancasters would be misty in the distance across the perimeter, their great wings gleaming in the slashing rain, their wheels standing in puddles of shining water which reflected their ebony undersides. The whole grass area of the field would be sparkling and jewel-bright, patches of water lying in the shallow folds between the runways. Beyond the perimeter the farms would be hazy and with a twilight look about them through the rain that came across the field in driven flurries as though from a waved hosepipe.

The office was stuffy and airless and Taudevin, nervy and irritable after a poor night, found it unbearable. He had left his wife and Eve Waltby eating breakfast in fits of flat conversation, finding it hard to be interested in anything when the only thing that lay at the back of their minds was the fact that Eve's husband was at best probably in a dinghy and that a gale was blowing.

He moved away from the window and sat down at his desk, resisting the desire to hurry upstairs to the Operations Room where he could learn only what he already knew. Nothing had been heard of the dinghy yet. Nothing, in fact, had even been heard of the launch which had been marooned not far from the Belgian coast with unserviceable engines. Messages kept coming in which were passed on immediately for his perusal, but they told him only that the launch towing the Walrus had had to report casting off the tow, that shortly afterwards the Walrus had been smashed below the surface by a wave catching its wing, and that naval vessels were beating their way out through the weather in the direction of the lost launch and the possible vicinity of the dinghy – if, indeed, there were a dinghy.

None had yet been spotted. That fact kept recurring to Taudevin with sickening insistence. He had no sure knowledge yet that Waltby and Harding and the others had even escaped from the aircraft. "No one got out." That phrase cropped up often enough in reports of aircraft ditching for him to know only too well what the chances were.

With the low cloud and beating rain, the Fighter people had not been able to get off the ground. They were willing enough to try at the first break in the weather and, while he itched to ask them to chance it, he knew their task was hopeless even if they reached the area of the search. They could never have seen anything – let alone a tiny yellow dinghy on the vast surface of the sea.

Taudevin lifted the papers on his desk and was perusing them when the door opened and Scotty entered.

"Good morning, sir. Wizard weather, isn't it?"

Taudevin pushed his chair back as Scotty slammed a sheaf of papers on his desk and started off in his normal boisterously youthful manner: "This bus service we're trying to start from the camp – " he began, when Taudevin cut him short with a wave of his hand.

"Not now," he said. "There's something else I want to talk to you about."

"Roger, sir," Scotty said heartily. He made a great show of being energetic and efficient, but he wasn't even efficient at that, and Taudevin could see he wasn't keen to have any more work pushed on to him that might cut short his tea-drinking and his morning chat with the station Adjutant. He pranced forward and, picking up the papers on the desk again, swept his moustache upwards with the back of his hand and waited with one foot splayed forward in a picture of interested attention.

"Tough about Harding's crowd," he said conversationally, waiting for the Group Captain to speak. "Rotten poor do, this thick stuff coming down just now."

"Scotty," Taudevin said. "I learn that one of the Mess WAAFs has been pestering the Sick Quarters about Ponsettia, Harding's navigator. She got the impression he was being brought back here last night. The girl was at her wit's end with worry, wondering where he'd got to."

"Really, sir? Tough luck. Ponsettia's popsie?"

"Yes. Ponsettia's girl. In fact, I've been making a few enquiries from her section officer and I gather they're almost engaged."

"Oh, tough luck!'

"It seems you told her he was about to be brought back." As he spoke Taudevin remembered uncomfortably his own white lies to Waltby's wife the night before.

Scotty's jaw had dropped. "*I* did, sir?"

"It seems she stopped you near Ops. Room and got the information from you there."

"Good God, sir!" Scotty exploded into noisy denials as Taudevin had known he would. "I wouldn't tell her that sort of nonsense."

Taudevin studied him with his still, expressionless gaze. "The fact remains, Scotty, that you did. Outside Ops. Room last evening."

Scotty searched back in his crowded mind and suddenly the memory of the tearful little WAAF came to him.

"Oh, good God, sir, that! Yes." He laughed shortly and nervously. "That! That was nothing. Heavens, I told her nothing at all. Nothing at all."

"You told her enough for her to feel quite certain about it."

"The stupid child." Scotty laughed again, trying to disengage his eyes from Taudevin's. "Silly little thing. Funny little girl. That's a fine thing to say, isn't it? Just the sort of thing to make me look a fool."

Taudevin stared at him. "As you know," he went on, "quite apart from the fact that you'd no right to tell her what was going on in the Operations Room, nothing was known about Harding's crew at that time. Nothing is known yet, in fact. We have no idea that they're even alive."

"Really, sir?" Scotty was beginning to realise by this time that he was in a spot and he was growing cautious. He tried to distract Taudevin with sympathy. "That's tough for them, isn't it?"

"It was tough for that girl." Taudevin's voice rose slightly.

"But, Heavens, sir!" Scotty gestured vaguely as he realised he had not moved Taudevin from his intentions. "I told her nothing. If she gets it into her stupid little head that I say things when I don't, surely that's *her* fault. I was only trying to stop her being too upset. That's the worst of WAAFS. Women and war don't mix. Too much emotion."

He was talking quickly to stave off Taudevin's anger, saying anything that came into his head. Taudevin cut him short.

"There's another point I learned in the Sick Quarters, too, Scotty. I gather the story about Mackay taking the petrol is all over the camp."

"Good God, sir, no!" Scotty gasped with a nicely simulated horror – the horror of a silly old lady, Taudevin thought angrily. "Those damn Station Police have been talking, I suppose!"

"I have gathered, rather, that you told the Met. Officer and one of his forecasters overheard the conversation. Probably you even told someone else."

"Good Lord, Sir!" Scotty shook his head vehemently. "I wouldn't do that. You know I wouldn't. You told me not to."

"Exactly. I told you not to."

"Those damn people in my office," Scotty snapped, his eyes flickering to hide his unhappiness. "That Sergeant Starr. I've been suspecting for a long time he's been watching all the stuff that goes across my desk. I believe he reads everything that comes through."

"Sergeant Starr was doing that job before you came, Scotty, and without complaint."

Scotty took a new line and plunged into a diatribe on the lack of support he received. "I don't know what it is," he mourned. "I seem to get no damn loyalty from my subordinates. If he could do the job for someone else, why the devil can't he for me – ?"

"One thing more, Scotty." Taudevin reached over his desk and tossed a sheet of paper towards the Administration Officer. "This."

Scotty picked it up and stared at it. Then his jaw dropped again. He flashed a quick glance at Taudevin and his face lost what was left of its jauntiness and became sagging and old.

"It's a charge sheet, sir," he gasped. "Made out against Mackay."

"Exactly."

"But..." Scotty gaped for a moment, his face reddening with his sense of guilt. "We'll have to go through with it now. The Special Investigation people won't let up on it – not with this made out. They're bound to have seen it. Our own police might let up but not those people. How the devil did they get it?" He searched frantically in his mind for an explanation.

"You dropped the file on the Station Warrant Officer's desk with some other papers," Taudevin pointed out "You asked his clerk to see that they were dealt with. Naturally, the man passed it on to the police who made out the charge sheet."

"*I* dropped – *I* dropped it on his desk?"

"Yesterday. Immediately after you'd left my office at lunchtime. Unfortunately, the SWO was out of the room at the time or it might have been stopped."

Scotty passed his hand underneath his moustache in an empty gesture of stroking it. He felt suddenly weary and sick as he remembered the missing file on Mackay and how he had puzzled over finding the folder about the accommodation in the hutted camp among the disorder on his desk after tea. He knew now what had happened. He had dropped the wrong file in the Station Warrant Officer's office.

"I particularly asked you to sit on that, Scotty," Taudevin was saying.

"Yes, sir." Scotty sought a way out. "I can't think how it happened. I'll have to clobber Starr about it. He never has a clue about what he's doing. I'll have to tear him off a tremendous strip – "

"For God's sake, Scotty," Taudevin snapped, irritated by Scotty's desperate dodging, "stop talking that infantile jargon to me."

Scotty gulped.

"Sir, it seems I can rely on nobody round here to do their jobs properly – neither Starr nor the Station Warrant Officer nor anyone. Those damn police should have known not to proceed with this thing – "

"Why? You asked the SWO's people to deal with it and they did so as they imagined you would want them to. And so did the police."

"Sir, you can't expect anyone in this place to use any initiative at all. It seems – "

"It seems to me they used their initiative remarkably well. Fortunately the Station Warrant Officer had enough sense to realise I'd be interested in this and he saw that I got a copy of it."

"Yessir." Scotty was floundering. "But it strikes me there are times when they might check back on me first before taking action. It seems they're only waiting for the opportunity to put one across me. I seem to get damn little loyalty anywhere."

"Oh, for Heaven's sake, Scotty, shut up about your infernal loyalty! You've had more loyalty than you realise. The SWO's been covering up for you for ages."

"Sir – "

"Nobody's to blame for this foul-up except yourself. You handed the wrong file over, I suppose. I expect you muddled the lot up in your office."

Scotty stood by the table, holding his sheaves of notes, his references to the bus service and the AOC's inspection, his figure crumpled, all the bounce gone out of him. Taudevin tossed in his direction Mackay's application for a commission.

"What about this?" he said. "I can't let that go through in the circumstances. He's earned it. He deserves it. But it can't go through now because of this charge – something I could have cleared up myself without having to make a charge of it. He's not a dishonest man. He's just been a fool. Now this has come to nothing."

"Sir – if only people…" Scotty swallowed, and his complaint died unborn. He swallowed again, his face twisted and broken, then he straightened up. "I'm sorry, sir," he said stiffly. "I seem to have made rather a cock of things."

Taudevin looked over his shoulder at him from the window, touched by Scotty's taut, pompous voice. Scotty seemed to have aged ten years suddenly, and Taudevin, a sensitive man, was immediately sorry for him. After all, he found himself thinking, Scotty was not a young man. Perhaps, he thought, when *he* was too old for the job some other war might break out and some whippersnapper might tell *him* to shut up.

He hardened his heart again. Scotty would have to go. There was no room for him on an operational aerodrome where the crews had the right to expect the best men to be looking after their interests. He would have to go to a recruit-training depot where they'd respect his rank and his medals and his age and not notice what an old duffer he was. It could be arranged without any loss of dignity.

Taudevin was about to continue speaking when there was a knock on the door and the Operations Room sergeant came in, holding out a message form to him.

"The Squadron Leader thought you'd like to see this, sir," he said. "It's from the launch."

Taudevin took the paper and Scotty stepped back a pace, suddenly forgotten and thankful for the break.

Dinghy sighted, Taudevin read. *Survivors on board. Position...*

Taudevin's face lifted for a moment and Scotty was relieved to see the anger disappear. Then Taudevin seemed to clutch at his gaiety and his brows came down again.

"Thank you, Sergeant. Tell the Squadron Leader I'll be up to see him in a moment."

When the sergeant had disappeared Taudevin turned again to Scotty.

"Since we can't withdraw this charge, Scotty," he said more gently, "we must at least do everything we can to see that someone else does. I'll deal with Mackay myself later. I don't want to lose him from flying. I want him to finish his tour of operations and I want him to have his commission. He might be of great value when the war moves to the Pacific. Get over to Felwell and see the Group Captain there. Tell him I want to borrow that KC chap, Ryder, he has on his staff. I must have him for Mackay. I want him to look into this charge and the facts that go with it and see if he can't find a loophole. If Mackay comes ashore injured, there must be no chance of any charge sticking. He's had enough."

He walked to the window, his raw hands thrust into his pockets. He was itching to go upstairs to the Operations

Room but he forced himself to conduct his business first. "If necessary, we must arrange for a posting here for Ryder for a while. They can have him back immediately afterwards. But we've got to put up a show for Mackay. Get off now, Scotty. If there's any difficulty, phone me, but I think the Group Captain there will play ball. For God's sake, don't slip up this time."

"No, sir, I'll not slip up."

"I'll get in touch with them myself as soon as I've sorted out this business of Harding."

Scotty turned away thankfully, determined to do his utmost, but at the door he crashed into the Controller as he entered.

Jones thrust him aside, almost rudely.

"Sir," he said to Taudevin, ignoring Scotty. "This message followed the other from the launch."

Taudevin glanced quickly at Jones and took the message form.

Dinghy inside sand-bank. Shore guns silent. I am going in... he read.

"There the message ended abruptly," Jones pointed out quietly. "There's now wireless silence. It was never finished and we can't get in touch with them. They've gone off the air completely. Something must have happened to them."

t w o

The dawn had come wet and cold and grey. The waves changed gradually from black to navy blue and eventually to a cold green-grey. First the white crests slowly became visible and then later the veinous streaks that marked the wind as it whipped off the crests. The water in the bottom of the dinghy changed from black to grey-yellow, a dirty colour that seemed symbolic of their position.

The sky was still covered from one horizon to the other by the close ridges of cloud, hard-packed together like old snow, and very low down. The rain fell in squally patches now, too, in a steeply slanting drizzle that blew into their faces, wetting them through and blurring the distance. It was difficult to tell the direction of the wind without looking at the compass, as the dinghy was constantly being whirled round in circles.

Waltby felt drunk with cold – as though he had been cold all his life. He felt as though he could never remember ever having been in any other state but this cheerless misery. He had begun to hate the sea with all the hate he possessed.

Whatever happened, he felt he could never look with kindly eyes on it again, not even on its gentlest day, no matter where he saw it – not even if it were the peacock blue of Cornwall or the rich ultramarine of the Mediterranean. Always he would remember it only as this ugly green-grey colour, turbulent, threatening, vast and utterly empty.

His arms ached with baling and his mind was stiff with worry and – away at the back – fear. All the time there was only this rhythmic surge of the waves, the slow climbing up the crests, the lurch over the top and the sickening slide down the other side to the valley where the water sloshed over them in icy jets.

He had never fallen asleep again throughout the long night. When his mind had cried out for rest and the others, even the determined Mackay, had fallen for a few minutes into a stupefied, frozen doze, he had remained awake, his spur the brief case between his legs which he must hand over complete with all its secrets. After that one horrifying slip away into nothingness he had sat rigidly upright, holding the case. Mackay had stayed awake, laboriously rubbing Harding's hands and arms, holding him clamped tight against his own great frame for warmth, until weariness and the frosty cold had carried him off into a sleep that was full of twitchings and protesting grunts.

As his mind came back to the present Waltby realised with a start that the other two were also awake and staring at him. Their faces were pinched and that sure hope that had been in their eyes the previous day had disappeared. Their eyes were sunken and dark-ringed with weariness, and their gauntness was accentuated by their beards; they looked as though the cold had eaten away the flesh from under their skin. Harding's lips were white now and Waltby well knew he couldn't last much longer, whatever his injuries might be – not without warmth to combat the shock.

He wanted to say something to cheer the others up, something to bring back the sparkle to Ponsettia's eyes, even the anger to Mackay's, but there seemed nothing intelligent he could say and, without speaking, they divided the chocolate and the biscuit with stiff fingers that wouldn't move properly.

As he chewed, Waltby thought of food with what amounted to nausea as the juices welled up in his mouth, almost choking him, and the lurch of the dinghy stressed the emptiness of his stomach.

"Well," Ponsettia said at last, "if that's breakfast, we've had it. How long do you reckon we'll last out on that in this weather?"

Waltby immediately remembered Harding's words soon after they had taken to the dinghy – days ago now, it seemed. "Exposure's as great a danger as running out of food," he had said, and Waltby became sickeningly aware how wet they all were.

He found he could not be honest, however, as he replied.

"Days, I imagine," he said, forcing the lightness into his voice in an effort to hide the listless indifference that he knew he must keep at bay. "One chap I heard of sailed for days in a one-man dinghy. No reason why *we* shouldn't."

Ponsettia smiled wryly and disbelievingly. The zest and the humour had gone out of him, as though he were tiring of the struggle with the cold. Mackay sat rigidly upright, one arm still round Harding, with the grimness, the unsmiling, humourless grimness, the unbending determination and the one-track faith of a Scottish covenanter. For all his eager energy of the previous day, he seemed during the night to have learned patience.

"Brandy seems to be indicated," Waltby said and they all had a sip and forced a little between Harding's teeth.

"I once read you couldn't get rheumatism from sea water," Ponsettia said wearily. "But the guy who wrote the book probably didn't include sitting up to your waist in it for twenty-four hours at this time of the year."

"Think we'll be picked up, Syd?" he asked after a while during which they all sat in silence, baling or slapping their chests or legs with an automatic hopelessness.

"Yes," Waltby said, realising what an appalling lie he was telling. By this time he no longer felt there was any likelihood of rescue. He felt they would inevitably succumb to the cold

– first Harding, then the others, probably Ponsettia next, then Mackay. He put himself last without thinking, taking as his source of strength his determination to deliver the briefcase, but he knew that Harding at least could not survive another night.

"Hope you're right," Ponsettia said. He was apathetic and slow speaking now. "I had a nightmare last night – I dreamed we were cast up on the shore and, just when we were looking forward to being warm again, it turned out to be the North Pole and we were colder than ever. Hey!"

He sat up sharply as he finished speaking, throwing off his lethargy so that the others involuntarily sat up, too, spurred by his excitement.

"The shore," Ponsettia continued, his voice higher. "Remember? The E-boats. I'd forgotten 'em. We must be within reach of land. We ought to be able to see it by now, I guess. Keep your eyes skinned. Let's have a look at the compass."

They all crouched over the swinging needle, Waltby miserably conscious of Harding's pale, silent face upturned away from them against Mackay's shoulder.

"Wind's still blowing from the north," Ponsettia pointed out. "That sets the Jerry coast over there, in the east."

He pointed and their eyes followed his outstretched hand.

They waited a long time in weary patience for the rain to slacken off a little. It was as though the squall that dragged their hair in limp strands over their eyes drew a curtain between them and the distance to shut off their view as effectively as if it had been solid.

"It's slackening," Ponsettia said after a while and they could see the white crests in the distance appearing again, blurred at first then gradually becoming more distinct. Then, as a wave lifted them, they all strained upwards, their tired eyes peering out of their salt-stiffened faces.

They saw it suddenly, just a long low shadow, blue-grey through the rain across the white-flecked metallic water, lifting upwards with them with slow deliberation above the intervening waves.

"There!" Mackay said sharply, flinging out an arm. "I saw it! There!"

As the rain stopped briefly they could see flat-fronted houses – even the blank windows which suggested they must be unoccupied by civilians – and the taller bulk of the trees behind. There was a long sea wall running along the shore with, here and there, the low humps of what appeared to be pill-boxes and sandbagged gun-positions. They could even see the yellow line of beach below the dunes with posts sticking upright out of it as though they held barbed wire.

"Houses," Ponsettia breathed. "Real houses! Jesus, don't they look warm?"

There was something reassuring about the solidity of the land, in spite of its hostile nature, and Waltby found himself marvelling at its stillness. After twenty-four hours of staring at the ever-moving sea the land seemed weighty and strong and, in spite of the thought of captivity, he found it hard to feel anything but thankfulness at the sight of it.

Its nearness now that they had seen it took their breath away.

"Hell, we're close in," Mackay said in shocked surprise. Then the rain came sidling along the sea again, like a grey fog, blanking out the view of the coast and even of the other waves, but they were oblivious of it this time, soaked as they already were and aware that they were almost in Occupied Territory.

Ponsettia, his face streaming, was trying to stare through the rain at the vanished coastline. "It must be Belgium south of Walcheren," he said. "As I thought. With the north wind and the tide setting south, that's about where we'd end up.

That'll be nice. Right in Jerry's lap. Wonder if our people have captured the place yet?"

They stared at each other, then Ponsettia shrugged.

"Ah, well," he said. "I could almost look forward to a nice cosy prison camp." He was silent for a while then he went on again. "I once heard of a bloke who survived four days in a one-man dinghy and then was washed up in Lincolnshire somewhere. He was killed when he tried to wade ashore. Land mines."

He was staring at his feet as he finished speaking.

"You know," Mackay said thoughtfully after a while. "If they spot us, at least the Skipper will soon be in hospital and warm. The war's almost over. It wouldn't be for long."

Waltby studied him, thinking, as he considered the warmth – even the warmth of captivity – with a sickening longing, of what would happen to the brief case full of documents if they were captured, and he forced his wearily protesting brain to try to work out some plan.

"At least," Mackay went on. "I should dodge a court martial. I'll bet some officious bloody Service policeman's got that jerrycan of petrol in the guardroom by now. If I get back I'll be down to sweeping the road outside the Flight Office."

"Such a pity," Ponsettia said dryly. "Flying pay's so useful."

"More useful than you think," Mackay said, and Waltby had a momentary picture of him banking every available penny for after the war to be put into that precious little business of his.

"Perhaps I could put in a word for you," he offered. "We've got to know each other pretty well, considering."

Mackay nodded, unable to get away from his tongue the thanks he knew he should utter, and they fell into an awkward silence.

As the light grew the baling continued, then Waltby stopped suddenly.

"Listen," he said. "What's that noise?"

They cocked their heads. "I can't hear anything," Mackay said. "Only waves."

"Yes, I know. That's what I mean. But listen – they're louder now."

"Christ, you're right," Ponsettia agreed, startled and suddenly apprehensive.

The rain cleared again and they saw they were moving steadily along the coast. The houses had disappeared and they were opposite sand dunes. But outside of them the sea was breaking wildly along a wide stretch of water, the waves leaping irregularly as though flung upwards from beneath.

"Sand-bank," Ponsettia said. "That's what it is. That's your noise, Syd. We're smack inside of it. And it's a big one. There's a good mile of it. I'll bet it dries out at low tide."

As the rain came down again, blurring the shore and the broken water, he prodded the yellow sides of the dinghy. "This damn sausage skin's getting soft," he said. "It'll be handy if it goes down. Better pump it up a bit." He turned, looking for the bellows, then he suddenly shouted – so unexpectedly that they jumped – his voice harsh and cracked with excitement.

"A launch!" he yelled, trying to stand up. "A launch! Oh, Christ Jesus Almighty God, a launch! They've found us! They've found us! They've found us!"

"Sit down, for God's sake," Waltby yelled, "or you'll have the dinghy over!" He found his own pulse was racing with excitement at Ponsettia's words, but his frantic relief stuck in his throat.

"Where? Where is it?" Mackay was demanding eagerly, half kneeling. "Where, man? Where is it?"

"Over there." Ponsettia was pointing wildly to the west. "Outside the bank. They're coming. I saw it through the rain just for a second. There. Just there. It bobbed up and disappeared."

They were all scrambling to their knees now, their eyes wild, desperate, clutching at the fragment of hope, praying it wasn't imagination.

"You're seeing things, man!" Mackay shouted. "You're going crackers."

All three of them were panting, their mouths hanging open, like exhausted runners.

"I tell you I saw a launch!" Ponsettia was shouting furiously. "Only just, but I saw it. And if it wasn't an Air-Sea Rescue job, I'm barmy."

"Well, where is it? Where is it?" They were peering through the rain, their eyes smarting with the wind and the salt water, all the time at the back of their hearts afraid of another disappointment. Ponsettia was almost in tears that they wouldn't believe him, and yet half laughing with hysterical joy.

"I saw it, I tell you. I did. I saw it. Where's it gone to?"

"Get the flare ready," Waltby reminded them soberly. "Just in case. And make sure it goes this time. We'll need it if Canada's right."

"I *was* right. I saw it, I tell you."

"Well, where the hell is it, you stupid fool?" Mackay shouted in a black disappointed fury.

While they were arguing and shouting at one another, by a trick of the sea they were lifted to the top of a huge combination of waves at precisely the same time as HSL 7525 was lifted up by another a mile away, and they all saw it before the rain came again, grey and indistinct but undoubtedly a launch.

"There! There!" Ponsettia's voice was almost a screech. "Oh, Jesus, ain't she pretty? Ahoy! Launch! Launch! For God's sake shout, blokes, we're saved."

He started to slap Mackay and Waltby with numbing blows on their shoulders. Choking with relief, Waltby fought down the desire to hug the little Canadian as common sense and the training of years told him to take every precaution first.

"They haven't seen us yet," he reminded them sharply. "Stop that yelling and for God's sake get the flare off, one of you!"

Mackay, who had been struggling with the tape of the flare, began to curse. "Oh, blast the cold," he was saying. "I can't hold it again!"

"Blow your whistle, Mac!" Ponsettia lunged forward and freeing Mackay's whistle from his lapel shoved it between his lips as he started to blow his own.

"Here, Syd," he said, diving for Harding's whistle. "You blow the Skipper's."

In a moment the three whistles were shrieking frantically, thin and reedy against the wind and the sea, only a thin pipe, like the lamenting of lost souls.

"The flare!" Mackay shouted, so that his whistle fell out of his mouth into the bottom of the dinghy. "I think I've got it! I have, I have! I've got the bastard!"

Dazed and stupid with the cold and the excitement, he forgot the flare and started to fumble instead for his whistle, and Ponsettia snatched it from his frozen hands and yanked at the tape. Immediately, with a hiss and a roar, they were enveloped in acrid crimson-tinted fumes as he held the flare as high as he could and began to wave it. The wind snatched away the blue-grey stream of smoke and carried it southwards.

Half blinded and choking, they peered again for the launch.

"They must see it," Waltby breathed. "They'll never hear the whistles over the sea."

"Suppose it's a Jerry?" Mackay said uneasily.

"It's not a Jerry," Ponsettia snorted with a confidence that was really only hope. "Hell, I can tell by the cut of the thing's

231

jib! She's an Air-Sea Rescue job. What else would she be doing here?"

"She might be an *E*-boat trying to find her way back."

Waltby was feverishly opening the brief case with clumsy hands and trying to stuff Harding's shoes into it to make weight. Then he felt for the blunt-ended, cork-handled knife from the dinghy equipment and stuffed it awkwardly into his belt, ready to cut the rope, which still tied the case to the dinghy.

"Suppose the shore batteries see it?" Mackay said, indicating the flare.

"The ASR boys'll have us out of here before that." Ponsettia was buoyed up by excitement to a near-hysterical expectancy.

The thinning rain cleared again for a moment and the three of them cowered in the lurching dinghy, soaked with spray staring over the tumbled water of the sand-bank, their hearts stopped with apprehension.

Then Ponsettia slapped Waltby's shoulders again. "She's stopped, Syd!" he shouted gleefully. "She must have seen us."

They watched again, then Ponsettia shrieked. "She has!" he yelled. "She's stopped! Oh, boy! I'll never say God doesn't listen to your prayers. I was praying last night enough to wake the dead." Tears were running down his face and mingling with the rain and the seawater there.

They could see the launch more clearly now. Although she was still greyish-blue and indistinct in the distance her outlines were recognisable. They could even see the silhouette of the gun on her stern, and her mast. As they watched, the beam-on outline shortened until she presented a head-on appearance to them, lifting slowly on the sea and disappearing again as both dinghy and boat dropped into troughs of the waves at the same time.

"She's heading towards us. She is! She's coming! There! A Verey light! See it? Shout, boys! Shout like merry hell to make sure."

Ponsettia's words died in the middle of his joy as he became aware of Mackay silent behind him, staring shorewards, his face taut and grim. Ponsettia's eyes lifted and over Mackay's head, as the dinghy breasted a wave, he could see the shore again. They had drifted past the sand-dunes once more and the houses were visible again, in a cluster along the fringe of the beach, and in front of them were those ominous huddles of sandbags which indicated gun-positions.

Mackay's gaze was cold and bitter as he stared at Ponsettia, his swollen, ugly-looking hand tucked into his battle-dress blouse. "You can stop your blasted celebrations for a bit," he said. "Until we've seen what that lot there have got to say about rescue."

three

It was Gus Westover who first saw the flare from the dinghy.

With the first light, Skinner had got his engines in working order again. He emerged from the engine-room hatch, the wind whipping at his trouser bottoms, and with both hands on the rail staggered along the heaving deck towards the bridge where Robb was hanging over the side on lookout, eating a corned-beef sandwich with vast enjoyment in spite of the rolling. His red face had a bovine, contented look as he chewed, and he was obviously free from worry or strain, a fact which infuriated the weary Skinner.

The engineer's face was grey with fatigue and his eyes were red with the staring he'd done in the poor light of the engine-room. His best jacket, which he had slipped on against the cold on deck, had a great black patch of oil across the front where it had fallen into the bilges and soaked up the dirt for half an hour before he'd noticed it. It was now seeping through to his best shirt

"Where's the Skipper?" he asked sourly.

"In his cabin," Robb said, half turning.

"Well, she's ready. We can start up."

Robb crammed the rest of his sandwich into his mouth and spoke with his cheeks full.

"Good!" he said. "Engines OK?"

" 'Course they're OK."

"We can make the inshore search?"

"Hell, I'd forgotten that!"

"Can we?"

"Have we got to? I rather like being alive."

"Can we?" Robb's voice rose to an infuriated shout.

"Oh, Christ, yes, if you're looking for a gong! The engines are all right now. Even the oil-feed."

"Whacko!"

Skinner missed the eagerness in Robb's voice as all his own pent-up fury burst out in an explosion that was touched off by Robb's lightheartedness. "After all the trouble I had to make sure that flaming oil-feed didn't let us down," he snarled. "And then the goddam, thrice-stricken water-pump keys had to shear off just because there was a cross-tide!"

Robb turned, half inside the wheelhouse, his bulk filling the door.

"Just goes to prove," he pointed out cheerfully. "Always make sure you repair your oil-feeds when they're in danger of packing up – instead of taking WAAFS to pubs – and then your water-pump keys won't shear."

Skinner gazed after him as he dived below.

To Milliken, who, exhausted by his long watch on the rolling bridge, had finally fallen asleep on the sick bay floor, the sudden explosion of the engines was the crack of doom; and he sat up, believing in the first moment he was awake that something else dreadful had happened to him. Then, realising with relief that Skinner had completed his repairs, he lay for a while dozing under the duffel coat which, he was surprised to find, had been thrown over him as he slept.

He was glad to see the daylight again. Nothing seemed quite so bad as when it was dark. Even the cold seemed less now that the harsh glare of the deckhead lights had disappeared. Never once during the long night had Milliken been able to draw any warmth or comfort from the light below deck after the wild darkness above. He listened to the pound and beat of the engines, then, as the boat rolled, swinging on to a new course, he began to slide across the deck and he sat up sharply, scratching his head and trying to rub the weariness out of his eyes.

By the time he staggered on deck the boat had been under way some time and she was plunging through cold grey seas that seemed always on the point of snatching her under, down into the dark fathoms below.

To his surprise, the rain was rattling on the port side. He had by this time got sufficient mastery of his directions to know that if they had been headed home the rain ought to have been beating at them from the starboard side, and the difference struck him ominously.

Then he remembered that last wireless message that had come through the previous night and he felt a sudden hollowness in his stomach and a dryness in his throat as he realised they were already on their way to the inshore search.

"Why aren't we going home?" he asked Knox, who was standing beside him on the after-deck, hanging on to the sick bay cabin top.

"Going for a look-see." Knox confirmed his fears with a tautly framed answer that made Milliken realise that everyone on the boat beside himself also knew what that message had contained. "Almost there by this time."

Milliken glanced towards the bridge where he could see Robb's red hair, and Treherne and Westover, and he noticed that they all wore Mae Wests. Although they should have worn them constantly at sea, this was the first time they had done so, and the significance of the fact made him swallow quickly.

There was no sign of haste or panic, however. Indeed, he could even smell the fumes of paraffin from the galley where Tebbitt was struggling with the stove again.

"Somebody making tea?" he asked, cheered a little by the thought of warmth.

"No." Knox's reply took the brightness out of him. "Hot-water bottles in case of shock."

"Oh!"

"Keep your eyes open," Knox warned him. "Might see a mine. We're inside their minefield now. Should be seeing the shore any time. It's only over there through the rain."

Milliken nodded, his eyes flickering about him across the wind-snatched water. The whole surface of the sea seemed to be rising to meet them now, in flying spray and skimmed foam, and the sky hung on the tattered flag, which had torn in the wind during the night into two long streamers. Dark grey broken clouds tumbled by overhead and to Milliken there seemed to be nothing but ridges of water, with the mast of the boat lying regularly parallel to the surface of the sea, so that he looked shudderingly into vast valleys.

It was after the wireless cabin had raised cheers with the news that 7526 had had to abandon the tow of the Walrus and leave her to her fate in the storm in order to reach safety herself, that Westover saw the flare.

His shout made Milliken jump.

"Skipper! Flight! On the starboard quarter! A flare! A red flare!"

Immediately Tebbitt's head emerged beside Milliken at the sick bay door and Knox, just re-entering the wireless cabin, turned at the shout and struggled up between them to watch.

At first they saw it only as a blur through the rain that came blowing across the bow, blotting out the surface of the sea, taking the jagged tips off the wave-crests and ruffling the hollows. Only for a second Milliken saw the glow, crimson and hazy through the rain, and then the boat had slid into the trough again, and the waves towered on either side of him, blotting it out once more. When they came up on the next wave he saw the glow again and this time the vague shape of what he knew must be a dinghy. In spite of his fear and his weariness he felt something bursting out of him, a joyous sensation of excitement that welled up and made him want to shout – that the dinghy they had been searching for, that elusive thing that had caused him so much wretchedness and had come to be nothing but a figment of Slingsby's fertile imagination, should be so incredibly real after all.

"It's the dinghy!" Robb was shouting on the bridge and everybody started to shout with him. "It's the dinghy!"

And Milliken found himself shouting and laughing, too. "Send them a Verey light to let them know we've seen them, Robby." Treherne's voice came thinly to Milliken before the wind whipped it away. "Come round, Flight. Round to starboard. Steady as she goes. Keep your eyes skinned, everybody. The shore's only just over there. There might be patrol craft about when this rain clears."

The red Verey light popped as he finished speaking and went hissing away into the gloomy sky to hang like a crimson sun.

"All right, Flight," Treherne said. "Shut down for a moment and come up here till we have a look round and see what's doing."

By the time the noise of the engines had died away and Slingsby had arrived on the bridge the sea seemed to have lightened as the wind blew a gap in the curtains of rain, and for the first time they saw the dinghy properly with its load of waving men. They could hear the screech of whistles and could distinctly see arms that moved like reeds.

"Four of them," Treherne said, staring through binoculars. "All there, thank God."

"And nearly on the beach," Slingsby added, peering grim-faced over the side of the bridge. "A bit further and they'd have been shrimping." He glanced round the empty sky. "Bags of air cover, as usual," he observed.

As the rain receded further the shore stood out startlingly clear, with white houses under red roofs and the green of trees beyond the dunes.

Treherne studied it There was no sign of life there but they all knew what the humped mounds along the fringe of the beach were – and that there were men in them probably already squinting at the launch through gun-sights.

Treherne gestured towards the broken water that stretched parallel to the shore between them and the dinghy.

"There's your sand-bank, Flight," he said.

Slingsby glared at it as though about to raise his iron voice to it. "Tide's falling," he announced. "Nice to be grounded on that with the water dropping." He peered at the dinghy again, assessing distances. "They're right inside," he went on. "Nice long run out again after we've been spotted."

"What do you think, flight? They're damned close in and there might be a hell of a lot of guns in there."

"Bound to be." Slingsby spoke thoughtfully. "But we've come a long way for these boys and we can't wait for anything bigger to be brought up. It'd be too late then and Jerry would have 'em if the sea didn't." He brightened a little. "There's one thing – we're too close in for the big stuff to bear on us."

"Right!" Treherne made up his mind immediately. "We'll go in up-tide round the south end of the bank and out at the other end. It'll slow us down but it'll make it more certain of being a first-time job. We can't afford to have to manoeuvre when we reach 'em. Give the bank a wide berth. Robby, tell Knox to get off our position. You know what it is. And state there are survivors. He can make out the message. I'm going to be busy. We'll send 'em another when we know a bit more about what's going to happen. That'll do for them at home to fix their position in case we don't pull it off."

As Robb disappeared Treherne turned to Slingsby.

"Ready, Flight?"

Slingsby grinned. "Aye, aye, sir. You can leave the deck to Robby. He can look after it."

Robb came down the catwalk alongside the sick bay, holding hard to the handrail on the lurching deck. "All right, doc!" he shouted as the engines fired again. "Now's your chance. This is what you're here for. Get your stuff handy. You know where the medical stores are. But for God's sake leave everything where it is till you want it or you'll lose it and you'll need to be smart off the mark if anybody's hurt. Tebby, get that kettle boiling whatever happens, then give a hand with the blankets and the survivors' clothing. We're going to need hot-water bottles. These poor devils will be cold."

Milliken felt a thrill of excitement as he and Tebbitt jumped below, a tenseness that overcame in the swiftness of movement his nausea and fear at the closeness of the enemy. He had forgotten his hatred of high-speed launches and his queasiness at the ghastly motion as he lurched busily about the sick bay, wedging his pack with its bandages and splints into a corner of the bunk. He was so engrossed, in fact, that he never even noticed the breath-taking roll as she started to turn on top of a wave, until she hung for a hideous moment or two on her beam-ends, and he was caught off balance and sent staggering one-legged to the bunk opposite.

Robb had progressed by this time to the engine-room and was bawling into the ear of Corporal Skinner. "Waste oil on deck, Skinner. Stand by to heave it over."

Skinner grinned. "All that fuss all night, and then *we* make the pick-up after all. Give Slingo my compliments and tell the little bastard that if it hadn't been for my engines conking we'd never have got them."

"We haven't yet."

Robb was back on deck by the time he had finished speaking, the wind beating on his face again, doubly cold after the heat of the engine-room.

In the wireless cabin, Botterill, his shoulders hunched, was pounding the Morse key and Knox was wrapping his lanky form with the Mae West he normally disdained to wear.

"Let's have one of you on deck," Robb called out. "We might need you."

"As soon as Botty's got the position away," Knox said, "I'll be up." His eyes were alight now with the same atmosphere of excitement that pervaded the whole ship.

Robb touched Milliken as he passed. "Stand by on deck as soon as you're finished, doc," he said. "We might need every hand we've got, in this weather. It'll be your job to get 'em in here once they're aboard. These boys are going to be too cold to help themselves much. Only for God's sake don't fall in the water."

By the time Milliken staggered on deck Skinner and Dray were hefting oil up through the engine-room hatch, the bounce of the boat slopping it in black splashes over Skinner, who was below.

"Hang on to that," Skinner said to him as Dray jammed an oil drum against the sick bay bulkhead. "And don't let go of it or it'll be in the drink."

Milliken nodded speechlessly. Robb and Westover had already loosened the ropes on the crash nets, he saw, and prepared them for immediate release. And the dinghy was still there ahead of them, distinctly there, blurred through the rain but definitely there, yellow now in spite of the poor light, rising slowly on top of a wave so that Milliken could see the men in it.

The launch crew were struggling on the swaying deck as the boat gained speed, working, on their knees and drenched by the spray that was flung upwards at them, to attach a metal ladder over the port side of the hull.

A moment later Robb swung himself through the bridge door and lurched up against the Skipper. "All ready, Skipper," he announced.

Treherne smiled faintly. "Good!" he said. "At least we can say we were sunk with everything ready."

Robb left the bridge again and took his place on the after-deck with Tebbitt and Westover and Milliken and Knox. Skinner had his head out of the engine-room hatch behind them, watching the shore where the guns were.

"Right, Botterill!" Treherne turned to speak into the wireless-cabin hatch. "Send off that second message I gave you. Everything's still quiet. We're going in now."

Nobody spoke as the launch manoeuvred slowly round the end of the sandbank, placing the broken water on its port side, between itself and safety. Once inside, there could be no fast run for the open sea if they were fired on. They would have to go all the way inside the sand-bank, parallel with the shore, or chance the danger of running aground.

"Here we go," Robb murmured alongside Milliken. "For what we are about to receive may the Lord make us truly thankful."

Milliken's eyes switched quickly to Robb's ruddy, cheerful face and, without being aware of what he was doing, he began to cower a little behind the sick bay cabin. Graven fear flooded over him suddenly, making his stomach cringe. His mouth was dry and he could feel a cold sweat on his forehead. His eyes straining for the first sight of the guns, he ran his tongue slowly over his lips. All his earlier desire to make contact with the enemy had drained away and he felt he was going to be seasick again.

The bow of the launch rose and fell with tremendous heaves, cutting into the waves like a knife-edged hammer so that the black-grey water sped backwards, hissing along the hull until it was drawn into the wake. Ahead of him, through the rain that beat into his face, Milliken could see the shape of the dinghy, the spray slashing across it and its occupants. To seawards he could see the broken waves over the sandbank, ugly and treacherous, throwing up gouts of water that smashed explosively into mist. It was as though there was something below the sea there trying to burst out and escape and, to Milliken's fascinated eyes, the bank seemed to draw them nearer with every yard they sped along its fringe.

"Port side to, Robby!" Treherne shouted. "Have the nets ready."

"Aye, aye, Skipper!"

As Robb answered with a wave Milliken, his weight against the oil drum, saw his eyes turn again to the shore and those ominously silent houses with their gaping windows. His head low behind the sick bay cabin, he felt every gun ashore moving slowly round to bear on them until he could almost hear the order to fire, and he bobbed sharply further down.

"Thank God the weather's thick," Knox said. He spoke as though his lips were stiff, his eyes never moving from the shore. Milliken, wide-eyed, hung on to his drum, his fear-addled brain knowing only one thing other than that eyes were watching them from behind parapets ashore – Skinner's instructions to him to see that the oil didn't go over the side.

Ahead of him, he saw the dingy heave slowly out of the sea again, like a submarine surfacing.

The engines were increasing revolutions and the thumping motion of the boat as it advanced in leaps across the waves became more violent. Treherne was obviously going all the way as fast as he dared.

As 7525 crashed into the next wave a shower of spray was lifted high into the air by the wind, in two vast plumes which sped faster and faster in a flattening arc along the length of the boat, slashing into Milliken's eyes and beyond him to rattle against the gun-shield of the Oerlikon on the stern.

"He'll break her back!" Skinner's head popped up like a jack-in-a-box through the engine-room hatch and he shouted before disappearing again: "The engines will be off their bearers in a minute!"

He made the announcement not in protest but as if the excitement had become too much for him.

Milliken wanted to shout, too – to do anything as he crouched behind the sick bay cabin with the oil drum. The nervous fears inside him wanted to burst out in sound, and words – any words – incoherent words – welled up. He felt he was looking down ten thousand barrels of ten thousand guns all trained upon him personally, and he wanted to screech his keyed-up apprehension into the wind.

"It's quiet," Robb said almost conversationally as they lurched against each other, bulky in their Mae Wests, and his voice had a steadying quality that calmed Milliken.

"This rain," Knox explained. "Can't see us.'

"Sunday morning lie-in, more like."

Milliken noticed they spoke in short syllables now. He could see the houses moving backwards on the starboard side, incredibly close, and the pill-boxes and the empty windows which might contain guns. He even saw a curtain flapping out of one gaunt casement, abandoned-looking and dejected.

"All asleep," Robb said.

"Bastards," Knox added by way of an amen.

Then Robb turned and caught sight of Milliken cowering behind the sick bay.

"Chin up, kid," he said with an unexpected grin. "The panic's not even started yet."

Milliken blushed and straightened up.

"Plywood won't keep out cannon shells," Robb pointed out.

His words oddly enough gave Milliken courage, and while he still stared down those ten thousand gun-barrels he found he was able to do so with his head up.

Then suddenly he saw red and green lights curving towards him and disappearing overhead with a whining noise. Even as he realised with a shock that they were tracer bullets he heard the rattle of a gun ashore.

"Here it comes," Robb said quietly. "They're rotten shots."

To Milliken, the coloured tracer seemed to have no malevolent design. It was just a string of coloured lights that gave no indication of danger, for the violent seas swallowed the splashes as the bullets fell. Then he saw another string appear from another point on the coast – and another – until the whole shore-line appeared to be shooting at him and he was amazed he wasn't hit and that he could be so detached and calm. Then he saw a string of larger tracer that whistled oddly as it passed them. These were not so close together as the others and he saw the flashes as they curved down and hit the water.

"Cannon shells," Robb said.

"Flak. Let's hope they've nothing bigger."

Then, with a suddenness that gave Milliken a sensation of annoyance that he was not ready for it and consequently did not see it properly, there was a flash at the base of the mast and the crack of an explosion. They all ducked together, Milliken banging his head heavily on the edge of the oil drum he was holding. Through the red flare of pain and the whirl of dizziness he heard a tearing, splintering crash above the noise of the boat smashing through the water and the roar of the engines. When he straightened up he saw Treherne had disappeared from the bridge, and caught the splash of the masthead hitting the water alongside, carrying the ensign below the surface. Instantly the roar of the engines ceased and the boat pulled up short as though it had struck something, and the little wave that the trailing masthead threw up died abruptly.

Slingsby was on the bridge before the boat stopped and Robb had emerged from the sick bay with the axe. Milliken had not even seen him disappear. The coloured balls of tracer were still passing over the boat.

"Get that lot clear, Robby!" Slingsby was shouting. "Come on, you set of bloody idlers there, bear a hand!

There's nothing wrong with the engines. We're not done yet."

In a confusion of impressions Milliken saw Knox running forward, careless of the lurch of the boat, with a pair of wire-cutters in his hands, and Robb swinging with the axe at the deck.

Skinner's head appeared through the engine-room hatch by his feet. "What's happening?"

"I don't know," Milliken panted with complete honesty, struggling with the coils of aerial wire that were looped round his shoulders. There was blood on his face, he realised, warm and sticky, and he thought he must have been wounded. But, since he felt all right, his only emotion was one of bewildered excitement and the desire to be free of that clinging wire before the boat sank and he was trapped.

Then Skinner saw the mast trailing in the water and the aerial strewn from one end of the boat to the other, and he started to climb on deck.

"Let's get out of here!" he shouted.

"You get below and shut your trap!" Robb bawled at him, swinging with the axe at the wire as it lay on the deck, so that Milliken saw the strands part as the blade bit into the planking. "The engines are all right, aren't they?"

Milliken caught Skinner's quick glance at Robb as he disappeared again, then Robb was shouting at him.

"Come on, you fool!" he yelled. "Don't stand there like a clot! Get this wire cut and get the mast free. We don't want it round the screws. Get it free of the Oerlikon."

Milliken was flung into nervous panic as two sets of orders clashed.

"This oil drum," he bleated. "I was told to hold it here. It'll go over the side."

"To hell with the oil!"

Milliken stared, patted the drum nervously, and left it with one final glance backwards to make sure it was safe, as he started to disentangle the aerial wire with Tebbitt. He had quite forgotten the shore guns in his excitement.

As he cut his hand on the taut wire he started upright at the pain, his hand to his mouth, and he was surprised to realise that the shooting had stopped. By the time they had freed the last of the aerial and the mast slid away, helped by a wild kick from Slingsby, Milliken saw Treherne had reappeared on the bridge, one arm stuffed into his battle-dress jacket, his hat gone, his face pale and twisted with pain, staggering blindly with the roll of the boat. 7525 was wallowing horribly by this time and swinging beam-on to the sea again and into those ghastly hanging lurches that almost swept Milliken's unresponsive legs away from under him and shot him into the sea.

"I'm all right, Flight," he heard Treherne say. "Something's broken, I think. That's all. The mast hit me as it went. I can manage here. Everybody all right?"

"Mast's free, Skipper!" Slingsby shouted, indicating the grey-painted spar that was drifting astern. "Engines are OK and the wire's well clear of the screws."

"Botty's stopped something," Tebbitt shouted from inside the sick bay. "He's bleeding."

"There's nothing wrong with me, you soft sod." Botterill's burst of bad temper was reassuring but Milliken, his job with the wire finished, slipped without thought below to where he was sitting on the deck, his eyes dazed, blood streaming down his face.

In the first instant of being inside the sick bay he realised he could see the swinging sky through a vast hole in the wireless cabin roof, and he saw also that the sick bay was pockmarked and torn with small holes. Slivers of wood and pieces of plastic from the wireless sets lay on the deck round Botterill in an untidy scattering.

"Get to hell out of it," the wireless operator said fiercely. "I'm all right. Splinters, I think. From the sets mostly. I'm only cut. I can see, can't I? I can talk. I'm not dead. You're bleeding worse'n me yourself. Go and do summat useful. Tell the Skipper the wireless sets have had it."

When he reached the deck again Milliken could see the dinghy ahead of them, tantalisingly close, its occupants quiet now. Beyond them, they could see the reason for the shore guns' silence.

Through the rain which rattled off the deck again and set the Oerlikon glistening, Milliken saw for the first time the shape of a trawler in the mist, slightly to port of them, blue-grey and blurred but ominously high and powerful. Between them, the yellow bag of the dinghy with its huddled occupants heaved slowly out of the water, then slid over to the next valley and out of sight again.

"Where did that come from?" Milliken had quite forgotten the blood on his face by this time and stood panting and horrified at the sight of the trawler.

"She's a Jerry," Robb said calmly. "They must have sent her out to the dinghy some time since. Well, now she's arrived. That's why the guns have stopped. They're frightened of hitting her."

"What are these trawlers like, Flight?" Treherne shouted. "Dead slow, Skipper." Slingsby sounded excited and more eager than normal. "Manned by scratch crews. I've heard they're dead rotten."

"Right, then," Treherne said. "We've not far to go. Let's get it over. They probably won't shoot any more for fear of hitting the trawler. Take it away. We've got to do this damned quickly."

The engines roared out again and the boat swung on to course for the dinghy and began to smash through the water once more. Milliken's breath was stilled in his throat. He couldn't have spoken then if he'd tried, for the excitement that left him tongue-tied.

Immediately their bows pointed to the dinghy they saw the flash of a gun on the trawler and a plume of brown-tinted water rose majestically up in a straight tower a hundred yards to port of them and hung there, apparently motionless, before the wind whipped the top off it and it seemed to disintegrate slowly and fall back into the sea.

"The bastards," Knox was intoning to himself like an incantation. "The bastards. Shooting at us when we're picking blokes out of the water. The bastards."

"We might do it if they don't get the range in time," Robb was shouting in excitement, jigging crazily on the after-deck. "If only those swine ashore hold off, we might. We might."

Almost before Milliken had realised what had happened they were on top of the dinghy, the great bow poised as though to smash it under. But Slingsby, with a skill that Milliken only half appreciated, had gauged it exactly and she dropped six feet away, crashing into a wave and drenching the occupants. The engines shut down abruptly and a heaving-line curled from Robb's flung arm across the dinghy which Milliken was surprised to see had arrived safely alongside them.

"Thank God for you guys!" a Canadian voice shouted, and Robb and Westover, crouching from the waves that exploded upwards into their faces along the hull, began to haul in the line hand over hand. "We thought we'd had it."

"Perhaps you have, chum," Knox retorted. "Perhaps we all have."

"Make it fast. Make it fast to the dinghy!" Robb was shouting in a cracked voice, and Milliken could see one of the men in the yellow raft fumbling with frozen hands to knot the line to one of the dinghy ropes.

Dray was slopping oil over the side of the launch forward so that the surface of the sea stilled a little as it drifted and spread, slimy, black, smothering the sides of the dinghy in an evil scum which drove the sea water into shining globules on its surface.

Then Milliken, dancing because he could no longer stand still, his senses functioning in a haze of blazing excitement from which all fear had disappeared, became aware that the shore guns, afraid of being cheated by the slowness of the trawler, were firing again. He could hear the rattle distinctly and the whine and hum of the bullets, and caught a glimpse of the flash of tracer passing over the boat.

The crash nets had splashed into the water by this time and Tebbitt was over the side, clinging perilously to the iron ladder that threatened with the motion to tear itself free from the boat.

Half a dozen hands reached up from the sea as Tebbitt leaned over, aware for the first time of an unconscious man in the dinghy. One of the survivors was yelling excitedly in an incoherent gibberish that was threaded through with a Canadian accent. "You first, Syd," he was shouting. "Then the Skipper."

"Never mind who's first!" Robb shouted. "Let's have you aboard. Come on, you're nearest. Look slippy."

Ponsettia glanced up quickly and reached out towards the ladder with frozen, clumsy hands.

"Can you make it?" Robb demanded. "Or do you want one of us down there?"

"We can make it." Ponsettia made a grab for the ladder Tebbitt was standing on, missed it and almost fell overboard. Tebbitt, magnificent with his worries forgotten in the urgency of the moment, his strength performing the task for which it was intended, grabbed him as his head went down and with a muscle-cracking heave hoisted him, one-handed, upwards to where he was grabbed by Robb and Knox and dragged sprawling across the deck. Immediately he jumped up and attempted a dance on the rolling deck, which ended as his cramped legs buckled under him.

He grabbed Milliken joyfully round the neck as he was hoisted to his feet again. "Oh, brother," he bawled, "am I glad to see you? You can have my cigarette ration for the next six months."

"I don't smoke," Milliken shouted in excitement, backing towards the sick bay with Ponsettia. "You get below," he ended with a show of authority that startled himself and he pushed the Canadian into the sick bay where he half fell down the steps and rolled sprawling on the wet floor, the water spreading from his clothes, while Milliken, clinging desperately to a lifeline again, watched Tebbitt over the side of the boat.

"Put a jerk in it!" Treherne was shouting. "She's beginning to swing. Go ahead a little, Flight!"

The panting men on the after-deck, their feet slipping on the wet planks, sprawling on their knees half the time among the coils of the heaving-line, hardly noticed the next shell-splash as it leapt up only fifty yards away, and the crack of the gun went unheard in the shouting and the violent slobbering, sucking noise of the water immediately below them.

Tebbitt, the oily sea sloshing up to his waist, half blinding him, made a quick grab at the unconscious man in the dinghy, got him with one hand in his collar and yanked him up in a strangling grip so that he hung downwards like a lifeless puppy for a second before he, too, was sprawling on the deck and being dragged clumsily towards the sick bay by Milliken and Westover.

They clattered down the steps together, Milliken thinking fearfully all the time of all the precepts of medical training that came into his mind about the careful handling of unconscious patients. But this was an emergency, he thought wildly, panting with excitement as he scrambled round the man. Even as he leapt back to the deck he heard the tap of bullets on woodwork and saw splinters whip upwards in front of him.

The third man, barefooted, his hand bound with a black RAF tie, was already on deck and diving for the sick bay, almost bowling Milliken over as he slid into his arms with a yell.

"My leg," Mackay was yelling in a voice that had more fury in it than fear or pain. "The bastards have got me!"

Then he dragged himself to his feet, somehow before Milliken, and fell into the sick bay.

The fourth survivor was hanging on to the ladder, grasping a brief case that was fastened to his middle by his overcoat belt.

"I can manage!" he was shouting in a welter of noise through which Milliken could still hear the insidious tapping of bullets. "I can manage!"

"Don't be a fool!" Tebbitt shouted back, heaving desperately as the sea threatened to carry the dinghy away from beneath Waltby's feet; then Waltby with his brief case was on the deck with Westover in front of Milliken, face downwards and gasping. Milliken grabbed him by the arm.

"Below, below!" he shrieked, pulling Waltby towards the sick bay and realising in amazement in the same wild instant that he was talking to an air commodore.

"Leave the dinghy!" Treherne was shouting. "Full ahead, flight. Hard a-port. Over the sandbank. We've got to chance it."

The boat leapt forward out of the oil-covered water with a jerk, sending one of Skinner's empty drums rolling along the deck with a clanking, rumbling noise before it splashed over the side into the sea. Robb and Knox were clinging to Tebbitt as the boat smashed forward, desperately heaving him up to the deck against the roll as she heeled over on her beam-ends to send the other drum clattering over the side and tear the ladder from its fastenings as it was plunged beneath the water.

Dray almost fell into the engine-room hatch as the stern came round to the weather and Westover opened fire with the Oerlikon. The noise startled Milliken but he felt an immense satisfaction as, in one brief instant before he was swamped with the work of medicine, he saw the tracers go curling over the sea towards the shore.

There was a last plume of yellow water a hundred yards away on the port quarter as the launch justified all the work that had gone into its designing and pulled rapidly away from the trawler.

"Hold your breath, boys!" Robb shouted as they smashed into the broken water over the sandbank. "Hope it's not low tide."

The men in the sick bay, just struggling to their feet, were all flung together again as the launch plunged into the spray. Water leapt high over the bows and sped over the wheelhouse in slashing spouts that somehow found their way below deck, and the boat leapt and bucked like a frantic animal for what seemed ages, all its timbers groaning, its doors wrenched loose and banging. Then, almost before Milliken was aware of it, they were in the open sea again and the bullets were falling behind them.

"Thank God," Robb breathed, flat on his face on the deck. "We did it! We did it! We bloody well did it!"

The roaring of the engines swelled as 7525 swung round and headed for home.

Milliken had thought several times during the past twenty-four hours that the sound of the exhausts as they beat towards England would be the sweetest music in the world when he heard it, but now it seemed more than that. It had a triumphant note in it, too – a blaring trumpet-song of defiance that heralded the end of his personal day of glory.

four

There was a big brown staff car standing on top of the slipway as 7525 turned slowly out of the chop of the river, her bow dipping as the way went off her. The staff car's matt-painted surface shone dully in the rain and on the wing of it a group captain's pennant fluttered. Beyond it an ambulance stood out, muddily camouflaged and drab, against the dark buildings.

As she turned into the sheltered basin, edging towards the jetty, the wind flung the last few waves under 7525's chine and the spray leapt outwards in a flat sheet. She looked low and fast without her mast, yet oddly crumpled and hurt, but Robb had found a brand new ensign in her flag locker and fastened it to the jackstaff aft so that it fluttered bright and blue and bold as the boat neared the shore. A destroyer had met them thirty miles out and offered assistance, but they had proudly refused it, asking only for their estimated time of arrival and a warning for ambulances to stand by to be sent by wireless. The holes in her sick bay cabin top and the stump of her mast were scars they were all anxious to show.

Milliken, still amazed to find themselves home and all alive, stood on the after-deck among the coiled ropes, watching the blue-clad figures moving down the black boards of the jetty. There seemed to be a reception committee to greet them and he saw a group captain's sleeve rings in spite of the steady rain, and at least one officer with the broad ring of higher rank. Then he recognised the Station

Medical Officer and the sergeant medical orderly, their shoulders hunched against the weather, and more than a dozen others – a few sailors from the motor gun-boat flotilla at the opposite side of the basin, and a few WRENS from the dinghies which lay aft of the launch trot. They huddled there together on the end of the jetty as 7525 came in closer, her engines popping noisily at low revs, her weary crew standing slouch-shouldered on her decks, their eyes haggard with sleeplessness, their faces covered with two-day-old beards.

Milliken's heart was singing a joyous song of triumph and self-esteem. He wore a bandage round his head and his hand was swathed in lint There was blood on his face, that he had purposely not bothered to wash away. He was not in any pain beyond a bad headache and he was thoroughly enjoying the spectacle he presented and the fact that he was still doing his duty, holding a fender. He was on deck more because he wanted to show his bandages than because he thought he might be useful.

Through his mind were running over and over again like a mad refrain the lines from *Henry V* he had learned at school not so very long before. They clashed in his brain like cymbals and drums and trumpets. *Then shall he strip his sleeve and show his scars, And say "These wounds I had on Crispin's Day."* And for the first time since he'd heard them read out loud by a bored English master he began to understand what they meant and the tremendous pride that lay beneath them.

The fact that both his injuries were superficial and that neither had been inflicted by the enemy meant nothing to him in his exalted state of mind.

He had been strapping up the wound in Mackay's leg when he had first realised that blood was dripping from his hand where he had cut it on the wire. Busy with his job, he had hurriedly wrapped his handkerchief round it and carried on.

"They hit you in the head, too, bud," Ponsettia had pointed out "That's a nasty gash you got there."

Milliken had put his hand up to his forehead and had stared at the bright smear on his fingers with surprise that he had been able to go on working. In his mind, immediately, he had seen the words he had read so often in the newspapers in citations for decorations. "Although wounded himself he refused to be attended until he had seen that all the other wounded were comfortable." It had a pleasant warming ring. The fact that he had not been in pain in no way detracted from his enjoyment of it, which had continued all the time he was working.

By the time he reached the bridge to attend to Treherne, the Skipper's arm had already been put expertly into a sling. Robb was there, eating his inevitable corned-beef sandwich, apparently unperturbed by the recent excitement.

"Better have a look at that head of yours, doc," he had said gravely.

As they dabbed away the blood Robb stared at the wound, puzzled. "What the hell have you been doing?" he asked. "Have you been banging it on something?"

Then Milliken remembered hitting his head on the edge of the oil drum, and his disgust knew no bounds as all his thoughts of heroism disappeared.

"Never mind." Robb grinned, enjoying some private joke that Milliken suspected was connected with the gash on his temple. "Let's put a bandage on it."

Grinning to himself he had put a swathe of linen on Milliken's head that was far more imposing than necessary.

"There," he said as he finished, "you look like a hero," and Milliken forgave him all his smooth sarcasm over the past two days.

As the boat turned slowly to thrust her nose towards the trot of launches that were sawing up and down in the wind, grinding their fenders to pulp, reminding Milliken of a set of jumping horses on a fairground roundabout, he saw 7526 lying there, clean, undamaged, but with nothing triumphant about her, none of the glow of heroism he seemed to see about their own scarred hull. Loxton stood on the bows, silently watching 7525 swing round. It was he who caught the heaving-line flung by Robb and hauled in the mooring-rope and made it fast. As he slipped the eye over a cleat he waved and grinned in a gesture, which admitted defeat.

Suddenly the after-deck seemed full of people, all talking at once, with Ponsettia's nasal Canadian voice joyous above the babble.

"Hell, brother," he said to Milliken, "when I saw you pressing on through that rain you looked like my goddam dream boat coming in. When we saw that son-of-a-bitch trawler we thought we'd had it."

"Get back," Milliken said with loud authority. "Give the crew a chance. Let the dog see the rabbit. Get into the sick bay till you're told to come out."

"Sorry, bud." Ponsettia dodged back humbly, pushing the others with him, as Milliken dropped his fender over the side with as much show of skill as the menial task could provide, and watched it ground flat as the two boats touched.

People from the jetty swarmed over 7525 immediately the ropes were ashore – the Group Captain and the broad-ringed brass hat with him, and the crew of the ambulance and the medical staff.

As they flooded round him, suddenly suffocating him by their numbers, Milliken flopped down on the edge of the Carley float, unexpectedly aware of his aching muscles and bruises and a sudden collapse of his elation in reaction. He saw the sergeant medical orderly standing over him and caught a glimpse of the doctor disappearing into the sick bay with Robb.

"How's the injured man?" the sergeant asked Milliken.

Unaware of the rain that was flung over the boat from the shelter of the jetty, and the drip of water and the slap of waves, Milliken answered without lifting his head which seemed suddenly to rest on his shoulders like a ton weight of weariness.

"He's OK. We got him just in time. He's bad, but he'll be all right. A couple of ribs, I think, and shock. The others are OK. A few cuts and a flesh wound."

The sergeant stared at his tired young face, suddenly grey with fatigue, and the dried dark blood on his cheek. "How was it?" he asked.

"Grim," Milliken said, experiencing as he spoke a feeling of vast superiority over the sergeant who had never been to sea. Fleetingly he wondered if it had really been as grim as he had thought, but he savoured the moment, nevertheless, getting the best out of it. "Grim," he repeated. "Bloody grim."

The sergeant patted his shoulder, as though to say he understood what Milliken had been through. To Milliken it was better than a medal. Then the doctor appeared in front of him and Milliken struggled to stand, but the doctor put a hand on his shoulder and held him down.

"Nice job you've done, Milliken," he said. "Nice job in the circumstances. How do you feel?"

"I'm all right," Milliken said.

"Better get into the ambulance and go up with the others."

"No. Honest, sir, this is nothing. I'm all right." Milliken had a moment of panic at the thought of the doctor's face as he removed the bandages. "I only bled a bit. I'm hungry. I'll come as soon as I've had something to eat."

The doctor grinned. "Sure?"

"I'm all right, sir. Honest."

"OK. Have it your own way. As soon as you've eaten, mind. You did a good job, son."

As the doctor turned away with the sergeant Milliken's proud heart was singing with pure joy. He had been to sea – and he knew suddenly he would be going again. He had been in action. He had fought the enemy. He had spoken sharply to an air commodore in the heat of battle. And, finally, he had been complimented for his part in it all. For all his youth, he was a man – now and forever.

The boat crew stood about the deck in their oilskins, coiling ropes with a slowness that spoke of fatigue, their hair hanging over their eyes, their bodies slack and weary. Skinner emerged from the engine-room, his best uniform ruined, his date gone, his eyes red with strain. "Thank Christ that's over," he murmured feelingly.

Then the boat began to empty. Ponsettia and Mackay appeared on deck, wrapped in blankets, helped by the station medical orderlies.

"Canada," Mackay was saying as he hopped towards the iron ladder up the jetty, one arm in a sling, "I reckon you were right. They say the Skipper's going to be OK. He'll be buying his greengroceries from my shop after all."

"Sure, he will, you soft clot. If I didn't have so far to come from River Falls, I would, too."

Ponsettia saw Milliken and slapped his shoulder as he passed. "S'long, doc," he said warmly. "I thought the cow was going to turn over when she rolled that time as we turned away from the trawler. Jees-us, give me flying any day. I wouldn't serve on these tubs for a fortune."

Milliken smiled faintly and watched them as they were helped on to the jetty and towards the ambulance, incongruous among the uniforms in their survivors' clothing. Then the Group Captain emerged with the other brass-hat and the Air Commodore from the dinghy who was looking more like a well-scrubbed tramp now, with the fatigue in his face and his civilian trousers and ill-fitting overcoat, his face dark with beard, and his hair awry in thin spikes on his head. He still clutched the water-blackened brief case in his hand.

"Anyway, thank God you're safe," Taudevin was saying. "Eve's looking forward to seeing you. She's waiting at home. We can send the brief case on, if you like, and you can get over it a bit before you need go."

"I'm all right," Waltby said. "I'll be fine in a day or so. I'm glad Eve took it all right and didn't knock herself up."

Taudevin helped him up to the jetty, then turned towards Treherne and the crew of the boat, standing huddled together on the after-deck round the stretcher they'd lowered for Harding.

"Good show, gentlemen," he said. "Thank you all very much."

Then he waved and disappeared along the jetty.

Milliken sat on the Carley float, too tired to stand up, letting the sergeant and the doctor and the others superintend the lifting of Harding to the jetty. Treherne and Botterill followed them to the ambulance in a little *cortège.*

Then, as he heard the ambulance door shut and the gears grind, he saw Slingsby in front of him with Robb. Slingsby was staring after Treherne. "You know," he said thoughtfully, "it wouldn't surprise me a bit if that Group Captain or the Air Commodore or somebody didn't recommend the Lad for a gong. That'd shove Loxton's nose out of joint with his lousy little Mention. Shore guns. Mast gone. Duff engines. Broken shoulder. No air cover. It was a good show, whichever way you look at it. It was worth a gong. Hell, what do they want for their money?"

Milliken was startled at the warmth in his tones. Then Slingsby turned round and seemed to see Milliken for the first time.

"Fag, Milliken?' he asked abruptly, and Milliken became acutely conscious of the fact that he had known his name all the time.

"Thanks, Flight," he said, quite forgetting he was a non-smoker. The offer made him one with the rest of the crew. It made him one with all those sly, wily, courageous men who were old in the Service. He had become a veteran.

"I hope you're grateful to us all," Slingsby went on in his harsh voice as he offered a match. "You've made a pick-up. You're one of God's chosen few."

Robb laughed. "Enjoy the trip?" he asked.

Milliken coughed over his first drag at the cigarette. "I never thought we'd get back," he said honestly.

"Get back?" Slingsby was once more the tough, vulgar little martinet with the taut frame and the iron voice, and Milliken jumped instinctively. "Get back? God, after a pick-up like that I'd have swum under the bastard, if necessary, and held her up all the way home."

Milliken grinned. "I'll bet you would, Flight," he said, meaning every word.

Slingsby stared unsmilingly, weary for the first time. "All in a day's work, son, all in a day's work."

His voice had lost its bark and Milliken felt no need to be humble before him any longer. Robb was grinning as they helped him up the iron ladder to the jetty, followed by the others. Tebbitt brought up the rear, in survivor's clothing, his shoulders hunched, his face flabby and old looking, and Milliken wondered what he was going to do with his worries.

Milliken's legs were aching with every heavy-footed step he took, and he walked along the hollow, echoing piles towards the land aware only of hunger and the desire for sleep, which lay on him, warm and cloying and comforting, making him indifferent to the cold rain that drifted into his face and the breeze that plucked at his hair.

Behind him, across the width of the river, the beat of the weather swept out to sea and across the Channel, where it harried the Continent and there died.

Milliken plodded on, weary but tremendously uplifted by triumph and the sensation he suddenly and joyously knew he'd cause among the WAAFS in the cookhouse. He wanted to sing, but then he remembered Slingsby's words, "All in a day's work, son, all in a day's work." He reached up, took off the neat blue side-hat he wore and, bashing it shapeless, shoved it cross-wise over his bandage and slouched after the others in a rolling piratical gait.

John Harris

China Seas

In this action-packed adventure, Willie Sarth becomes a survivor. Forced to fight pirates on the East China Seas, wrestle for his life on the South China Seas and cross the Sea of Japan ravaged by typhus, Sarth is determined to come out alive. Dealing with human tragedy, war and revolution, Harris presents a novel which packs an awesome punch.

A Funny Place to Hold a War

Ginger Donnelly is on the trail of Nazi saboteurs in Sierra Leone. Whilst taking a midnight paddle, with a willing woman, in a canoe cajoled from a local fisherman, Donnelly sees an enormous seaplane thunder across the sky only to crash in a ball of brilliant flame. It seems like an accident... at least until a second plane explodes in a blistering shower along the same flight path.

John Harris

Live Free or Die!

Charles Walter Scully, cut off from his unit and running on empty, is trapped. It's 1944 and, though the Allied invasion of France has finally begun, for Scully the war isn't going well. That is, until he meets a French boy trying to get home to Paris. What begins is a hair-raising journey into the heart of France, an involvement with the French Liberation Front and one of the most monumental events of the war. Harris vividly portrays wartime France in a panorama of scenes that enthral and entertain the reader.

The Old Trade of Killing

Harris' exciting adventure is set against the backdrop of the Western Desert and scene of the Eighth Army battles. The men who fought together in the Second World War return twenty years later in search of treasure. But twenty years can change a man. Young ideals have been replaced by greed. Comradeship has vanished along with innocence. And treachery and murder make for a breathtaking read.

John Harris

Take or Destroy!

Lieutenant-Colonel George Hockold must destroy Rommel's vast fuel reserves stored at the port of Qaba if the Eighth Army is to succeed in the Alamein offensive. Time is desperately running out, resources are scant and the commando unit Hockold must lead is a ragtag band of misfits scraped from the dregs of the British Army. They must attack Qaba. The orders? Take or destroy.

'One of the finest war novels of the year'
– *Evening News*

The Unforgiving Wind

Charting the disastrous expedition of Commander Adams, this novel follows the misfortunes of his men across the Arctic after his sudden death. Whatever can go wrong does go wrong as transport, instruments, health and sanity begin to fail. The team seems irretrievably lost in the dark Arctic winter, frightened and half-starving even when it finds a base. Only one man can rescue them, the truculent Tom Fife who must respond to the faint radio signals coming from the Arctic shores. A powerful and disturbing novel, this story aims to take your breath away.

TITLES BY JOHN HARRIS AVAILABLE DIRECT
FROM HOUSE OF STRATUS

Quantity		£	$(US)	$(CAN)	€
	Army of Shadows	6.99	12.95	19.95	13.50
	China Seas	6.99	12.95	19.95	13.50
	The Claws of Mercy	6.99	12.95	19.95	13.50
	Corporal Cotton's Little War	6.99	12.95	19.95	13.50
	The Cross of Lazzaro	6.99	12.95	19.95	13.50
	Flawed Banner	6.99	12.95	19.95	13.50
	The Fox from his Lair	6.99	12.95	19.95	13.50
	A Funny Place to Hold a War	6.99	12.95	19.95	13.50
	Getaway	6.99	12.95	19.95	13.50
	Harkaway's Sixth Column	6.99	12.95	19.95	13.50
	A Kind of Courage	6.99	12.95	19.95	13.50
	Live Free or Die!	6.99	12.95	19.95	13.50
	The Lonely Voyage	6.99	12.95	19.95	13.50
	The Mercenaries	6.99	12.95	19.95	13.50
	North Strike	6.99	12.95	19.95	13.50

ALL HOUSE OF STRATUS BOOKS ARE AVAILABLE FROM GOOD BOOKSHOPS
OR DIRECT FROM THE PUBLISHER:

Internet: www.houseofstratus.com including synopses and features.

Email: sales@houseofstratus.com
info@houseofstratus.com
(please quote author, title and credit card details.)

TITLES BY JOHN HARRIS AVAILABLE DIRECT
FROM HOUSE OF STRATUS

Quantity		£	$(US)	$(CAN)	€
	THE OLD TRADE OF KILLING	6.99	12.95	19.95	13.50
	PICTURE OF DEFEAT	6.99	12.95	19.95	13.50
	THE QUICK BOAT MEN	6.99	12.95	19.95	13.50
	RIDE OUT THE STORM	6.99	12.95	19.95	13.50
	RIGHT OF REPLY	6.99	12.95	19.95	13.50
	ROAD TO THE COAST	6.99	12.95	19.95	13.50
	THE SLEEPING MOUNTAIN	6.99	12.95	19.95	13.50
	SMILING WILLIE AND THE TIGER	6.99	12.95	19.95	13.50
	SO FAR FROM GOD	6.99	12.95	19.95	13.50
	THE SPRING OF MALICE	6.99	12.95	19.95	13.50
	SUNSET AT SHEBA	6.99	12.95	19.95	13.50
	SWORDPOINT	6.99	12.95	19.95	13.50
	TAKE OR DESTROY!	6.99	12.95	19.95	13.50
	THE THIRTY DAYS WAR	6.99	12.95	19.95	13.50
	THE UNFORGIVING WIND	6.99	12.95	19.95	13.50
	UP FOR GRABS	6.99	12.95	19.95	13.50
	VARDY	6.99	12.95	19.95	13.50

ALL HOUSE OF STRATUS BOOKS ARE AVAILABLE FROM GOOD BOOKSHOPS
OR DIRECT FROM THE PUBLISHER:

Tel: **Order Line**
0800 169 1780 (UK)
 800 724 1100 (USA)
International
+44 (0) 1845 527700 (UK)
+01   845 463 1100 (USA)

Fax: +44 (0) 1845 527711 (UK)
+01   845 463 0018 (USA)
(please quote author, title and credit card details.)

Send to: **House of Stratus Sales Department**   **House of Stratus Inc.**
Thirsk Industrial Park   **2 Neptune Road**
York Road, Thirsk   **Poughkeepsie**
North Yorkshire, YO7 3BX   **NY 12601**
UK   **USA**

PAYMENT

Please tick currency you wish to use:

☐ £ (Sterling)   ☐ $ (US)   ☐ $ (CAN)   ☐ € (Euros)

Allow for shipping costs charged per order plus an amount per book as set out in the tables below:

CURRENCY/DESTINATION

	£(Sterling)	$(US)	$(CAN)	€(Euros)
Cost per order				
UK	1.50	2.25	3.50	2.50
Europe	3.00	4.50	6.75	5.00
North America	3.00	3.50	5.25	5.00
Rest of World	3.00	4.50	6.75	5.00
Additional cost per book				
UK	0.50	0.75	1.15	0.85
Europe	1.00	1.50	2.25	1.70
North America	1.00	1.00	1.50	1.70
Rest of World	1.50	2.25	3.50	3.00

PLEASE SEND CHEQUE OR INTERNATIONAL MONEY ORDER
payable to: HOUSE OF STRATUS LTD or HOUSE OF STRATUS INC. or card payment as indicated

STERLING EXAMPLE

Cost of book(s):..................... Example: 3 x books at £6.99 each: £20.97
Cost of order: .... Example: £1.50 (Delivery to UK address)
Additional cost per book:.............. Example: 3 x £0.50: £1.50
Order total including shipping:.......... Example: £23.97

VISA, MASTERCARD, SWITCH, AMEX:

☐☐☐☐☐☐☐☐☐☐☐☐☐☐☐☐☐☐☐

Issue number (Switch only):

☐☐☐

Start Date: Expiry Date:

☐☐/☐☐   ☐☐/☐☐

Signature: _____

NAME: _____

ADDRESS: _____

COUNTRY: _____

ZIP/POSTCODE: _____

Please allow 28 days for delivery. Despatch normally within 48 hours.

Prices subject to change without notice.
Please tick box if you do not wish to receive any additional information. ☐

House of Stratus publishes many other titles in this genre; please check our website (**www.houseofstratus.com**) for more details.